Mad Love 2

by

Colet Abedi

"The great question that has never been answered and which I have not yet been able to answer. . . is, "What does a woman want?"
—Sigmund Freud

The Cataloging-in-Publication Data is on file at the Library of Congress.

Cover Photograph: Isaac Matthew White Photography
Cover Design: Afshin Toussi

e-Book ISBN 978-0-9967088-0-7
Paperback ISBN 978-0-9967088-1-4

For my father, Hedy Abedi.
I know you're the brightest star in heaven.
I love you, daddy

Acknowledgments

This book is dedicated to my father, Hedayat Abedi. My hero. The man who taught me to dream. The man who taught me that I could be anything I wanted. That the sky was the limit. That this country, America, was a land of opportunity and we were blessed to be here and to become anything we wanted. Daddy, I don't know how to thank you. You left your home when you were so young and dreamt of something greater and you accomplished it. And not only that, you taught your daughters to do the same. Papa, you used to say that we were your universe and your hopes . . . well, *you* are mine. I can't believe I have to wait to see you again. To hug you. To embrace you. To just hold your hand. . .. Which was everything. *Everything.*

I love you, dad. I miss you more every day. Thank you for being the best father. Ever.

To my agent, Lisa Gallagher. You walked through hell with me and actually came out with a smile. That is a miracle in itself. Thank you for believing in me. Championing me. And most fun, cussing people out with me. . ..

To Jane Cavolina. My editor. But more importantly, my friend. Not only are you a beautiful soul but you're an incredible critic. Your opinion is invaluable to me. I don't know what I'd do without your talent and support. Thank you for sticking around through everything. For listening to me cry like a baby and for just being there. Everything happens for a reason and I know you're my reason from *Mad Love.*

My husband. I love you. I don't know what I'd do without you or where I would be. Thank you for supporting me. For believing in me. For pushing me. For holding me through my endless tears. I love you more than words can say. You're my soul mate and my love. What a year we've had.

Mommy and Jasmine. We are united in grief and love forever. Not just that, you're my core family now. I love you both and would do anything for you. Thank you for your support and love. I know Papa is holding our hands and guiding us along in this next chapter of our lives. But even so, I *really* wish he was here. I love you guys.

Ellajoon. You were very upset that you didn't get a thanks in book one and I ask that you forgive me for that. You are my angel. My daughter. My love. My khaleh. My beautiful niece with a heart of gold. You are the light in our life. You are our gift. You are my love forever and ever. You are always first and never, ever forgotten, my love. My biggest wish is that you find your very own Mad Love. He just has to pass through the Auntie test first . . .

Giuliana and Bill. Together you're a force, individually incredible energy and beautiful friends/family. Bill, thank you for pushing me. For telling me not to give up when I thought the world was so dark. You are a wonderful man and I'm blessed to count you as my friend. Jules, what can I say? We've been through it all together. And you've always been there as my bestest friend and biggest supporter. You never hesitate when I ask and you always push me to believe in myself. I love you forever, sister from another mister. #bffsforever. Where would we be if we hadn't met at that fax machine?

Annalynne. Cover model. Book critic. Past life family member ☺. I love you. You're an incredible, loyal friend. I am so lucky to have you in my life. I honestly can't imagine it without you in it. Your kindness and endless generosity is something I admire so much. I believe you when you say the best is coming. #nothingrealcanbethreatened

Nicky. Aussie lady. We've been through it. Oh boy, have we. Thank you for taking me to steam, for caring about my health, for letting me cry like a baby. Bringing me wine. Letting me drink wine ☺. And for never ever judging. Your heart is gold, lady. GOLD. I love you. Isn't life funny? Thank God we met . . .

Ariana, Andrea, Christina, Tanna, Brenda—my biggest book critics! And my loves. You ladies are Mad Lovers and the ones I trusted to read my book and tell me your honest opinion. Not only that . . . you're my family. Forever and ever. Always. I love you guys.

Giannina. My friend. Mentor. I love and thank you for all of your support and belief in me—in everything I do. You've taught me true strength and I learn more from you everyday. #QueenofHearts XXX

Jorge Serrano. Not only do you do the best sex hair there is but you're incredibly kind, giving, loving, and have the most beautiful heart I know. I love you.

Carlton. My soul sister. I love you. You're my protector. For realz. I know I have nothing to worry about with you on my side. You and David are the best and thank you for letting me use your amazing fireplace. #ChurchofGebbia

Cathea. How long has it been? You are and will always be my get out of jail call ☺. Literally. Your friendship means the world to me. You are so loyal and wonderful. And you're always there if I need you. I love you, beautiful lady.

Lauren. Thank you for being such an amazing friend to me. You shared my grief and checked in every day. And you let me know it was okay for me to be sad. I will never ever forget it. I love you.

Erik and Orie. Ummm . . . you are Sophie's BFFs. Drinking partners. Eating partners. Laughing partners. What more can I say? Love you guys.

Rana, Sally, Noonoosh—the Persian posse. Utah. Barbies. The H Rock. OPP. France 2000. Munich. DSV. Bathtub shots. Wine. Martinis. Food. Lots of food. Everything in between. I love you, girls.

Nina, Sahar, Nedda, Bahman, Shawn, Uncle Massoud, Minajoon, Uncle Mojee, Marlene, Mamanjoon, Bubajoon, Manjehjoon, Firoozehoon, Irajjoon, Babak, Mahnazjoon . . . family. We are lucky to have each other. This year has taught me that more than anything. You're my glue. Forever.

JD, Megan, Male Model, Arash, Bob, John, Mary, Matt, Amy, Angel, Esme, Amanda, Laya, Mona, Shirin, Trace, Lily, Majeed, Rizzotti, Staci, Mark, Matt A.—friends. You all mean so much to me and bring me such joy. My life wouldn't be complete without all of you in it.

To my incredible fan base . . . Mad Lovers Worldwide—Kristen Cambensy, Kerry Ann, Kerry-Lee, Elaine, Alicia, Nic, Logan, all the FAE fans who became Mad Love ones, NWA Gossip Girl, Nina Literary Gossip, Jacyln, LA_Fandom, Romance Addict Book Blog, Nazarea Andrews, Inkslinger PR, and the rest! You guys waited so patiently and were so supportive and loving. I can't ask for a better team on my side. This book would be nothing without you.

My wish is that everyone finds their very own Mad Love ...

1

"Alright, Sophie, in a moment I'm going to count to three. And when I do I want you to take a deep breath in and then slowly exhale," Dr. Goldstein, my hypnotherapist, says to me in a soothing voice. "And when you release your breath, you will let go of all your pain. All your anxiety. And you will forget you ever knew Clayton Astor Sinclair."

I take in a shaky breath and prepare myself.

"One."

My eyes flutter like a butterfly and before I can stop myself I see a flash of Clayton pulling me into his arms.

"Two."

His lips crush mine with savage intensity.

"Three."

His tongue moves into my mouth to take full ownership and—

Dr. Goldstein snaps his fingers.

"Uh-hum," Dr. Goldstein coughs loudly. "I said, *three.*"

It takes me a moment to remember where I am and more important, *why* I'm here. And when that happens the memories hit me hard.

When I open my eyes I'm pretty sure my cheeks are on fire.

"How do you feel, Sophie?" Dr. Goldstein asks me with a raised brow.

I think about lying to him, but wonder if he's a mind reader, too. He's the hypnotherapist that Erik recommended to get rid of bad habits. People usually saw him for smoking, alcohol addiction, or binge eating. Not to forget sex with a man they met in the Maldives.

"Good." I hope I sound convincing.

Dr. Goldstein brushes a hand through his silver hair and stands up to walk behind his large glass desk. I sit up from the couch I've been lying down on and smooth out my grey sweat pants. I watch Dr. Goldstein pace. His office could be the poster child for minimalist perfection. The walls are winter white, with three large, framed, iconic Ansel Adams photos. A simple black leather sofa with a single metal chair for the doctor are placed in front of his enormous desk. It is sparse, but strangely comforting in a nonthreatening kind of way.

I watch as Dr. Goldstein moves to stand in front of the window that overlooks Santa Monica pier. He crosses his arms and stares down at me from behind his thick dark frames. The look reminds of the kind my dad would have when he was disappointed in something I'd done. A feeling of dread washes over me as he frowns at the view.

"Honesty is a requirement in this office," he says. "Without honesty how do we know this is helping?"

I think about his words before I reluctantly answer.

"Well," I begin slowly, "I guess when you told me to forget Clayton, I saw a flash of his face. Then I thought of his arms around me and kissing him, then—" my voice starts to get choked up, the tears, those damn tears of mine, are dangerously close to falling. Again.

Dr. Goldstein waves his hand in the air.

"I get it. You *see* Clayton even though I keep telling you to *stop* seeing him. Same way you've been seeing him for the past three weeks." He turns away from the window and sits down at his desk. He leans back in his chair and twirls his silver mustache between his fingers as he stares at me.

It feels like an eternity.

"I can't believe I'm going to say this, but since you've been coming here three times a week with no improvement whatsoever, I'm going to have to say that I think you're a classic case study."

Classic case study?

I wonder what mental issue he's about to diagnose me with.

"Tell me, Dr. Goldstein," I say softly, ready to hear his conclusion and learn how to forget Clayton forever. "I can handle whatever you're going to tell me as long as there is medication for it."

I think Dr. Goldstein rolls his eyes but I can't be sure because my eyes are blurry from the tears that I'm determined not to shed. Not anymore.

"There is *no* medication for what you have, Sophie! You don't want to forget the damn guy." He throws his hands up in the air when he says the last bit.

But I'm trying. I really am.

The last person I want to be with is a serial philanderer, always focused on the next conquest. Someone I can never trust and will always wonder about.

But the problem is that I've not been able to forget him. *Not yet.* The man who introduced me to passion. Who introduced me to love. The most perfect man in every way— *Okay, except for one glaring flaw. Okay, more than glaring, try* epic *flaw— Oh whatever, Sophie! You're the one who fell for him!*

Clayton. *The Cheater.*

My plane ride home from Singapore four weeks ago was like something out of a nightmare. Between the wine and the tears, I was sure I drove Erik and Orie crazy. The two of them were staring at me like I needed to be admitted to a mental institution. We were in first class and I didn't even notice the luxury, I just cried my heart out and drank an obscene amount of red wine.

Erik, my dear beautiful best friend, tried his hardest to talk me out of the hole of darkness I had buried myself in.

"Get a goddamn grip! You need to be strong! You're a woman now in every sense of the word. This is real life, Sophie."

Real life? Was this my only choice?

"What Erik is trying to say," Orie chimed in with his usual gentle demeanor, "is that unfortunately this is part of the ups and downs of life. Of relationships."

I turned my gaze away from Orie and stared blindly out the plane window.

"Sophie," Orie continued, "I think the best way for you to handle this is to pretend like it's a death. You can never go back because it's gone. *He's gone.* For good. It's done. It's over. It's dead—"

"I think she gets it," Erik interrupted. "But Orie's right. If you look at this like a death you can give yourself real closure. Like, pretend a shark ate him in the Maldives. Or, I don't know . . . something just as gruesome and painful because that's exactly what the bastard deserves."

But he wasn't dead, he was alive and well at the resort. And probably zeroing in on his next victim. Moving her to the villa next to his. Getting ready to wine and dine—

"Jesus. Look at your face," Erik said as he grabbed my hand. "It's not going to be easy. But we're going to be right here next to you the whole way. You *will* get over him. I promise you. You will. And one day, we'll look back on this and laugh. The way I'm silently laughing at you right now."

Erik put a small mirror in front of my face and I gasped in horror at how frightening I looked because the wine had stained my teeth and lips.

"You look like death becomes her," he said, trying his hardest not to smile.

He did finally manage to get a giggle out of me. But it didn't last long.

And that feels like ages ago.

I'm all cried out now. Exhausted. Trying not to think about him even though I can't stop dreaming about him. Hoping that I wake up and the pain will at least be a bit less. Something that I can deal with. Not this horrible feeling that no one will *ever* be as perfect as him. But there is no way I can be with a man who is unfaithful. No way. I remember a girl at school whose father always had affairs. It was awful and the worst part was, after her mother had spend twenty years putting up with his shit, he ended up leaving her in the end. No way I would let myself go down that road.

When I got home from the trip I locked myself up in my apartment and refused to see anyone for two days. My parents tried to force their way over but I avoided them by claiming I had a horrible flu and just wanted to sleep. I got a two-day reprieve and then made myself go to their house, or else I knew they'd have the police breaking down my door. Thankfully my tan hid the fact that I was such a mess inside.

I managed to get through dinner without crying and even forced myself to eat a few bites. Luckily, no one had noticed my lack of appetite. After, I sat on the couch in the family room and stared blindly at the TV. My dad was watching CNN and my mom was in the kitchen cleaning up the dishes from dinner. We had opted to stay in so we could catch up. I was grateful because I was able to wear what had become my uniform since I returned: sweatpants and sweatshirt, with my hair tied up in a bun. My parents were dressed casually as well, but they were wearing nice tracksuits that didn't have old stains on them. My dad looked relaxed, sitting back on the cozy white sofa with a glass of wine in his hand. His silver hair was brushed back from his handsome face and I could tell he was enjoying the broadcast. I felt good when my dad was at ease. At least there was something in the world that could still make me happy.

Dad had occasionally broken the silence by asking me a question about my vacation. My answers were abrupt and I'm sure he could tell that I didn't want to talk about it. So he had stayed silent for most of the evening. I was happy for that because it gave me the opportunity to obsess about Clayton and analyze every single moment we had together.

"God what a frightening thought," my father said out loud.

"Uh huh," I replied automatically as I relived the moments on the Remington's yacht when I first met Amelia Von Peters, the model.

"Just awful," he went on.

"Sure is," I nodded blankly as I realized I should have known from the looks Amelia gave Clayton that something was going on.

"To think we had the alien mothership in our backyard this entire time and didn't know it."

"Yeah."

Huh. Aliens. Amelia's beauty reminded me of an alien. It was like something from out of this world–

"Sophie Walker, have you heard a word I've said?!"

Crap.

My dad gave me a knowing look. I was so busted.

"What's wrong, honey? Talk to me. This silence is so unlike you." The caring tone in my dad's voice was nearly my undoing. He looked so genuinely concerned about me. I wanted to tell him— a big part of me wanted to throw myself in his loving arms and hear him say that it would be okay, that he would keep me safe, as he had when I was a child. But I was so afraid of the disappointment I thought I would see when I told him everything, that I couldn't bring myself to.

"Nothing, dad."

"Don't lie to me," he said. "You know I can tell. Something *is* wrong. You've seemed off. Didn't you have fun in the Maldives, honey?"

Fun? Try, it was the time of my life until I found out—ugh, I didn't want to go there again.

"It was great, dad."

"Is it a financial thing? Are you in trouble because of the trip?"

I almost laughed. Even though we had paid for the villas in advance, Clayton had gone behind our backs and taken care of our entire bill. He had paid for our villas, meals, activities, spa, the whole trip. I guess I could thank him for giving me a month of financial freedom I didn't think I'd have when I'd left on my vacation.

But now I needed to start making money. And fast. There was no way I would ever ask my parents for any help because that would lead to them arguing that I needed to go back to law school.

"I'm really okay, dad," I lied. "It's not money, it's just jet lag."

"Is it a boy thing?" He pushed.

I almost started hyperventilating. My dad, being the perceptive lawyer, could see it on my face.

"It's Jerry, isn't it, Sophie?"

Jerry?

I had almost forgotten about him.

"It's not a relationship thing, dad. I told you, I'm just tired."

I knew my dad didn't believe me but I also knew that he would let up for a while and probably call me the next day to see what was going on.

Thankfully, I'd be able to fake happiness on the phone much better than in person.

"Sophie?" Dr. Goldstein's voice interrupts my revere. "Have you heard anything I've said?"

"Yes," I lie, then shake my head. "No. No, I haven't heard a word."

"I asked if he was still calling you from an anonymous number."

Right. Since Clayton wouldn't stop calling and texting me I blocked his cell. Then I started to get calls from a private number. I never picked up. And then he stopped leaving text messages. The last one he left was a week ago. It was simple. To the point. And final.

It appears that my desire to speak to you and explain what you saw means absolutely nothing to you. There's nothing left to say than goodbye, Sophie.

"No. He has stopped calling me."

"How does that make you feel?"

Like my life is over.

"It's getting easier," I say with false bravado. "I know this is going to take time."

Dr. Goldstein gives me a sympathetic smile. "Heartbreak is the hardest experience to go through, especially the first time. But chin up, Sophie. Life is long. You're bound to have your heart broken at least a dozen more times."

I will never date again. Never.

I leave Dr. Goldstein's office twenty minutes later and dread going home to my apartment. My entire existence has turned into either obsessing about Clayton or obsessing about finding a job. And in between freaking out about both topics I usually call Erik and burden him with my problems. I owe him and Orie big time for putting up with me lately.

They must cringe when they see my phone number on the caller ID.

I can't believe I've become that person.

So instead I flick through my iPhone while I'm driving and find the Audiobooks app and quickly hit play. Since getting back from the Maldives I've forced myself to listen to every single self-help book that I can get my hands on. I'm currently hoping that Dr. Wayne Dyer's *Miracles Happen* will somehow magically make a miracle happen and I'll wake up a whole new person.

"Okay Sophie, you've got this," I say out loud as I begin the *I AM* mantra that Dr. Dyer says really works.

My caller ID flashes on the dashboard. It's Erik.

"I am strong," I call out.

I hit the button to accept his call.

"What you are is *crazy*," Erik's loud voice rings through my car.

"You weren't supposed to hear that," I say.

I don't even have the energy to be embarrassed.

"Too late. Cat's outta the bag," he says sarcastically. "So what are you doing besides driving around LA talking to yourself? How was Dr. Goldstein? And I'm only asking because it's the polite thing to do. From what I just heard I'm thinking it didn't go so well."

"Dr. Goldstein was fine," I tell him. "I think I need a few more sessions."

Erik's snort is telling.

"You're rude," I say.

"Stop, you're hurting my feelings," he says with a laugh, then, "Wanna come over? I have some news."

"Good or bad?" I ask.

"Do you honestly think I would give you bad news right now? You can barely handle watching a

Tampax commercial without having some type of meltdown."

True.

"Alright, see you in a few," I say.

Ten minutes later I pull into the driveway of Erik and Orie's house in the Hollywood Hills. Their home is a large three bedroom, built in the 1940s and is Spanish style. They renovated the entire interior but kept the original old-world charm of the exterior. The floors are Spanish tiled and paired with comfortable but modern furniture, a collection of pieces the two have found on their travels around the world and at local antique shops.

I ring the doorbell.

Erik answers, looking perfect as usual. He's wearing gray baggy sweat pants and a white t-shirt that says, *I Got This.* I watch as he checks out my outfit. I can tell he's not happy.

"Were you working out?" I ask, hoping to distract him.

"Orie and I were at the gym," he says as I follow him through the house.

"I just made some fresh green juice. You want some?"

"I'm not really thirsty."

"I'll pour you a glass," he says, ignoring me as we walk into his ultramodern kitchen. I sit on one of the barstools and lean on my elbows over the Carrera white counter to watch as he pours me a large cup of juice. He sets it in front of me. There's nothing about it that looks appealing.

"Where's Orie?"

"In the shower," Erik says. "You should try one sometime."

"Whatever," I say as I roll my eyes. "So what's your big news?"

I watch as Erik's eyes light up. I can tell it's going to be good.

"So here it goes—unbeknownst to me my agent put me up for this *huge* job overseas. Some super wealthy Russian oligarch's son is getting married and is having a two-week extravaganza in Provence. There are over one hundred guests and everyone's staying at this one property that is supposed to be sick," Erik says excitedly, then admits, "Okay, I know it's sick because I Googled it. I'll show you the pictures later."

He rushes on.

"So I'm supposed to shop for the fiancée's wardrobe here, then go out to Provence and dress her for each event she's hosting with the oligarch's son. He wants her to look perfect every day for pictures and media stuff. I guess his family is some kind of big deal. Super rich. And yes, in case you're wondering, I did have to look up the word oligarch because I had no fucking idea what it meant," he says. Then asks me, "Do you know?"

"A business magnate," I say.

"That's why you're in law school," Erik says with a smile.

"I dropped out," I remind him.

Erik waves my comment off.

"But you got in."

True.

"So wait . . . you got the job?" I ask in excitement.

"Yes! We spoke on the phone the other day and they hired me!"

"Holy cow!" I stand up and run around the bar to hug my friend. "This is a huge deal!"

"With a huge paycheck to match," Erik says as he lifts me up in his arms. "They're paying me more than my day rate and letting me bring an assistant."

I know the answer as he sets me down. "Orie."

"You guessed it! It's too long for us to be apart and since it's the holidays and most of his clients go out of town for the break he won't miss much here."

I'm so happy for my friend. To get such a great job sounds almost unreal—and Provence of all places? It's too good to be true.

"I'm so happy for you," I tell him sincerely. "This sounds incredible. When do you leave?"

"Two weeks. So we'll end up there over the holidays, which has always been a dream of mine. Christmas in Europe. Could you just die?"

"It's amazing," I say, but I'm not going to lie, I do feel a bit depressed that he's going to leave me for Christmas and New Year's. What will I do with myself?

I can picture myself depressed and dressed in sweatpants, wandering the streets of Beverly Hills like a homeless person. I shiver at the thought.

"But wait, have a seat my friend." Erik interrupts my mental image as he rubs his hands together. "Because there's more."

I take a cautious step back and sit down on the barstool.

"So remember those portraits you painted of me and Orie?" Erik asks.

"Of course. How could I forget? We had the best time doing those."

Erik nods in agreement.

"Well, apparently rich people like to have their portraits done, especially before they get married. It's like a gift the brides give to their husbands-to-be," Erik begins slowly. "And when I spoke to the oligarch's people—"

"Why do you keep referring to them as oligarchs?" I interrupt.

"Because I can't pronounce their last name, it's really long and Russian and I like saying oligarch. Sounds shit hot."

"Okay," I nod. "So the fiancé makes all the decisions for the bride-to-be?"

"I guess," Erik shrugs. "Or his people do. Can I finish my story or do you want to interrupt me one more time?"

"Go ahead," I say.

"So they told me about this portrait that the wife-to-be has to do and what the fiancé wants her to wear, which is bizarre. I hope for her sake it's not some kind of fetish."

"Why?" I ask curiously.

"He wants her to dress up as Marie Antoinette."

I nod in agreement. That's definitely weird.

"Yeah, I know," Erik says as if he can read my mind. And then he continues. "So then after they told me about the Halloween costume the fiancé wants her to wear for the portrait, I told them about you."

"Me?" I'm confused. Or slow. I didn't know which.

Erik rolls his eyes.

"Yes, *you!* I told them that's what *you* do and that you're incredible. And then I sent pictures of your stuff so the oligarch's family could see for themselves." He pauses to be sure he has my attention, then says, "So, you're welcome, because I got you the job."

I'm pretty sure my mouth is hanging open.

Erik says slowly, "You are going to paint a rich Russian chick. You are coming to come and hang out with us in Provence. You are going to get paid to do it."

I don't know how to respond.

"Ummm, I'm *waiting?*" Erik says as he impatiently taps his fingers on the counter.

"Thank you?" I say weakly. I still can't believe it.

"Thank me with a gift," he says with a smile. "Preferably one from John Varvatos."

And then it hits me. I'm going to make money doing what I love and get to spend time in Europe with my best friends.

It's like a miracle just happened.

Huh.

Thank you, Wayne Dyer.

2

Two weeks later Erik, Orie, and I find ourselves headed east, not quite knowing what to expect but open to adventure. We arrive in style at the airport in Marseille and are picked up by the oligarch, aka Lobonav-Dostyanevsky, family's personal driver, Sergei, who will be taking us to the chateau in Avignon.

Since I've never been to Provence I'm beyond excited and actually am not plagued by incessant thoughts of Clayton. Before we left I promised myself I would push him out of my mind and focus on the trip ahead of me, which is really a dream come true. Here I am, about to start my first real, paid job as an artist. If it goes well, which I have every intention of making sure it does, one good painting can get me into the wedding portrait business. That would give me a steady income and the financial freedom to be able to work on my passion art projects on the side. This is my once-in-a-lifetime opportunity and I plan on making the most of every moment of it.

The L-D family (I refuse to call them the oligarchs like Erik) let me know via e-mail that I wouldn't have to bring any painting supplies, as they would make sure that I was fully stocked with everything I would need. I did, however, bring a few of my favorite brushes and my camera to take photos of the wife-to-be, because I figured it would be highly unlikely that she would sit for hours during the day. Realistically the portrait would take two to three months for me to complete, which meant that I would have to have all my work shipped back to the States. The L-Ds seemed amenable to all my requests.

It's kind of insane how generous they are.

Considering that I'm an unknown artist , the amount of money they're paying me is staggering. A paycheck that will sustain me for at least three months of my life.

Ten thousand dollars.

I'm still reeling from the thought of it.

I remember seeing the number in the body of my e-mail and feeling like someone was pulling a fast one on me. I had actually written back and said, "Are you sure?" They didn't respond right away so I immediately went to the dark side and cursed my stupidity for bringing the amount to their attention. Lucky for me, they replied the next day with a simple, "Yes." I didn't want to push my luck so I just offered a polite thank you.

So here I am, in a chauffeur-driven Maybach (*could you die?)* on my way to a chateau on a vineyard to basically start living my dream. It feels too good to be true.

I look over and watch as Erik presses the button on the side of his chair to make it lean back the way one does in an airplane. Orie was generous enough to let Erik and I take the backseat; he was sitting in front with Sergei.

A Mercedes Benz van with all of our luggage and the fiancé's new wardrobe is following us. We're used to the warm weather in Los Angeles so we figured we'd freeze in the Provence winter and probably overpacked warm clothes.

My phone beeps with a text message.

I pull it out of my handbag and am not surprised to see that it's from Erik. Orie is also copied.

I read: *What's Sergei's deal? He's so quiet. I'm a little scared.*

I look over at Erik and shake my head. My phone beeps again.

ORIE: I tried to talk to him three times and he didn't seem very friendly. He definitely gives off the "I can kick your ass vibe."

ERIK: He IS Russian.

I turn my phone on silent so it's not so apparent to Sergei that we're texting each other, even though I'm pretty sure he knows.

ME: You guys, this is so obvious. He knows we're texting each other.

ORIE: You think?

My gaze meets Sergei's in the rearview mirror and from the smirk on his face I know I'm right. I'm sure my cheeks are flaming red from guilt so I immediately turn my phone off and stare blindly at the passing trees outside my window.

"Sergei?" Erik says politely.

"Yes, Mr. Johnson?" His accent is thick.

"Can you turn the music on?"

"Of course."

In a second One Republic's "Apologize" fills the silence. Erik looks at me nervously and I immediately know what he's thinking.

"Can we find something a bit more upbeat?" he asks.

"I'll find us a station, if you don't mind," Orie tells Sergei as he takes over the controls. He settles on a song from Ellie Goulding.

"Is this safe?" Orie turns around to ask me. His smile is mischievous and Erik finds his comment vastly amusing.

"You're rude," I tell Erik as I roll my eyes. "I appreciate your concern, Orie, but I think I can handle hearing a love song."

"Doubtful," Erik replies as he studies my face.

I decide I'm not going speak to him for the rest of the ride to the chateau. It's easier this way. I'm pretty sure he has a whole bag full of comments ready to hit me with about how I need to be strong and get a goddamn grip. He's right, but I finally feel like I *am* getting a bit more of a grip, so I hope he lays off. The smell of croissants in the airport actually gave me hunger pangs and I haven't felt hungry for weeks. I've actually lost five pounds, which is a lot for my me. I guess there's a silver lining to every cloud.

After we've been driving for forty-five minutes and I take in the winter ambience. The vineyards are dried out but the layout and symmetry of the land is still spectacular to see. I can only imagine what it's like in the summer months, when the vineyards are filled with leaves and the lavender is in full bloom. French lavender is the best in the world.

Sergei says, "We'll be arriving at the Chateau de Comte Clare in less than five minutes."

"How's the weather been?" Orie asks.

"It's been a mild winter. We haven't had a Mistral wind yet so we feel lucky. But I am sure it will be very different from your Californian winter."

"What's the Mistral?" Orie asks.

"Fierce winds that come down the Rhone Valley. If we have Mistral winds the temperatures really drop."

"I think wind is romantic," Erik says as Orie turns to give him a smile.

"For some." From the tone of Sergei's voice I doubt he agrees with Erik's view of the terrible winds.

"We have arrived," Sergei tells us as we drive through two enormous gates and down a long winding dirt driveway lined with olive trees.

I'm looking out to see where we'll be staying for the next two-plus weeks, and when the chateau comes into view my mouth drops open. As the car slowly makes its way up the wide path and I see what can only be described as a castle. Like a fairytale. Real people in the real world don't live in places like this.

"Welcome to Chateau de Comte Clare."

"This is unbelievable," Orie says, his voice expressing his complete awe.

"It is very incredible," Sergei agrees. "The family owns over one hundred acres of land. There are five different homes on the estate but this is the main residence."

"How many bedrooms does it have?" Erik asks.

"Twenty-five."

Erik whistles.

As Sergei pulls into the enormous circular driveway, I take in the magical beauty of Chateau de Comte Clare. A central stone staircase leads up to the entrance. There are vaulted archways around the white stone residence and pale blue shutters flank the windows. It looks exactly like the kind of homes I saw online when I Googled Provence. For the ultra-rich, that is.

And I mean really, *really* rich.

As Sergei pulls to a stop in front of the staircase, he says, "Please don't worry about any of your luggage. We will have someone take them up to your rooms. Ms. Abigail is eagerly waiting to meet you."

Erik and I turn to each other and mouth *Abigail*? I think we were both expecting an Ekaterina or Anastasia.

I grab my fluffy crème oversized beanie out of my bag and pull it over my head. Erik opens the door and the cool air rushes in.

"It's so cold!" he mutters before he slams the door shut. I open mine and step outside, grateful that I'm wearing warm UGGS and jeans. Erik and Orie are happily looking around while I pull my black wool jacket on so I don't freeze.

"This way, please," Sergei says as he motions toward the stairs. We follow him.

I'm suddenly kind of nervous about meeting Ms. Abigail. Since she obviously comes from a very upper-class world, I wonder if she'll have the same demeanor as Jane or if she'll be more like Elizabeth. I pray the latter.

The thought of Jane and Elizabeth leads to thoughts of Clayton, and I'm hit with a wave of sadness. It's stunning. I wonder when I'll stop feeling like I'm suffocating whenever he comes to mind. I know I need to be grateful for the experience—for him being a considerate lover, for the romance, for his extraordinary generosity. I just have to start thinking about the positive part of my time with him, not this awful side of being without him. And somehow I have to figure out how to forgive him. Because when that happens I know I'll be able to let go of my pain.

Erik yanks my arm and brings me back to reality. We are at the top of the stairs.

"Are you looking at this?" he says as we walk through a the pebbled atrium that leads to two enormous, ancient pale blue wooden doors that are being held open by four people.

"In my next life I want to come back as a Russian oligarch's wife," Erik whispers.

"Why wife?"

"All the perks and none of the responsibility," he explains.

I burst out laughing.

"Your thank-you gift to me is looking better by the minute," he continues.

I link my arm through his and lean in to his side, so grateful for having him in my life.

"I promise it will be good."

"Have Orie pick it out."

"You don't trust my taste?" I ask in mock anger.

"I don't think you want me to answer that, Sophie."

I turn my gaze to the incredible surroundings. Erik is right. I'm going to need to get him a very good gift. We walk down a hall of gothic-style limestone arches. Black wrought-iron chandeliers line the ceilings, creating a dramatic entrance to the home. I don't know where to look first. Everywhere I gaze I see a statue or a painting I'd like to stop and stare at. I know that every item I see is probably worth more money than the average person makes in a year.

The wealth is mind-blowing. To think that this is someone's home is unreal. We're shown into what I assume is the drawing room and I marvel at the high ceilings. The room is painted in a powder blue that fits the Provencal setting perfectly. Two identical long creme, gold-rimmed couches are set opposite from one another across a marble coffee table that is fit for a king. An enormous fireplace crackles with life and practically begs you to sit down and enjoy the ambiance. And I don't think I've ever seen a bigger Persian rug; it practically takes up the large room. Dramatic French windows overlook the impeccably landscaped grounds.

I have to stop taking inventory, since Ms. Abigail is seated on one of the couches. She gets up with a warm smile as we enter the room. She's the exact opposite of what I pictured in my head, and I like her instantly. She's an extraordinarily pretty, petite brunette with a friendly face and reminds me a lot of Elizabeth. She's dressed conservatively in a long, gray wool skirt and blue turtleneck. Her hair is swept away from her face and I'm surprised by how young she is. She can't be older than me. She walks straight over to me and extends her hand.

"You must be Sophie," she says in a posh English accent. "It's so lovely to meet you."

"It's wonderful to meet you," I say, I guess I'm still surprised that she is not Russian. And hearing her upper-class English accent has thrown me.

She turns her attention to Erik and Orie.

"I'm so thrilled to have here," she says. "You must be exhausted."

"We slept a good portion of our flight so we're feeling okay," Erik tells her. "And the service on the plane was just great."

"That pleases me to hear."

"Your fiancé and his team have been incredibly generous," Erik tells her. "Please thank them for us."

"I won't hear another word. There are no thanks necessary," she says, as if spending ten thousand dollars on first class tickets for three people is no big deal.

From the look of things it's probably not, Sophie, my inner voice chimes in.

"Would you like to freshen up in your rooms or shall I give you a quick tour before? Whichever you prefer," she says.

"Actually, I wouldn't mind a tour before we settle in," Erik answers for us then looks at Orie and I. "Are you guys okay with that?"

We both nod in agreement even though I would have loved to splash some water on my face. And shower. I'm dying to just get clean.

"Fantastic. I'll show you the dressing room I'd like you to use, and of course I want to show Sophie where I'll sit for the portrait," Abigail begins. "I'm having the three of you stay in the main house with me. Your rooms are upstairs and I'll show them to you as I give you a tour. Some of our other guests are staying here, too but mostly they are in the other homes on the estate. You'll see many of our friends coming and going between the activities we have planned. So please don't be surprised or alarmed. Almost everyone comes up here for breakfast in the morning. We keep it refreshed from seven until eleven, but you can always ask for something if you're hungry. An itinerary for each day will be delivered to your room. Whenever you are free, you are more than welcome to join us."

Itinerary? It's like a hotel.

"It's such a beautiful setting for a wedding," I tell her warmly as I motion toward our surroundings.

"It is lovely, isn't it?" she agrees with a smile. "It's very romantic. I do love this home. It's always been one of my favorites."

One? How many more like this are there? I can't even fathom it. For the obvious reasons it's a world apart from the Maldives but it feels just as romantic.

Crap.

Did I just go there again? *Yes, you did.*

I force a big smile.

"I would love to see the room I'll be working in, and I'm sure Erik is just as anxious to start steaming the clothes he brought for you," I say to distract myself as my thoughts start to go down a path I can't afford to take right now. I need to focus. Just on my job.

"Follow me," Abigail says as she leads the way out of the room.

Ten minutes later I'm standing in a room that looks like it belongs in Versailles. Even though the room is bare except for a few pieces of furniture, it is regal, in Louis XIV style with lots of gold and royal blue colors. Abby, as she insists we call her, told me that she had the room cleared of most of the furniture so that I could have plenty of space to work. They moved a long blue and gold fainting sofa against an enormous window that overlooks the vineyard. I'm happy with her choice. It's a great setting for her portrait. She'll look beautiful and ethereal with the sun shining in.

But the thing that really wowed me was the extensive supplies set up for me. They really weren't joking when they said they'd have everything covered. My painting station is enormous, and contains an easel, raw canvas, hundreds of different colored oil paints and more brushes than I've ever seen in my life. They thought of literally everything I might need and made sure it was at hand. It's like an art student's wet dream. Looking at all my supplies makes me anxious to get started. I can't wait.

We decide that she will sit for me the day after tomorrow, so she can choose from the few costume dresses that Erik brought and pick her hairstyle and make-up. I'm happy about the wait because it means I have enough time to get ready for my debut performance and get over any possible jet lag I might have. For now, since I'm not at all tired, I've asked Abby and the guys to let me stay in the room and do a little bit of prep work while they head to Abby's dressing room. I figure I'll work for a little bit before I head over to my room and shower.

I walk around and familiarize myself with the space. The colors, the depth, it's just so perfect for Abby. I can picture her lying on the lounge dressed like Marie Antoinette.

That's the weird part, I'm not going to lie. But whatever, it's her choice. Or her fiancé's.

I find an iPod dock, pull my phone out of my back pocket, connect and play some music. I switch on one of the lights, which is pretty dim but will do for now, and pull off my beanie. I throw my jacket on one of the chairs and push up the sleeves to my black thermal top. It's strange, but I'm not at all nervous about painting Abby. I probably should be, given the circumstances and the pomp and pageantry of this place, but instead I'm so eager. I walk over to the oil canvas and begin to size and support it.

The song changes and Chris Martin's sexy voice floats through the room. Coldplay's song "Magic" is one of my favorites. Within minutes I'm immersed in performing the necessary steps to prep for doing what I love most in the world. It's definitely therapeutic, because my focus has changed, I'm lost in my work, and I can't think about anything else.

And then something happens.

I feel the energy in the room change.

I feel a crackle in the air. Like all the oxygen is slowly being sucked out. I get goose bumps all over my body and I know, I just *know* that I'm not alone anymore.

I know *he's* in the room with me.

It's *his* energy that has invaded my space.

I feel his eyes on my body. Moving over my head, down to my feet. The back of my neck tingles at the thought.

He's here.

I slowly turn around, and I see I'm right.

Clayton. Astor. Sinclair.

Sitting on a chair in the corner of the room by the door. Wearing jeans and a black sweater, leaning back casually, holding a glass of what I'm sure is his favorite whiskey, Dalmore. Staring at me.

Oh my god is he staring at me. I wonder how long he's been watching me.

I forget to breathe.

I don't even think I remember how. He's here. Clayton is *here*. The relief I feel from just seeing him is staggering. Like there's a reason to live again. I think I might fall to the ground from the force of my feelings.

We stay like this for a long while. Staring at each other. I watch him slowly look me up and down, then that sapphire blue gaze of his meets mine.

Oh. My. God.

So many thoughts race through my mind. So many different thoughts, some ugly, some beautiful, some just nonsensical.

He sets his drink down, gets up and makes his way toward me.

My mouth goes dry.

I feel like I'm cemented to the ground. I can't move.

He stops when he's just a foot away and I have to tilt my head to look up at him. I forgot how tall he is. How he towers over me. How hot he is. But different now. Darker. Brooding. This close, I can see the tell-tale signs of someone who hasn't slept. He looks tired, a dark stubble lines his jaw, but nothing can detract from his devastating good looks. His broad shoulders fill out his black sweater perfectly and he was definitely made to wear jeans. I feel like I've been lost in a desert for months and he's my first taste of water. He's so incredibly gorgeous that I want to jump in his arms and forgive him.

But that's not going to happen.

It can't happen.

I search his face, looking for answers that I instinctively know. There's no hiding from it.

I state the obvious. "You planned this."

He doesn't have to answer because I know I'm right. Everything rushes into my mind at once.

"Chateau de Comte Clare?"

"Chateau de Comte *St. Clare*. This is my home," he says and I can't help it, his voice, that lyrical sexy voice, is like music to my ears.

This is his home? Holy shit.

But I can't be weak. So I continue in what I hope is an assertive voice.

"Are you related to Abigail?"

"She's my cousin."

He's diabolical.

"I planned only one part of it. Erik. But not you," Clayton says softly. "You have your friend to thank for that, as do I. You being here is entirely his doing."

"I don't believe you," I say immediately.

I watch his eyes turn to ice. "Shocking."

Right. Suddenly I think of Amelia Von Peters and his betrayal and I just have to get away from him. I turn to find my jacket and grab my iPhone. I need to go tell Erik the truth and then find the first plane out of Marseille and head home. Like pronto. With any luck I can get on a flight tonight.

I knew it was too good to be true.

Before I can get into a giant internal argument with myself, a strong hand on my arm stops me in my tracks. The jolt of electricity I get from his touch is the best thing I've felt in weeks.

God help me. I need to be strong.

"Let go of me," I tell him forcefully. I can't look at his handsome face even though it's all I want to do.

"Unfortunately that's not a possibility."

My heart drops and my eyes flick up to his.

"Please don't hurt me anymore than you already have," I plead. "If you have a heart, just stop."

He loosens his grip but he doesn't let go.

"The situation we find ourselves in is entirely your doing, Sophie," Clayton says quietly.

I want to close my eyes like a child and pretend none of this is happening. Unfortunately real life doesn't work that way.

"I'm not having this conversation with you," I tell him. "I'm jet lagged and exhausted—"

"Fine," he interrupts in that autocratic tone of his. "Go take a nap and enjoy the rest of your day and we'll talk in the morning."

"Don't tell me what to do."

I watch his eyes narrow at my words. I can tell he doesn't like what I say. But *tough.* Screw him. He's the cheater. Not me.

He meets my gaze and I hope I don't look as nervous as I feel inside. But I'm not going to lie, I'm a bit unnerved by the intensity of his stormy eyes. He has the look of a predator. *A wolf.*

Crap.

And then the last or the first thing I want to happen does. His eyes go from looking annoyed to something else. To being filled with something else.

Desire.

And now I know I really have to run. Because if this man leans in and kisses me, I'm done. So done. I think he can sense how he's affecting me because he gives me a smug smile.

"Scared?"

"Hardly." I swallow audibly.

"You should be."

Warnings again.

"Of what? Of you? You've already done the worst thing you could do to me."

Unless he tells me he's married. Now that would definitely be the worst thing.

I think I see a flash of hurt in his eyes. But it's quickly masked. And let's be real, I'd be delusional to think he'd even be capable of that emotion.

"Fuck it," he whispers, then he leans down and throws me over his shoulder like a sack of rice and marches out of the room.

For a moment I'm too shocked to even scream out at the indignity of it, then I get over it.

"Put me down, " I whisper furiously as I hit him on the back. He answers by smacking me hard on my ass.

"Oww!" I'm pretty sure my shriek is heard through out the chateau.

"Lower your voice unless you want my entire staff to see you in your current position. I don't think that's how you want to meet them for the first time."

I close my mouth and watch the ground change from black-and-white checkered marble floors to crème carpet. A door shuts. And I know I'm in a bedroom. A second later my hunch is proven correct because I'm thrown rather unceremoniously on a large bed and Clayton quickly traps me between his arms and leans in close. I have no idea where I am. Not that I'd know anyway, the place is so damn big and I opted out of the full tour to get ready for my art debut. *What a mistake that was.*

I look up at his angry face. Okay. His pissed off face. Like, really *really* pissed off.

"Take a bath. And just rest," he says in a commanding voice as his gaze lowers to my mouth. His eyes get that steamy look and I think he's going to kiss me.

I *wish* he'd kiss me. He stays like that for a minute almost like he's playing with me. And he is. Because this is pure torture. He's so close I can smell his cologne. The Clayton smell that is singularly his and is so delicious I don't even know what to do with myself.

But he doesn't kiss me. Instead he draws back.

"We'll talk tomorrow morning after you have the day to yourself to unwind."

"I won't be here tomorrow," I tell him, furiously angry that he can dismiss me so easily. Angry that I am so turned on by him even after everything.

But he gives me an imperious look, like my comment is meaningless.

"You'll be here."

"In your dreams, Clayton Astor Sinclair!" I say confidently. "*Only in your dreams*!"

The look on Clayton's face softens.

"You're right, baby," he tells me. "You're finally right about something."

3

You're right, baby. You're finally right about something.

Am I hallucinating? Is my mind playing tricks or did Clayton just say those words to me and then walk out of the bedroom and shut the door? Is he really here? *Am* I *really here?*

Are you really still lying on the bed?

Well, shit. Yes. Because I'm too shocked to move. Because seeing Clayton makes me not want to move. Seeing him makes me want to hold him, breathe him in, and remember all the delicious parts of our time together. Seeing him gives me hope.

Before I can even sit up from the bed, the door bursts open and slams shut. Orie and Erik rush over to me and stare down at what I'm sure is my shell-shocked face. But they both have the same look as me.

"What the fuck is going on?" Erik asks incredulously.

Orie brushes a hand through his thick black hair then looks like he's going to break into a cold sweat. "I'm seriously having a panic attack

I stare up at them. My eyes are wide and unfortunately I'm still incapable of putting a coherent sentence together.

"Since you're not going to talk, I will." Leave it to Erik to fill any uncomfortable silences.

"Clayton, aka *asshole*, just walked right into the dressing room that Orie and I were busy putting together for fucking Abigail. He said one sentence to us: 'Sophie's in the room with the double doors, straight down the hall.' Then he walked right out."

Erik is clearly outraged. "Do you have any idea, *any idea* how incredibly fucked this is? I thought I was seeing a ghost from Christmas past."

"It was full on," Orie agrees. "Like the movie *Shining* kind of full on."

I start to giggle. I can't help it. The looks on their faces are priceless. Hysterical.

Erik does not appreciate my amusement. "Do you think this is funny? This isn't fucking funny, Sophie. I'll tell you what this is—it's *crazy*."

"Talk to us," Orie demands in a calm voice, "before Erik spontaneously combusts. And tell us what the hell you're doing laying on this bed," Orie's obviously pulled it together.

I sit up and quickly fill them in on what happened. I don't leave anything out. I tell them everything. Every word. And when I'm done, I just sit back and wait for their reactions. I know I won't be disappointed.

"I feel so used," Erik says.

"Erik—" I begin.

But he goes on before I can say anything else. "I can't believe the Russian oligarchs didn't hire me because of how amazing I am."

"You are amazing and they know it." I say hurriedly, hoping to placate his bruised ego. "Abby for sure knows it now."

"Easy for you to say," Erik snorts. "Apparently you're the *only* one here because of her talent. I'm just a tool. A means to an end. A ying to someone's fucking yang."

"Oh for God's sake quit being so *dramatique*!" Orie says. "This isn't about you."

"Well, I'm sorry. But I'm the one with the hurt feelings here. I would hope you'd be more sensitive to my situation," Erik says indignantly.

I can sense a fight coming.

"Guys—" I interject.

Erik holds up his hand.

"I can't believe I didn't see this coming," he says. "I can usually smell a conspiracy a mile away. In retrospect it was so obvious."

"Was it?" Orie asks. "I mean, we just thought it was a great gig."

"Had I known Abby's full name we wouldn't be in this situation because I would have Googled her, too," he continues, ignoring Orie.

"That's why they didn't give it to us," I tell him.

Orie switches gears and looks over at me.

"How are *you* feeling?"

I shrug.

"I don't really know."

"What do you want to do?" Orie asks gently.

Erik has already made the decision. "We're leaving," he says, but Orie ignores him.

"No. This isn't about your ego. It's about Sophie. What *she* wants to do," Orie says with a wave of his hand at a visibly upset Erik. "This is her one chance to have real closure *or* something else."

"Something else?" I ask, as hope grows inside. *What am I thinking?* I squash it immediately.

"Yes," Orie says. "Sophie, think about it. Put your anger aside and just look at all the trouble he went through to get you here at his fucking unbelievable chateau. I mean, really? I had no idea how rich the son of a bitch was, but goddamn. *He's sick rich.*"

"I really don't care about that part of him, Orie," I say honestly. "It's nice, obviously. But it doesn't matter. Actually, to be frank, this kind of rich scares me."

"Doesn't scare me," Erik says without hesitation as he sits down on the bed and leans back.

"I could definitely acclimate," Orie agrees.

I close my eyes and try to think rationally. What do I want to do?

Run back into his arms and beg him to take you to bed.

Shit.

"Honestly, Sophie. Don't you want to know? He wouldn't have gone through all this trouble if he didn't give a shit about you," Orie continues. "And maybe nothing happened between him and the whore. Maybe we all overreacted and made assumptions. You're the one who's always telling us about that book *The Four Agreements*. Isn't never making assumptions one of the cardinal rules?"

A nagging seed of guilt begins to grow.

I hear Erik sigh. "Orie's right," he says. "We could be wrong about him. And what he's done now is pretty damn extreme. I'm still pissed off at him for using me. I mean, he could have called, because that would have been a hell of a lot easier. But I do think you have to talk to him. Think about how miserable you've been. How utterly fucking rock bottom and depressing as shit—"

"Erik—" Orie says gently.

Leave it to Erik to sum up my behavior perfectly. I can't blame the guy. Especially when he only speaks the truth.

I have been pretty rock bottom.

"And don't forget that Abby actually wanted you for your *mad* skills. I'm the token hire here," Erik reminds me sarcastically.

"Erik's right," Orie says as he nods in agreement.

"Jesus. That's harsh," Erik says.

"Sorry, babe."

I look at both of them and think about how I will feel if I never know what really happened between Clayton and Amelia. Then I also think about the job and how much I need it for so many reasons. And then I make my decision.

"Alright," I say halfheartedly. "We'll stay."

"And that doesn't mean you get to hide in your room and avoid a confrontation," Erik tells me. "It means you act like a goddamn woman, take a nap

Unpack. Eat something and then you'll get your ass downstairs for the cocktail party tonight."

"What cocktail party?" I ask.

"The one we're invited to, downstairs in the ballroom—have you ever? They have a goddamn ballroom in this place," Erik says in awe, then reverts to his commanding voice. "And I'm pretty sure *everyone* will be there, and by everyone I mean *him*. So you're coming." He stands up and looks around at my room. "Wear the navy dress."

"Jesus," he sounds outraged. "I hope our room looks like this. Look at her view."

"It's probably Clayton's room," Orie says to placate him. "It has a master suite kind of vibe."

I sit up immediately and finally take in my surroundings. The four-poster antique bed is huge. Giant. And the room is extremely masculine, done simply, too simply compared to the rest of the house, in whites and dark navy blues. A navy couch sits at one end, flanked by two navy cushioned chairs. A large mahogany desk faces a window that looks out on the land and there is a hall that I think must lead to the bathroom and closet. Erik is right. The room is enormous. And incredibly masculine.

My body lights up at the thought of being in his personal bedroom. Sleeping in his bed.

"Whore," Erik interrupts my thoughts with a laugh.

I know I'm blushing when I look up at him.

"What?" I hope I don't look guilty.

"Go ahead. Imagine having sex with him in that massive bed. But be ready by six which is only a few hours from now,," Erik says as he grabs Orie's hand and the two walk out.

"Wait—" I call out, suddenly unsure about it all.

"You made your decision," Erik calls out before leaving me alone.

"Take a shower and definitely straighten your hair," Orie says as he shuts the door.

For the first time I immediately do as I'm told.

We're led by attendants through a massive library, through a sitting room, and toward the ballroom. Some of Abby and her fiancé, Dimitri's posh friends are in the various rooms. They're talking amongst each other and sipping on champagne that servants are busy passing out. They are clearly at home in these surroundings. A woman's soulful voice echoes down the corridor. She sounds a lot like Cesaria Evora, who has always been one of my favorites. There are flowers in every room and all are white and very elegant. In fact, everything is very tastefully done.

We stop just outside the ballroom, and my gaze searches for Clayton among the guests. But he's nowhere to be seen. I turn to Erik, who's on my right, and whisper under my breath.

"How do I look?" I ask, even though it's the third time I've inquired since we left my room.

Erik looks down and gives me a huge smile and doesn't make an issue out of it. "Gorg. Aren't you glad I packed for you?"

"Oh, my god, yes," I tell him as I look down at the short, navy blue lace dress that he chose for me to wear tonight. It's long-sleeved, with a high neck in the front that scoops low in the back. The dress fits like a glove. Because it's cold, I chose to wear nude nylons with nude Louboutin heels. As directed, my hair has been straightened and falls way past my shoulders. Orie came and helped me with my make-up, using golden colors and thick black mascara to enhance my green eyes. I'm not going to lie, I do think I look good. I'm definitely confident enough to confront Clayton.

Erik takes two champagne glasses from a passing waiter and hands one to me. I smile at him gratefully. He then picks one up for Orie.

"Liquid courage," he tells me before clinking my glass. "Bottoms up."

I take a healthy sip before we walk into the ballroom. I'm literally blown away by the opulent room. The walls are all frescoed with Renaissance imagery. Tall tables are set throughout the room, covered in fabulous white lace cloth and elegant white flower arrangements. The band is playing romantic French music in the corner, and I spot Abby and the man I assume is her fiancé, Dimitri, dancing to the soft ballad. There are more than fifty people in the room and it doesn't feel remotely full. It's big enough to fit at least another hundred people.

"Gorgeous," Orie says as he takes in the ambiance.

I agree, but I'm too busy searching for Clayton to get the words out.

And then like in a movie, the crowd moves apart and I spot him.

My heart stops.

He's standing at one of the tables with a cocktail in hand, dressed in a black fitted suit with a white-collared, cuff-linked shirt underneath. The top two buttons are undone, making him look more roguishly handsome. His light brown hair is brushed back from his tanned face and his blue gaze is focused on a blonde bombshell who looks to be hanging on his every word.

Confident, Sophie. Be confident. You are no shrinking violet, I tell myself.

Erik and Orie spot him and immediately turn to me with worried looks, probably thinking that I'm about to have some form of a nervous breakdown because he's talking to another woman. Given my behavior in the past, I can't blame them.

"I'm good," I say with a forced smile, even though I really am not great. I'm far from it. *Why did I put myself in this situation again?*

"Want another glass of champagne?" Erik asks, nodding at my empty flute.

Wow. I didn't even realize I drank the entire thing. Go figure.

"Yes, please. And maybe we should hang out in one of the other rooms because it's—" I try to finish my sentence but I'm interrupted by Orie.

"Too late. He's staring right at you and is making his way over here right now."

"He's wearing Tom Ford," Erik whispers. "The man really does have impeccable taste."

I know.

My heart goes a mile a minute. Erik hands me his champagne flute and I take a sip, hoping the bubbles will work their magic. Lord, do I ever need it.

"Gentlemen," I hear his husky voice as he greets Erik and Orie.

"Clayton," Orie says.

And then I want the floor to open up and swallow me whole because Erik literally makes me break out in a cold sweat.

"I can't tell you how thrilled I am to see you," Erik says, and gives him a fake smile before adding: "Clearly that's sarcasm at its best."

I can't even bring myself to look up at Clayton. I just stare at my friend with what I'm sure is an incredulous expression on my face.

"What?? Erik says. "Do you want me to lie or tell the truth?" he asks me. "At least I didn't say I almost threw up in my mouth when I caught sight of him. Now *that* would have just been rude."

My mouth is now hanging open.

"Fair enough," Clayton says smoothly. "Allow me to repair the damage to my character. But first, Sophie and I need to talk privately, if you don't mind."

Before I know it he's grabbed hold of my arm and is leading me away from the safety of my friends. His touch causes shock waves to rush through my body.

I need a drink! I need to be drunk for this!

As we walk, I say the first thing that comes to mind as I quickly glance up at his inscrutable face. "I thought we decided that we weren't going to speak until tomorrow."

"That's when I thought you had jet lag and would just rest in your room." I can't tell what he's thinking, if he's angry or annoyed that I've come down to the party.

We walk out of the ballroom and I pull my arm from his.

"I can follow you just fine."

He looks down at me and I see the icy resolve in his eyes. Now I can tell he's pissed. I meet his gaze evenly.

"This way," he says as he moves his hand to the small of my back and we walk down a hall. His hand rests against my bare skin and I feel like I'm burned by fire. Before I know it we are in a room that looks like a smaller version of the giant library we walked through on the way to the ballroom.

I hear the ominous sound of the door clicking behind him. And now we're all alone. He crosses his arms and lean back against the door, as if guarding it from me making an exit. As if I could outrun him? I feel like a trapped bird.

His gaze sweeps over me.

From our previous encounters I'm guessing he doesn't like the length of my dress, which I'm not going to lie, is part of the reason why I wore it tonight. Yes, I was looking for a reaction from him, and yes, I did just get one.

"Well?" I say, when it's clear that he has no intention of breaking the awful silence. His eyes hold mine and I see the anger flash through them again.

"I'm so furious with you I don't even know where to begin," Clayton says in a dangerous voice.

I instinctively step back in fear.

He gives me a smile that doesn't quite reach his eyes. And then takes a step away from the door.

I cross my arms, too, and do my best to look irritated. And confident. I hope I'm not failing miserably. I finally say, "*You're* furious with me?"

Clayton takes another step toward me then looks at his cuff and picks off an imaginary piece of lint. He takes his time, methodically turning me into a giant piece of mush. Intentionally unnerving me. My heart is pounding so hard I don't even know what to do. He's so gut-wrenchingly gorgeous that I want to lose myself in him, want to believe that I made one god-awful assumption. But then there's the other side of it, the one that makes me remember Amelia and what she looked like, and their past, and then I'm deathly afraid that I'll believe a liar.

He finally looks up at me.

"Furious doesn't even begin to fucking cut it, Sophie."

Shit.

"But right now I just need to take what's mine. What I've been dying to have since the moment I watched you upstairs."

I don't have time to think. Or breathe. Because in less than three seconds I'm pulled into his arms and his lips capture mine. I don't have the energy or the desire to stop him. My arms curl around his neck as I allow him to cup my bottom and pull my body up against his. I can feel how hard he is for me and I instinctively grind my hips into his.

It's heaven.

It's hell.

And everything in between.

Because I want more. Crave more. Need more.

His tongue sweeps into my mouth as he unleashes the force of his passion. I respond just as fiercely as my fingers move through his hair and I pull his mouth harder into mine. God, I've missed him. Missed the warmth of his skin. Missed the intimacy. Missed the way he took control of me. Held me. Like he cherished me. And so I pull him even closer.

Our kiss is openly carnal and wild. I've lost all ability to care because I just want more. And he answers my need with a passion that perhaps even surpasses my own. And even though there is so much between us, so much that probably will never be, there is something about his touch, his smell, his *being* that speaks to my soul. My body knows it. And somewhere in my heart, so do I.

He finally pulls back from me and sets me down, stepping away, robbing me of the magic of his touch. I almost cry out in frustration as I take in deep breaths and try to get a grip. And pull myself back to reality.

What did I just do?

I notice with some satisfaction that Clayton is breathing just as heavily as I am.

"I want you in my bed."

And just like that he sucks the breath right out of me. I look up at him, trying to get my thoughts in order, but it's a bad idea. The look in his eyes is so full on that it robs me of even more of the little sanity I have left. But I close my eyes and hide from it. Take a deep breath in and calm my raging hormones. Try to turn my heart to ice.

And remember the feeling of seeing that magazine in the airport after he made me believe in a crazy kind of love.

When I meet his gaze I'm strong Sophie again. I remember the line from Marianne Williamson's *A Course in Miracles*: "Nothing real can be threatened." If this was real or if my love for him was real why had a picture in a magazine threatened it?

"That's too bad for you," I tell him.

His narrows his eyes.

"Is it?"

The way he enunciates those two words gives me the chills, but I don't back down.

I continue to meet his cold gaze.

"Nothing happened with Amelia."

Talk about engine failure. If I were a plane I would plummet to the ground right now. I realize I really don't want to have this conversation with him. Not now. Not ever. But I know I have to. Because I have to look in his eyes and know either way. This is me, Sophie Walker, wearing my big girl pants.

"Have you heard of the saying, where there's smoke there's fire?" I ask him.

I see his jaw tick. I'm guessing he doesn't like my comment.

"I told you I was there for business. I had a business lunch at the Ritz and Amelia happened to show up. And if you remember, I rushed back to see *you.*" He sounds annoyed. "You know, Sophie, I have never explained myself to anyone in my life. And I don't particularly enjoy doing it."

I get a rush from his words.

"I'm not asking you to explain anything," I say, hoping I don't sound breathless.

"If I don't explain we can't move past this."

He's slowly chipping away at my wall and I know I have to build it back quickly before he seizes the castle.

"I've already moved on," I lie boldly.

"Really?" Clayton asks as he takes a dangerous step closer to me. His possessive gaze sweeps over my face and stops on my parted lips. Yes, they're parted. I can't help it. The man turns me on.

If he touches me I'm a goner. So I hold up my hand.

"Please don't come any closer." I'm sure he can hear the plea in my voice.

"Nothing happened with Amelia. She was in Singapore on business. The Ritz-Carlton is where she always stays."

Oh, does she? The irrational thought that he knows where Amelia always stays in Singapore pisses me off.

"You two looked extremely cozy in that picture," I blurt out before I can stop myself.

"We were together for a year, Sophie. She's not an enemy." Clayton's voice is harsh.

"How convenient for you."

"Goddamnit!" Clayton curses and runs a hand through his hair. "I'm through defending myself against an indiscretion that *did not even happen.*"

My adrenaline rushes at the sight of his anger. But the thought of him believing he has a right to be even remotely upset at me goads me on.

"Listen, Clayton, does it really matter if something happened or not? Let's say you're telling the truth and I was wrong. It still doesn't change our circumstance," I tell him softly. "It doesn't change the fact that you live in another country clear across the world and I live in Los Angeles. And not to mention," my voice trails off.

"Not to mention what?" His voice is cold, devoid of emotion.

I motion around the room. "This place," I begin to say, knowing I sound incredibly gauche. "We come from two completely different worlds."

"Sophie—" he begins.

"And it's not just that," I rush on. "It's that I don't even know you—"

"You know me in the most intimate of ways," Clayton says.

I know I'm blushing now.

"No," I continue. "I don't *know* you. I don't know what makes you tick—"

He takes a step toward me, invading my space. His gaze captures mine and my pulse flutters at the intensity I see in them.

"Right now, *you* are. You are what makes me tick."

There goes my heart again. Why does he have to say something so damn perfect? I look away from him, knowing my eyes are about to well up with tears from the emotion I feel from his words. From the absurd feeling of happiness they give me.

"For how long?" I ask, pushing on. Knowing that this is the best thing I can do for myself. This is the best way I can protect my heart from him.

There's an awful silence after I ask him this question and I know that I've thrown him.

"I don't know," he tells me honestly. "I've never felt this way before. I've never lost sleep over a woman before. No one has ever made me so furious and so fucking turned on at the same time."

I stare at him.

"But I don't know what that means," he admits, his eyes bright with confusion.

His confession thrills me. It does something to my insides. It makes me feel powerful. And desired. *So desired.*

But still.

"I don't know what to say to you," I say. "I don't know what you want me to say."

"I want you to believe me."

I stop breathing as he holds my gaze. Do I trust him? Do I think he actually slept with Amelia? Or have my massive insecurities led me down this sick path?

"I don't know what to believe."

He hates my answer. I can see it. Feel it all around me. And his reaction to me proves it. He takes a step back.

"If you don't trust my word after all that I've done, I don't know what else to say to you." His translucent blue eyes burn into mine.

His words sound so final. Is this what I want?

Wake the fuck up, Sophie, my mind shouts at me. *This is not what you want! You don't want him to turn around and leave your life forever.*

While I continue on with my inner dialogue I hear Clayton speak again.

"I'm sorry for inconveniencing you," he says politely as he turns around to walk out the door.

And then I react.

"Wait!"

He stops, his back still toward me. I step close to him and touch his arm and my fingers tingle from the brief intimacy. I can feel the muscles tense under my hand and it pleases me to know that my touch affects him just as much as his affects me.

"I just," I say frantically, "I just need time. Everything that happened between us happened so fast, and maybe that was, or *is*, the problem. I don't understand how to ride this storm."

When he turns and meets my gaze, his look is guarded.

"Let me show you."

And then he walks out of the room.

4

I slept like shit.

After Clayton left me I went back to the ballroom to let Erik and Orie know that I was going to bed. There had been no sign of Clayton in the ballroom, so I guessed he had excused himself from the party as well, which did secretly make me happy. I took a long bath in his rock crystal bathtub. Yes, a rock crystal bathtub. I took a picture of it after I filled the thing with water because it was so incredible and I wanted to memorialize the experience. I never even knew that such a tub existed. It was completely unreal, but to be honest, I was grateful for the extravagance because it was amazingly relaxing. One thing was for certain: the man clearly liked the finer things in life.

I sat in the scented water for over an hour and replayed our conversation in my head.

I've never felt this way before.

Was that the truth? My gut instinct told me it was. My gut instinct told me that I had been so wrong about everything,, needlessly torturing myself and screwing things up. But still, even if that was the case, it didn't change the fact that we were from two different worlds. With two different lives. And we literally led those lives across an ocean and a continent from each other. Maybe *that* was my problem. Even in the Maldives I had thought about what came after for us. And he still didn't have an answer to that. If I chased after another fling with Clayton, it would still have the same outcome. Me, in Los Angeles. Him, jet-setting around the world.

Then I pushed all the thoughts out of my head and tried to go to sleep. But my mind was plagued all night—and even now, in the morning—by one all-consuming fact.

My desire. The *need* I have for him is staggering. How am I going to stay away from him for two weeks? How am I going to control myself?

It's very early and I'm wide awake, so I decide to shower and get dressed. I put on jeans and a camel-colored sweater and go to my work room. After a while of prepping, I get antsy and take another tour around Clayton's home for a closer look. It's very Old World, of course. There are oil paintings that look as if they date back to the thirteenth century and in some parts of the chateau even the floors feel antique. I feel like I've stepped back in time and am in another era. All I need is a long, heavy medieval dress and I would fit right in.

I wonder if he knows how lucky he is to have grown up surrounded by so much history. The home is so inspiring. It calls to my creative soul. And of course, I'm obsessed with all the art I see as I wander around. The paintings I've seen are all remarkable.

I get lost down one of the long corridors and find a painting of the chateau in the summer and I can't bring myself to move away from it. It's big, ten by ten at least, and it looks so real. The artist really captured the exact likeness of the home. I simply love it.

I finally force myself to walk away and do a bit more exploring. I enter what I think must be Clayton's study, where there is a massive desk with a breathtaking view of the vineyard behind it, and I can literally picture him working there. I suddenly feel like an intruder. Even though I know this is probably only one of his many homes, I kind of feel like I'm encroaching on his personal space, sort of spying on him, and so I quickly leave. I decide to grab my camera and go for a walk outside around the estate. I find my room, put on my warm oversized wool beanie and black puffer jacket, and go down the stairs and out.

It rained last night, so there is a nice dewy smell in the air that is super refreshing. I find the Olympic-size pool, walk across manicured lawns that remind me of Russell Crowe's home in *Gladiator*, and then I find myself on a dirt path that is shrouded by trees. I follow it and it takes me up a hill. I wish I brought my iPod so I could listen to one of my self-help tapes. I'm currently on *Only Love Is Real* by Dr. Brian Weiss. It's about past-life loves being reincarnated together again and again. I wonder if Clayton and I are karmically connected through our past lives. I can just picture his face if I asked him that question. Ha! Now that would definitely send him running for the hills.

I reach an area where the greenery is cleared and I can take in the view of the valley that's now below me. The clouds sit low over the chateau and though the sky is gray there is a feeling of romance that makes me feel alive. I take my camera out and start to photograph the beautiful vista. I'm so lost in the moment that I'm completely caught by surprise when someone behind me grabs my arm. I can't stop my shriek of fear. I turn around and stumble a bit but am steadied by a pair of strong arms.

I look up and stare at eyes as blue as the ones I've come to obsess over. But Clayton's hair is light brown, and these eyes are framed by jet-black lashes and onyx hair that is long and held back by a rubber band, revealing his startlingly handsome, but very rugged and masculine face. His five o'clock shadow only adds to his good looks.

"Are you okay?" he asks me in a deep voice. His accent is eerily similar to Clayton's.

I manage to nod that I'm okay as I take him in. He's wearing a North Face black puffer jacket and a pair of old jeans. He seems to be as tall as Clayton and to have the same kind of build.

"Are you a friend of Abby's or Dimitri's?" he asks.

"Neither," I say as I shake my head.

"Neither?" He seems surprised by my answer.

Shit. He must think I'm trespassing. Nice one, Sophie.

"I mean, I've been hired to paint the portrait of Abby," I explain.

"An American artist?" he says, and his smile is flirtatious.

God. He's gorgeous. But he doesn't make my heart skip a beat the way Clayton does.

"Yes," I say.

He holds out his hand and I take it.

"I'm Michael Sinclair."

My mouth drops open. Clayton's brother. Fuck. Of course he is. Look at those wolf eyes. The gene pool in this family is out of this world.

"Have I grown horns? Because the look on your face just beat the hell out of my ego."

"I'm sorry," I rush out, hoping I don't sound like a big idiot. "I just, I've met your brother. I mean... I know him."

Intimately.

Oh, my god.

Michael's brow goes up as he looks me up and down before his gaze settles on my face.

"Clayton does have amazing taste, I'll give him that."

I am positive that my face is bright red. Positive. Like one hundred percent sure.

"We're not... I mean, we're," I stammer out. "We're just friends—or, I don't know, acquaintances."

Mortifying.

Michael's knowing gaze meets mine.

"Does that mean you're available?"

What is it with these men? Who are their parents? What was in their food growing up? How did they become so confident?

Umm, they're gorgeous, you moron!

"No— I mean, yes." I officially sound like an idiot.

"Yes or no?"

"No. Yes." Arghhh!

Michael throws back his head and roars with laughter and I'm not going to lie, it's pretty damn sexy. He seems much more free-spirited than Clayton, but if I remember correctly, this is the brother who is off saving the world.

"So you're the one," he gives me a soft smile.

"I'm sorry?"

"The one who has my brother tied up in knots," he says. "I'm happy to finally meet you."

Hope blooms like flower petals opening up to the sun.

"You know, you shouldn't come out here alone," Michael admonishes me. "We have security on the land, but sometimes hunters illegally cross the lines and it can be unsafe. Let me escort you back."

Now he sounds like his brother.

"I'm a big girl," I tell him.

"My brother would kill me if I left you out here alone. I won't allow you to refuse me."

I decide not to argue because from experience I'm pretty sure it won't do any good. Michael Sinclair will have his way.

He is incredibly easy-going and polite. He's also an expert at small talk, and fills the silence by telling me about the non-profit wildlife animal rights foundation he's started and his work to clean contaminated ground water. He's pretty passionate about it all and his relaxed attitude puts me at ease, too. He asks me a few questions about my work, about dropping out of law school, and thankfully steers clear of any questions about his brother. I'm grateful. He also mentions that he got in last night after the party and spent many hours in the study with Clayton, drinking whiskey and catching up.

When we reach the chateau he says, "You must be hungry. Let's grab some breakfast."

"Sure," I say, because I am a little hungry and he happens to be great company.

He escorts me down a corridor into the dining room. There's a long, large, dark wood table that seats at least twenty. Across from it is a mouth-watering buffet set for a king. Workers move about the room filling coffee and tea for the few guests who are sitting at the table eating.

"Davis," Michael nods in the direction of a blond-haired man drinking tea.

"Michael," Davis replies with a fake smile. "Good to see you."

The man's brown eyes settle on me and I watch him check me out.

Michael puts his arm around my shoulder and pulls me close. "This is Sophie."

I smile awkwardly.

"Pleasure," Davis leers. I'm grateful for Michael's possessive arm. It makes me feel safe from Davis's gross behavior so I lean into it.

"She's fetching," he goes on to say as he undresses me with his eyes.

I feel Michael's body tense. There's a shuffling noise at the entrance to the dining room and we turn to see who it is. My heart skips a beat. It's Clayton. Looking too incredible for words. In the Maldives I only saw him in shorts and t-shirts, mostly with his shirt off, which was a sight to behold, for sure. But sophisticated Clayton is another kind of glorious. He's wearing dark blue jeans and a navy sweater with brown scruffy boots that give him a bit of an edge. He could model. Seriously. There is no doubt that he looks as good in clothes as he does without them.

His gaze holds mine then settles on the arm Michael has around my shoulder. If looks could kill Michael would be toast. But he meets his brother's gaze without fear. Clayton finally walks toward us.

"Clayton," Michael says warmly. "Sophie and I have spent the whole morning together."

I can feel my cheeks burning.

Clayton's face is perfectly composed but I can tell there is something savage brewing underneath. His hot stare finds mine and the look he gives me is one of pure ownership. Clearly the man still thinks he owns me.

He might.

"Having fun?" he asks.

"Yes," I tell him. "Thank you for asking."

Clayton gently pulls me away from Michael's hold.

"If you don't mind, Michael, I'd like to have a word with Sophie."

"Can't it wait until after she eats?" Michael asks evenly. "She's famished after our hike."

I don't miss the use of the word "our." Clayton's jaw ticks.

"It won't take long."

Right. He always has to get his way and I don't feel like arguing with him in front of his brother even though every encounter I've had with him in France starts with him leading me to a secluded room. I look apologetically at Michael and then we walk out of the dining room and down another hallway. Moving too quickly for me to react, he corners me against a wall. I have nowhere to go. Not that I want to. He leans in nice and close, his eyes intense.

"Don't you have work to do?" There's a definite edge to his voice.

"I prepped this morning, Clayton," I say, irritated. "And besides, even hired help can go on walks."

His eyes widen at my words.

"That's not what I meant—"

"Then what did you mean?" I glare at him.

"My brother is a charmer," Clayton says slowly as his eyes sweep over my face. I feel the heat from his proximity. I can't help but stare at his lips. Why do I always have to be so obvious?

"He's nice," I agree.

Clayton is silent for a moment. Our faces are inches apart, and his scent, his closeness is driving me crazy.

"Is he?" he whispers as he moves his hand up to the wall, essentially trapping me again. His mouth moves down close to mine. He's literally a whisper away. I can almost taste his lips.

I barely manage to nod.

If possible, he moves in closer. "So did you think about what I said?"

Huh? What is he talking about?

"Last night, Sophie," He sounds amused. "Us."

It takes me a moment to regain my bearings and remember what it is he's referring to.

"I don't know," I whisper back. "I want—"

My voice trails off because I forget what it is I want as he seductively moves his body closer. He rubs his cheek against mine; his lips brush my skin, teasing me mercilessly.

"What do you want?"

You. I want you. Now. Upstairs. On your giant bed. Or in the rock crystal bathtub. Or in a hole. I'll take it however I can get it.

"Umm," is the only word I can manage.

"Tell me," he commands.

"I want more, Clayton," I finally say. "I want to know everything about you." And that is the truth.

That is what I want right after he takes me to bed and has his way with me.

He moves his lips against mine but doesn't kiss me. No, he just whispers into my mouth. The man is a walking sex god.

"You want to know me?" he says. "Then you need to know what you do to me first."

And with that he pulls me up against his body so I can feel *exactly* how I affect him.

My traitorous body burns with desire. I'm overcome by him in every way. An ache begins to build inside. One that I know only he can satisfy. His translucent eyes sear into mine, begging me to let him in.

And oh how I want to.

"Clayton—"

"Sophie."

I close my eyes against the intensity I see in his.

"Don't hide from me."

"I can't help it," I whisper back.

"Please," he says, surprising me, "open your eyes."

And I do.

I look up at him and all the memories of our time together flood through my mind and body. I relive snippets of every moment in the Maldives. Everything. From the time on the private island to the time we spent alone in his bungalow. Everything.

"I want to show you something today," he says intensely.

The logical thing to do is to say no. To stay far away from the possibility of being alone with him at any time. That would be the smart thing to do. Which is exactly why I'm going to do just the opposite.

"Okay," I tell him. "But I have some more prep work to do and I need to sit down with Abby and talk to her about what she has in mind."

He lifts his hand and looks at his silver Rolex and I can't help but think how well it suits him. I never knew a watch could be so sexy on a man's wrist.

"Is three hours enough time? That's just about when lunch will be prepared."

I can only nod.

The smile he gives me is dangerous. "Shall I come to your bedroom to collect you?"

Yes. I'll be waiting in my bed. Naked.

"Sure."

"Dress warm," he commands, then brushes a kiss on my forehead and leaves me.

So much for naked.

After my run-in with Clayton I skipped breakfast and asked Clayton to give my apologies to Michael, then came straight upstairs to tell my friends about everything that just happened.

"I sincerely hope you got a bikini wax in LA," Erik said.

"We're not having sex, Erik. He's taking me somewhere," I tell him as I lounge on the sofa in the dressing room they're using for Abby's wardrobe. Erik and Orie are busy putting outfits, matching jewelry, and shoes together.

"To pleasure island," Orie says with a laugh.

"At least have the decency to blush," Erik admonishes me.

"That's not happening."

Yet.

"You're a bad liar, Sophie. I'm really disappointed in you," Erik says as he holds up a crème Herve Leger dress. "This would look great on you. Fit your body like a glove."

"Can't afford it but nice try," I say automatically.

"She'll be eating ramen noodles in no time with that outlook," Erik mutters to Orie as he puts the dress back on a rack.

"What's that supposed to mean?" I ask.

"It means I'm sick of your depressing-as-shit attitude. It's time for you to wake the fuck up and be happy and be goddamn grateful for what you have. I've got to be honest, lately I feel like when you walk into a room you need your own depressing soundtrack."

My mouth drops open in outrage.

"Erik, that is the rudest thing you have ever said to me!"

"Doubtful," he thinks about it. "I've definitely said worse."

I cross my arms and try to remember all the quips I've heard from him over the years and then it hits me.

"Freshman year in college," I remember now.

Erik nods. "When you had a muffin top."

"That was a blip in time—" I argue as I remember the freshman fifteen that I almost put on.

"Only a blip because I prevented you from becoming a *blimp*," Erik says pointedly. "I deserve a thank you. I'm only trying to protect you from yourself. Sometimes you're your own worst enemy."

I look at Orie,,"Is it true? Do *you* think I need my own soundtrack?"

"Like a James Blunt song maybe," Orie admits.

"Oooh, that's a good one." Erik clearly agrees.

"You know, I really resent your comments. I was a twenty-three-year-old virgin who gave it up on a vacation to the world's most perfect guy who turned out not to be so perfect, or so I thought," I start to rant. "And I was and maybe still *am* in love with him. And all of it happened in eleven days! Eleven days! So forgive me if I haven't been the picture of happiness. I think all things being said and done, I'm doing pretty damn well."

Erik and Orie stare at me.

"Finally!" Erik shouts out after a minute. "You've grown some balls! Do you have any idea how long I've waited for this day to come?"

I get up and make my way to the door.

"I'm going to leave now."

"Use some of that fire in the bedroom. Clayton will love it," Erik calls out after me as I slam the door shut.

I quickly walk toward my workroom determined to be happy and jovial just to spite Erik and find Abby waiting there.

"Oh, hi, Abby," I say with a bright smile.

"Hi, Sophie," Abby replies politely. "I'm actually surprised that you're greeting me so kindly."

"What do you mean?" I ask as I step into the room and face her.

"My little part in Clayton's plan," Abby says. "He told me you know the truth. I plan on going to see Erik right after I sit with you."

"Abby," I begin, hoping to put her at ease, "I know how convincing Clayton can be. I've experienced it firsthand."

"Yes, well, my cousin always gets what he wants," Abby says. "I didn't realize that it was all about you until I saw you."

"What do you mean?" I ask confused.

"I was asked to hire Erik as a favor to Clayton and he told me he'd foot the bill, which was very generous of him. And Dimitri and his family didn't mind."

The Russian oligarchs.

"Clayton is letting us use his chateau for the wedding and has been beyond giving," Abby continues in an apologetic voice, "so I agreed. Dimitri had his people book Erik for me so it wouldn't be so obvious. And after seeing Erik's portfolio and meeting him in person, I'm so happy that I did go along with the plan. His demeanor, as I'm sure you know, is extremely fun to be around."

"Very," I agree.

Except when he compares your energy to a depressing song.

"Then Erik sent pictures of your paintings and the rest is history," she says. "I just want you to know that I did hire you because I genuinely love your work. When I told Clayton about it, he was so pleased. At the time I couldn't understand why, but then I saw you in person and it all clicked in my head."

"What do you mean?" I ask her.

"You're beautiful," Abby says with a smile. "I don't know. I'm a woman. I just had a feeling."

I can't believe Abby is revealing all this to me. She must really be feeling guilty. But Lord, do I appreciate it.

"So please don't be mad at me," Abby says gently.

"I'm not mad at you at all," I tell her honestly. "I swear. But I have to admit that I am thankful you've shared this with me. It definitely makes everything feel a bit better."

I can see that Abby is relieved.

And then in a flash she's back to being extraordinarily polite. It's a trait I noticed in Elizabeth and Jane, even Clayton. One second you could completely read a face, whether it showed disdain or friendliness, and the next there was an aloofness, like all the posh training that occurred in childhood was back in full force.

"Well, then, if you'll excuse me I'd like to go and speak to Erik. I was hoping I could sit for you tomorrow around noon and we could go over everything then? I don't think there's much we have to discuss in terms of what Dimitri wants. I think you'll get the idea when you see me tomorrow in my costume."

"That sounds perfect."

Abby walks to the door but pauses when her hand is on the doorknob. She turns to face me and asks, "Can I tell you something, Sophie? Woman to woman?"

"Anything."

"I've never seen my cousin like this before. And I mean *ever*. There have been many women in his life, but he's never gone to this extreme. I don't know what's going on between you or what transpired in the past," Abby says, "but don't give up on him. He's not easy, I know. And he's a bit intimidating. But he's a good man. And the Sinclair men had an unusual childhood," Her voice trails off.

I wonder if she's referring to the shuttling back and forth between their parents. Something inside says no. There's a nagging feeling in my gut that tells me there's more to it than what little Clayton has shared with me of his childhood.

"I've said too much." Abby looks horrified by her words. "I'm sorry."

"I won't say anything, Abby," I reassure her. "I won't betray your confidence."

"Thank you, Sophie." She smiles at me. "I'll see you tomorrow then. Enjoy the rest of your day."

5

There's a knock on my door at exactly noon.

I take a quick look in the mirror and am happy with what I see. I've left my hair down and I'm wearing dark blue skinny jeans with knee length brown suede boots. I have a brown turtleneck on and a short brown coat. Lucky for me, I'm pretty well prepared for any situation that's thrown my way.

I take a deep breath and open the door.

Clayton hasn't changed. He's just added a long navy wool jacket and scarf, which he looks divine in. Gorgeous. The best part? He's holding a long-stemmed red rose in his hand.

My heart is beating a mile a minute. I wonder if he can sense my excitement or how incredibly happy I am to see him.

"Hi," I say.

I see a flash of pleasure in his eyes as he takes in my appearance.

"You look beautiful," he says.

That single look makes it so worth me changing three times. I take the rose from him and our fingers brush against each other, causing fire to burn through my body.

"Thank you," I tell him.

"Shall we?" he asks, and extends his hand. I hesitate for a brief moment before I let him lead the way.

We're both quiet as we make our way through the home. Sergei is outside to greet us.

"Miss Walker," Sergei says formally as he opens the door to a black Range Rover for me.

"Hello," I reply nervously. I'm really not used to this in-your-face wealth. It's kind of crazy.

I step inside and Clayton follows. Sergei gets into the front seat and drives us away. I look at Clayton's profile and know there's a good chance I'm probably drooling.

"Sergei picked us up in a different car before," I comment lamely, trying to fill the silence and distract myself from his incredible looks.

"The Maybach is Dimitri's car. He had it shipped over," Clayton says. "This one is mine."

I think the Range Rover suits him more. There's definitely a cool factor to it.

"So where are we going?" I ask.

"It's a surprise," he says with a smile.

Beautiful memories wash over me from the last time he surprised me with a trip. I stare out the window to avoid his knowing gaze even though I don't really need to look at him to feel the energy that's always pulsating between us.

Clayton's hand covers mine. He entwines our fingers and gently rubs my skin. The contact is all I need to get me hot and bothered in no time.

"Unfortunately, I'm not kidnapping you again," he tells me.

I wonder if he's a mind reader, too.

"Yet."

Holy shit.

His confidence only adds to his appeal. He's good, I'll give him that. He sure as hell knows how to knock any reservation I might have.

"Your brother is really nice." I change the topic to something not sexual. I turn to look at his handsome profile again.

"He's a heartbreaker," Clayton agrees as he pins me with his gaze.

"Like you?" I ask softly as I arch a brow.

In two point five seconds his demeanor changes from playful to aloof and I silently curse myself.

"I'm sorry," I say quickly. The last thing I want to do is start some type of weirdness and ruin what could potentially be a nice day.

He nods ever so slightly and looks straight ahead.

"We've arrived," he tells me as Sergei pulls into the parking lot of a huge medieval building.

"Where are we?" I ask curiously.

"Le Musée du Petit Palais," he tells me in the most perfect and sexy French accent. Clearly, he's a master of the language.

Let's be real, Sophie, I'm pretty sure he's the master of the universe.

"They have an incredible collection of Renaissance paintings that I thought you'd enjoy," Clayton tells me almost hesitantly, his eyes guarded.

"This is amazing, Clayton. Thank you. What a wonderful surprise," I say quickly because it's true. I'm taken aback and touched. So touched that he would bring me to a museum to show me an art collection.

Clayton smiles with pleasure. "I thought you would like it."

Sergei opens the door for me and I get out and make my way to Clayton. As if it's the most natural thing in the world, he takes my hand in his and kisses me lightly on the forehead. It's almost like we're a real couple.

Except we're not. We're in this weird limbo-land trying to figure everything out. But I tell myself there's nothing wrong with holding hands. It's safe. Okay, maybe not the way *he* holds hands, always rubbing my skin, drawing circles and caressing me, but I just want to be close to him.

"I know I shouldn't admit it but I do have a soft spot for Renaissance art," he says breaking my chain of thought as we begin to walk to the museum entrance.

"Why shouldn't you admit that?" I ask.

"I don't know if it's very masculine," he says with a wolfish smile.

Ummm, hello? He's like the most masculine man I've ever encountered in my life. What is he talking about?

"I think it's hot," I tell him instantly then look away in embarrassment.

Nice one, Sophie.

Talk about desperado.

"Well, in that case, I'm happy to show you around the collection," he says as he squeezes my hand. "I'll show you my favorite piece."

We spend the next two hours having an amazing time. I linger in front of paintings that I become entranced with and surprisingly Clayton appreciates the work as much as I do. I'm shocked by how much knowledge he has and how familiar he is with all the artists. It makes him even more appealing.

We find ourselves near the museum coffee shop, and the smell of the baguettes is seriously making my mouth water.

"You must be famished," Clayton says.

"I am pretty hungry, but I can wait until we get back home—" I say, then quickly add, "I mean, back to your chateau."

Did you really just say that?

"I like that you called it home." My heart slams inside my chest as I look up at him. "But we're not going back. I'm taking you to lunch and to taste some wine," he says. "If the plan had been for us just to come to the museum I would have driven myself."

Wine tasting.

Just the two of us.

Alcohol and Clayton in close proximity. *Bad idea, Sophie. You should go back to the chateau and be safe.*

"Sounds great," I say enthusiastically.

Believe it or not I have never been wine tasting before, even though I've lived in California all my life. I've definitely *consumed* plenty of wine, from French whites, to New Zealand, to a Bordeaux or an Italian Brunello... but I've never actually sat down and consecutively tried wine after wine after wine. And for the life of me I don't know why I've robbed myself of such an incredibly awesome experience.

The cheese.

The bread.

The buzz.

The man...

Crap. I don't get to taste or eat him but I can look. Oh, can I look.

We're in a quaint restaurant in the small town of Avignon eating, drinking, and laughing and really enjoying each other's company. There is no awkwardness, no references to the magazine article or to our relationship. We're both carefully avoiding any topic that might ruin our moment.

"Merci," Clayton tells the waiter as he sets another two glasses down.

"This is a Sancerre," he tells me as he pushes another taster glass toward me. "Try it. I think you'll really enjoy this—"

I gladly take it and have a sip. More than a sip, but who's paying attention?

"This is delicious."

He hands me a cracker with brie and a dollop of fig jam that is truly incredible. Honestly, I really think I've died and gone to cheese and wine heaven.

"This is decadent, Clayton," I say, savoring every bite.

We're side by side in a small booth in a secluded part of the restaurant. After the first glass of wine I began a pattern that has continued with every new glass: I scoot about half an inch closer to Clayton. At the rate I'm going I will be sitting on his lap in no time.

Of course he hasn't moved at all. But that hasn't stopped me. Something about alcohol and the false sense of confidence it gives has made me utterly bold. Our legs are now touching under the table, lightly grazing ever so often. It's such a turn-on. It's crazy that a single brush of a jean-clad leg can make me so hot. I feel like a teenager, not an experienced woman who's had mad sex with the man who happens to be sitting next to me.

"It's hard to believe that you've never done this before," he says as he picks up his glass. "But I am glad that so many of your first times are with me."

Talk about needing another glass of wine. Like pronto.

"So you and Abby must be close," I change the subject. Clayton laughs devilishly. I know he's enjoying my discomfort.

"She's a lot closer to Michael," he admits. "Michael is six years older than Abby and has always been very protective of her. She worshipped him her entire childhood, followed him around like his shadow. Actually, she's more like our little sister."

"Is she from your father's side?" I ask curiously.

"Yes. She's my uncle's step-daughter."

"So you're not blood related?" I'm surprised.

"No. But that doesn't change a thing," Clayton says. "We would do anything for her. She had a very lonely childhood. My blood cousin, her older brother, Davis, is a lot to handle."

I thought of the Davis I met early with Michael.

"Was he in the dining room this morning?" I ask.

Clayton gives me an inquisitive look. "Did you meet him?"

"Yes." I try to sound cool. I definitely know why Abby had such a tough childhood. Who would want him as an older brother? He gave me the creeps.

"So do you like Dimitri?" I ask, diplomatically changing the subject. I didn't get to meet him at the cocktail party last night, and only saw him from a distance, so I'm curious to know what Clayton thinks of him.

He shrugs. "Abby's marrying him, not me."

"Does that mean you don't like him?"

"It means I'd rather not talk about him," Clayton says seriously.

Definitely doesn't like him. His more-than-generous gesture of offering his chateau and all the perks that I have no doubt he's given to Abby seems even sweeter. He must really love her.

"Abby seems lovely," I tell him.

"She is wonderful," Clayton says. "That man is lucky to have her."

I don't miss the tone he takes when he refers to Dimitri as *that man*.

"So I take it your entire family is coming to this wedding?" I enquire, though I'm nauseous at the thought of being surrounded by the Sinclair clan.

"If my father can spare the time," Clayton says indifferently. "And my mother wouldn't miss the wedding for anything. She adores Abigail and she'll also use this as an opportunity to pester me about getting married."

Of course she will.

She must just be dying for you to procreate. I can just imagine what his kids will look like. Little boys or girls with those blue eyes, those lips, and that perfect symmetry... *Just stop, Sophie!* Picturing his children, or maybe what *my* children with him would look like is probably the worst thing I can do. I stop myself from going down that dangerous path and throw out the obvious question, one I'm dying to know the answer to, and one that the wine has made me daring enough to ask.

"Well, do you want to?" I ask, boldly throwing caution to the wind.

"Do I want to what?" His gaze is hooded as he stares at me. I know he's fully aware of what I'm asking and it irritates me no end that he won't answer, but I arch a brow in challenge.

"Get married."

"Are you asking me?" His voice is quite polite.

Oh. My. God.

My entire body turns red. From the tips of my toes to the top of my head. I just know. I sputter and try to come back with a suitable reply but the devil that is Clayton saves me.

"I'm only joking," he says with a laugh. "You should see your face."

"I wasn't aware you had a sense of humor," I tell him.

"Sometimes." His gives me a sexy smile then, "I've never given marriage a thought."

Meaning he's never *met* anyone who's made him give marriage a thought.

"And there's the answer," I say, hoping my voice doesn't sound dejected.

His blue eyes burn into mine. The look is so intense, it causes my breath to hitch.

"I didn't give a definitive reply."

"You didn't have to," I tell him with a playful smile.

"I take offense," Clayton says as he leans closer to me. "I could be the marrying kind."

Only in my dreams.

"Please," I try to laugh it off. "You're a thirty-something-year-old bachelor."

"You don't remember how old I am?" he asks curiously.

"I forget," I lie, shrugging my shoulders as if I have no idea what his date of birth and sign is.

Born in November. Scorpio. He's thirty-four. If I knew his time of birth I could figure out his rising sign, too.

"Liar."

The way he says it softens the sting.

I unconsciously lick my lips and watch with some satisfaction, okay, *a lot* of satisfaction, how his eyes flash with desire.

"I'm glad you're enjoying yourself," he says as his eyes darken.

"Aren't you?" I ask, suddenly uncertain because of the edge I heard in his voice.

His gaze slowly moves from my lips to my eyes and back up to my lips. I feel like I've been branded by fire. The look isn't just about desire. It's about ownership. Pure, male, Neanderthal-like ownership. And I realize I don't mind one damn bit.

"There are other things I'd rather be doing," he says softly. "But no one else I'd rather be with."

As if on some magical cue Brian Ferry's "Slave to Love" starts to play softly in the restaurant.

Holy cow.

Talk about the hottest song on the planet featured in one of the hottest movies ever made, *9½ Weeks.* I realize that the film is strangely reminiscent of my nine and half days with Clayton in the Maldives. Interesting. I can't wait to share that piece of information with Erik and Orie.

"What are you thinking about?" he asks.

Mickey Rourke and Kim Basinger having sex in front of the refrigerator and kind of wishing that we could have the same experience.

"Nothing."

Coward.

To my surprise he reaches out and cups my jaw in his large hand. He pulls my face up to his and I think he's going to kiss me. God, I want him to kiss me.

Instead he uses his other hand to bring a piece of chocolate to my lips. I open my mouth and he places the candy inside. I brush his finger with my tongue. His eyes light up.

"Do you like the way it tastes?"

The chocolate is fine. Whatever. His finger tastes so much better. I can't even answer him and I know my eyes say it all. He gets up suddenly and takes my hand, pulling me after him to the back of the restaurant, where there's a dark hall that leads to the bathrooms and a phone booth.

Before I know what's happening he pulls me into the phone booth and shoves the curtain shut and engulfs me with the sheer size of him. He grabs my hair and tugs hard, tilting my head up before his mouth consumes mine. His other hand reaches out and lifts me up against his body and I gladly wrap my legs around his waist and pull him closer with all my strength. The kiss devours me. Consumes me. Owns me. His tongue moves into my mouth and I feel like I've died and gone to sweet, Clayton Sinclair heaven.

I can feel how hard he is for me. I die. Literally. Die. I want him so badly I hurt. He rubs up against me as he deepens the kiss, moving his hand to cup my ass and pull me even tighter to him, using the friction, the seductive movement, to drive me insane.

It's madness.

But I realize it's the kind I need. And want more than anything.

He pulls his lips away and moves to kiss my neck. "God, I missed you."

"I missed you," I admit.

He still holds me up but pulls back so he can look at me.

"Nothing happened with Amelia," he says. "I will not say that again."

I search his face for evidence that differs from what my heart knows and then I nod.

"Okay," I say.

"Sophie, I don't know where we're going," he goes on to say, his voice uncertain, lacking the usual authority I'm accustomed to hearing. "I don't know why I can't get you out of my mind. Why I feel like you're in my blood. I didn't sleep for weeks. I didn't want to eat. To see anyone," he says. " I was so fucking furious with you, and with myself for even caring. But then you weren't going away. You weren't leaving my thoughts. And I had to have you back. No matter the consequence. *I had to have you back.*"

I can feel the moisture on my cheeks and I know tears are streaming down my face because I'm overcome by his words. He lets me down and uses his thumbs to wipe my tears away as he leans close to me.

"Play this out with me," he continues. "Let's see where the ride takes us."

He kisses me on my forehead and I have to close my eyes. All the feelings I have are consuming me. The love I have is flooding my heart and practically choking me. I knew this in the Maldives and I know it here. This is a man who can ruin me for life. Eleven days with him already proved that. He is a huge risk.

I've never enjoyed gambling.

But with him I want to roll the dice.

He kisses my eyes, my cheeks, my nose, my jawline. He protects me with his body, embraces me and pulls me into the warmth that he exudes and I let him.

"I'm not a patient man," Clayton says. "I've told you this before. I'll tell you again. I will have you."

I take a brief moment before I respond.

You've always had me. From the moment you set eyes on me. You can have me for as long as you want because no matter how hard I try to be strong there's something about you that makes me want to say yes.

That's what I want to say.

"Let's see how this time together goes," I answer instead.

"Fair enough," he says. That's not the best answer. Not exactly the declaration that I was hoping for but it's something.

"No more tears?" Clayton says gently.

"Don't make me cry and you won't see them," I say with a smile, praying to the gods above that I won't shed another tear over him again.

Somehow I know that is as likely as me voluntarily getting in a great white shark cage for fun.

6

"He's like a Mr. Darcy who walks, talks, and fucks like a porn star," Erik says.

He's in my room and we're lying on the bed facing each other. When Clayton and I got back to the chateau he told me he had work to do and would come find me after he was done. He also invited me to be his date tonight at a dinner that some count is throwing in honor of Abby and Dimitri's wedding. I was thrilled he asked and honestly, I can't wait to spend more time with him.

"Where do you come up with this shit?" I ask with a giggle.

Erik shrugs.

"How did Einstein come up with e equals m c squared? He just did," he says. "It's like me. I just do."

I can't help it. I burst out laughing. Erik sees the humor in it and joins in. His eyes obviously catch site of something on my teeth because he reaches out to brush it away, and says, "Are you saving this piece of food for a snack later?"

I laugh and shake my head.

"Did you get it?" I ask.

"Hard not to," he tells me. "So you're happy we stayed?"

"I am, but I'm still scared," I admit.

"So the whole Amelia magazine story is behind us?"

I nod.

"Dr. Goldstein will be thrilled," Erik mutters. "You should e-mail him."

"No doubt."

I smile then study my friend's face. "How are you?"

"Shit hot."

"I'm serious, Erik."

"I am, too," he tells me.

"Erik—" he knows I don't believe him. I know every single one of his moods. And I know when something isn't right.

"Alright," he begins slowly. "I'm not going to lie. I'm a little jet lagged and Orie and I have been bickering, which is unlike us, as you know. But I think we're both just cranky and tired."

"Are you sure that's it?" I ask, concerned, as I try to figure out if he *is* lying to me.

"I promise, Sophie. Jesus. This is what a real relationship is. You don't always get along," Erik tells me as if he's explaining it to a child. "But you love and fucking desire each other. And you know that even if you get into a fight you've got great make-up sex to look forward to."

Now that I know firsthand. But still—

Erik studies my face. "You're staring at me with crazy eyes."

"I am?"

"Full on cray town," Erik says.

God, he knows he me so well. Even when my mind is wandering and I'm going to kookoo land he can tell.

"What makes men stray?" I blurt out.

Where did that come from? Umm—*insecure city?*

"Why? I thought we were past the point of thinking he cheated with Amelia."

"I'm just asking," I say. "You were a player before Orie..."

"You cheat when it's not right. You get a wandering eye when the person you're with doesn't excite you mentally, physically, and emotionally. That's when you start to look for something that will make you feel alive again. But when you find the one, then you're good. No more searching. Because the thought of losing the one you're with makes you want to die."

The one. The infamous fabled partner who is supposed to be your other half. A mate your soul recognizes the moment you gaze into each other's eyes.

Dare I believe Clayton is *my* one?

"The odds of finding the one are not great," I tell him. "Do you know how lucky you are?"

"I do. Most people are in fucked relationships just going through the motions," Erik says. "But that's not going to be the case with you either."

"How do you know?" I ask softly.

"Because look at the first real sexual relationship you've attracted into your life. The man is crazy for you."

I can't stop my grin.

"He has to be, right?"

"Obviously," Erik tells me as he gets up to lean on his elbow. "By the way, I have a new favorite word. And it's French."

"I'm sitting on pins and needles."

"Trés."

"Trés?" I ask confused. "As in *very?*"

"Yes, but in French it sounds so much cooler, trés chic, trés gorg, trés pissterical."

We both bust out laughing.

"Try it," he urges.

"Trés stupide?"

"I'm telling you," Erik says with excitement, "I'm kind of obsessed."

There's a knock at the door before I can try out another trés phrase.

"I'll get that," he says jumping up in a flash. I wonder if it's Orie. I sit up and see Erik let in a woman carrying a tray of tea and yummy-looking pastries.

"Did you ask for this?" he asks me as she walks in the room and places the large tray on the coffee table.

I shake my head as the woman turns to face me.

"Monsieur Sinclair asked that I bring you some tea and sweets," she says pleasantly. "He thought you might be hungry."

I feel warm inside and touched that he is so considerate.

"Merci," I tell her. She leaves and Erik closes the door.

"He's not just crazy for you, Sophie," my friend tells me as he walks over and grabs a pastry. "The man has to be in love with you. The only thing is he might not know it yet."

I spend the next few hours before the dinner party obsessing about Erik's words to me. Can Clayton be in love with me? Do I dare even hope? Old Sophie would doubt that any man that hot could feel that way for her, but the new Sophie, which is who I'm desperate to be, keeps trying to tell myself, *why not?* It could happen. I mean, I'm kind of a catch, right?

I'm employed—

My evil twin's inner voice creeps up before I know it...

For now. Who knows when you'll find your next job?

That's beside the point! I'm smart—

You dropped out of law school. How smart can you really be?

But like Erik said, I got in! And I'm attractive—

You're no Amelia...

My inner voice sucks!

For every positive attribute I think about myself I instantly insert a negative point to counter it. Clearly, I have many more self-help tapes to go through before I'm my perfect self.

I decide to change my train of thought and think about something much more pleasant. Like my afternoon with Clayton. But before I can really get into it my phone vibrates with a text message.

I reach over and see the international number. I'm guessing it's one person.

And I'm right.

CLAYTON: Will you unblock my main number now?

I smile as I write back.

ME: Yes. But I have to ask Erik to do it for me.

CLAYTON: Bring your phone this evening and I will do it.

Control freak.

ME: Where are you?

CLAYTON: In a guest bedroom. Not too far from you.

I sigh and text.

ME: Did you give me your room?

CLAYTON: Yes.

Butterflies dance around in my stomach.

ME: Why?

CLAYTON: Because I want you to be in the best room in the chateau.

I take a moment before I type.

ME: You must miss your room.

He types quickly.

CLAYTON: Not my room, the beautiful woman who's sleeping in my bed, yes. Without a doubt.

God.

ME: Do you want it back?

CLAYTON: Only if you come with it.

He really is the master of the universe. I don't know what to write back. If Erik and Orie were here they would do it for me. Luckily, my phone vibrates again, saving me from having to reply.

CLAYTON: Of course with one stipulation.

ME: What's that?

CLAYTON: Naked. In my bed every night. Fucking hot!

The crazy in me wants to write, YES in all caps and with twenty-five exclamation points. But the cool in me knows that I have to pretend to be at least a tad demure.

ME: I get cold very easily. Remember, I am from Los Angeles.

I don't even have to wait a second.

CLAYTON: Don't worry baby, I'll make sure you're hot every night.

I'm one hundred percent positive he would make good on that promise.

ME: I don't doubt it.

CLAYTON: Then that settles it.

My heart is beating a mile minute.

CLAYTON: See you in a few hours, sweetheart.

That settles it? Does that mean what I think it means? It has to, right?

Clayton is moving in with me.

Shit.

Like double. Triple. Quadruple shit.

Way to play hard to get.

Oh shut up!

Later in the evening Clayton, Erik, Orie, and I are being driven by Sergei to Comte Georges de Banville's home. Clayton filled us in that Georges prefers to go by Georgie and that he's an old friend of Abby's. They went to boarding school together and are very close. We're also told, or warned, don't know which, that Georges has a great love for the finer things in life and that everything he does is excessive. I have no idea what Clayton means by this but I'm looking forward to finding out.

I'm not really surprised that Georgie is a comte or count given Clayton's own lofty title of viscount. Clayton told me that as the eldest son he carries the title until his father passes away, at which time he becomes an earl. His other brothers have the title of honorable. After I found out in the Maldives about him being a lord he told me all about the English peerage system and how a lord was the informal title, used instead of calling him viscount. It's still out of this world to think he has an actual title like the ones I read about in period romance novels. Since he doesn't act like it's a big deal I just go with it, even though to me it kind of is.

I look at him and think again how handsome he looks in his midnight blue three-piece suit with black lapels. It fits him like a glove and does wonders for his broad shoulders. I'm in the backseat of the Range Rover between Clayton and Orie. Erik's taken the front. Clayton casually touches my arm but hasn't reached out to take my hand. I wonder if it's because Orie is next to us.

I'm wearing a knee-length black dress that I feel like Audrey Hepburn in. It has a bit of a poof in the skirt and is sleeveless. It's one of my favorites and paired with platform Louboutin high-heeled black suede shoes it feels really sexy. Orie did my hair; he pulled it back in an elegant low ponytail, giving me a very classic look. I know Clayton loves what I'm wearing because his mouth practically dropped open when he saw me, and he said only one word, "Stunning." He definitely has a way of making me feel like I'm the most beautiful woman in the world.

But I do think we all look pretty great. As usual, Erik and Orie look incredible, both in black suits. According to Erik, his is in Saint Laurent and Orie is wearing Dior Homme. What else?

"Here we are," Clayton says as he motions toward the enormous medieval castle.

"Holy shit," Erik swears.

"It dates back to the eleventh century," Clayton tells us.

"It's really quite remarkable." When he says this he looks over at me to give me a special look.

"You're remarkable," he whispers.

"Thank you," I say with a blush. "So are you."

Orie coughs uncomfortably, probably to disguise his laughter and Clayton actually gives me a tender smile.

"I don't know if I told you, but Elizabeth, Jane, and Eduard will be here. They just arrived today and are staying in one of the homes on the estate."

Sour Jane? Ugh. Talk about buzz kill.

"I can't wait to see them," I say. *Just two of them.*

"It's like a Maldivian reunion," Orie says.

"That sounds so shit hot," Erik turns to smile at us.

The car pulls up to the entrance, where a long staircase is lit by torchlight. I suddenly feel like I'm Elizabeth in *Pride and Prejudice* arriving at a fancy ball. Except at this party the pulsating sound of the DJ spinning music and the crowd screaming can be heard inside our car.

I look over at Clayton with a raised brow.

"I warned you," he tells us. "Georgie loves to throw parties."

"I like him already," Orie says with a good deal of excitement.

Clayton pulls my black wool cape over my shoulders and helps me out of the car. He takes my hand in his and Erik and Orie follow.

He lifts my hand and brushes his lips against my knuckles.

"I can't wait to get out of here," he says in a low voice.

"We just arrived," I whisper back.

"And I'm already done sharing you," Clayton says as I look up at him. "I want you to myself."

God, I can just get lost in those eyes of his—

"Careful," he chides as I literally trip over my own two feet and almost fly head first up the stairs. Clayton has to help me steady myself.

Trés embarrassante! That's French for very embarrassing. Erik might have a point with his whole *trés* obsession.

But then I'm not embarrassed anymore because the double doors are opened and we enter what can only be described as a Versace circus. There are medusas and lions everywhere. Medusa statues, medusa paintings, lion emblems, lion statues, and all are in the shiniest gold I've ever seen. The couches, tables and chairs are done in either deep purple, green, or gold, and it's so loud and totally over the top that I think Gianni Versace would be jumping around in glee.

The party is in full swing and is packed with people who seem like they are already intoxicated and having the time of their life. I'm pretty sure that Count Georgie invited the whole country of France.

The DJ's music is thumping as people dance, drink, and pick food off the appetizer plates that are being passed around like candy. Everywhere I look I see a waiter holding a tray of appetizers, champagne, or shots. Yes, shots. This party is very different from the one at Clayton's home. It's like the polar opposite. Erik and Orie turn to me and smile. I know they love it. And I'm not going to lie, so do I.

"Clayton Sinclair, you just made my party."

We all turn around.

"Georgie," Clayton says dryly.

Count Georgie is drop dead gorgeous. Like seriously perfect. He has thick, dark, brown hair and amber-colored eyes. He's got a total Calvin Klein underwear model vibe going for him. If he didn't have a thick French accent, I would think he was from Greece or Italy. He's dressed in a killer white tuxedo and I notice he's got a gold ring of a lion's head on his pinky. I wonder if he's a Leo.

"In all the years I've known you, I don't think I've *ever* seen you hold anyone's hand," Georgie observes. "Right after we do shots, I want an introduction to this beauty."

"*Venir ici*," he commands the waiter holding a tray of shots and quickly gives us each one.

"*A votre santé!*" He chugs his. I feel Clayton's body stiffen as I quickly down mine, too, but then he, Erik, and Orie do the same. I'm know he doesn't like the fact that I did a shot and he's trying to control himself from saying something to me in front of his friend, which I'm proud of him for. The shot was awesome and it burns through my body making me feel warm already.

"*Alors*," Georgie says as he looks at me. "Now you may introduce us."

"Sophie Walker, please meet Comte Georges de Banville," Clayton says with a smile. "Or Georgie, as he prefers to be called."

Georgie takes my hand and kisses it while bowing low.

"*Enchanté.* It is an honor to meet a woman who can tame the wolf."

Tame the wolf? Now that's funny.

I decide I like Georgie.

"He can't be tamed," I tell him. "But it's a pleasure to meet you. The party looks great."

He gives me a big smile and starts to blatantly analyze my face. It' a bit uncomfortable, I'm not going to lie. I'm pretty sure he's picking it apart and looking for flaws.

"You're scaring her, Georgie," Clayton says as he pulls me into his embrace.

"*Il est impossible*," Georgie waves his hand. "This one has fire in her eyes."

His gaze then settles on Erik and Orie. I watch him give them an appreciative once-over. Clayton quickly introduces them.

"Thanks for having us," Orie says. "Your place is fabulous."

"Merci, it is what I call home," Georgie says graciously, then motions for us to follow him. "Now it is time to celebrate the future marriage of my belle Abby to that awful, common Cossack."

I'm happy I don't have food or liquid in my mouth because I would be choking on it right about now. Without a doubt Georgie just insulted Dimitri.

"Georgie," Clayton chides, "*il n'est pas approprié.*"

I think he just told him that his words are not appropriate.

"*Vous savez que j'ai raison,*" Georgie says as he turns to look at Clayton. "We are standing by and allowing her soul to be taken by a dragon into the pits of Russian hell."

Clayton is unusually silent.

I wonder what kind of man Dimitri is. The only thing I know is that he's absurdly wealthy, makes all the decisions, and wants Abby to dress like Marie Antoinette for her portrait. *That is so weird!* And that neither Clayton nor Georgie like him.

Georgie has led us to a large room that looks like it was cleared out for the DJ and dancing. The dance floor is packed with people, and others are sitting on the purple and gold couches set up around the floor, with small tables in front, all set with what seems to be full bottle service. It's insane. It looks exactly like a club in Hollywood.

"I like Georgie's style," Orie leans in to whisper in my ear. I can only nod at him in agreement because I'm still trying to digest everything I'm seeing.

Georgie takes us right to the biggest of the couches, which Abby and Dimitri are already occupying. Abby is dressed in a short, skimpy white dress that leaves little to the imagination. I'm shocked that Erik chose this for her. Completely shocked. Her hair is down and wavy and she's wearing full make-up. She looks really beautiful, but very different from the way she usually dresses and, to be honest, kind of uncomfortable. I finally get a look at the mysterious Dimitri. He's not tall and he's not short, and pleasant looking enough, but he seems super serious and very aloof. Abby seems relieved to see us. She stands up with a big smile.

"Sophie, you look beautiful," she tells me as she embraces me warmly.

"I think you're the belle of the ball, Abby," I tell her honestly. "Wow. You look so sexy!"

"Abby darling, at least wait until *after* the wedding to start looking so Russian," Georgie says loudly.

She turns bright red and I quickly realize that Georgie and Erik have a lot in common.

"Dimitri likes this kind of look," she answers a bit defensively.

I look over at Erik, who dressed the poor girl, and he is for once stunned or shamed into silence. I don't know which. And I'm pretty sure that he totally agrees with Georgie's comment, which makes this dress all the more bizarre.

"What about Abby? What does she like?" Clayton asks sharply. I look over at him and notice how his eyes have gone cold as they settle on Dimitri. It's impressive. The look is even effective when it's not directed at me.

"I like it," her voice sounds small and almost unsure.

"If you were a figure skater I could see why," Georgie says glibly.

I wonder what is going on with her. Shouldn't she be glowing? She's the bride-to-be and she's marrying the man of her dreams, or at least I think she is.

Dimitri, on the other hand, is completely uninterested in our conversation. In fact, he hasn't bothered to introduce himself and he's even texting on his iPhone. I'm not going to lie, it's really rude.

"You're beautiful," Erik finally finds his voice. There has got to be a part of him that's insulted by Georgie's comment about her outfit. But he doesn't let on. And that's the thing with Erik as opposed to me—in public he has his game face on point.

"I love everything about you right now," Orie agrees as he smiles at Abby.

Abby nods in thanks then embraces Clayton and pulls him aside to say something to him in private.

Erik takes the moment to whisper in my ear, "I want to die! I did not bring that for her. She pulled it out of the closet on her own!"

"Why was it in the closet in the first place?" I ask curiously.

"I brought it for *you*," he admits. "There are a few more dresses like that in the wardrobe that I guess I'm going to have to hide. I was hoping to turn you into a slut in Europe. Get you laid. Help you get more experience so you can compare and choose what you want in life with a few more notches on your belt. Orie and I wanted you to be sexually liberated."

I have heard little more than his first sentence. "Me?" I look at him in horror.

"Yes. I thought if you had a few one night stands you'd get over stalker-lover boy." Erik eyes the dress. "That's the perfect kind of outfit to do it in. It screams, 'Come and fuck me...' then I've gotta admit, 'Skate with me.'"

I sincerely hope that Clayton can't hear what Erik is saying, but I can't be sure because he is standing dangerously close.

"To be honest," Erik continues, unaffected by the look on my face, which is still registering shock.

"I don't want her walking around telling people that I picked that for her. It's kind of embarrassing."

Erik has the good grace to look a bit horrified himself.

"What's *embarrassing* is that you think that if I put that on I would magically want to have sex with a random stranger," I retort sharply.

"Nothing wrong with that," Orie interjects, clearly having heard every word of our conversation. "Look where sleeping with a stranger in the Maldives got you."

God almighty, I don't know why I even try to have a civilized discussion with these people.

Thankfully, Georgie starts to pass out glasses of champagne and I subtly step back to Clayton's side.

He doesn't acknowledge me, and when I look up at his face and take in the aloof look he has going on my stomach sinks in dread. I really hope he didn't hear Erik talking about me having sex with random strangers.

I take note of how Georgie sets Dimitri's champagne on the table in front of him, without saying a word. Dimitri doesn't seem to care one bit. He's completely immersed with his cell phone. I wonder what has him so riveted.

"He's playing Angry Birds," Erik whispers in my ear. He's clocked the whole scenario, too.

I try not to look surprised.

"Have you ever?" Erik says dramatically.

Umm, no.

"A toast to my girl," Georgie says loudly as he stares at Abby with love. "I only want the best for you."

"To a lifetime of happiness with Dimitri," Erik adds.

Georgie gives Erik a strange look but we all toast. The champagne tastes great and loosens up the mood. Everyone starts to talk to each other so I look up at Clayton, trying to gauge his mood but I can't read him.

"Is your brother here?" I ask him softly.

"He said he'd be late, but he should be arriving any minute." His answer is abrupt, like he doesn't want to engage in conversation with me.

I look at the crowd on the dance floor and feel the energy pulsate through my body. One thing's for sure, Georgie definitely knows how to throw a party.

I look at Clayton again. He's busy scanning the crowd, completely ignoring me. His body language screams that he's angry about something. With me. I place my hand on his arm and feel his muscles clench from my touch.

"Is there something wrong?" I ask him.

"Why would there be?" His voice is cold, his jaw rigid with tension. I feel my heartbeat flutter; even riled up, he's hot.

But something is *definitely* wrong.

Even though the music is blaring the silence between us is palpable. Shit.

"Clayton," I say in a calm voice, "talk to me."

He looks down at me for a long second then takes my hand and walks me over to a set of empty couches so we can have some privacy, even though we have to speak loudly to hear each other over the music.

"You're not *fucking* anyone but me," he says crudely, his eyes ablaze with fury.

My jaw drops. He definitely heard what Erik said.

"Erik was just being a friend," I tell him.

"Turning you into a whore is being a friend?" His voice cuts.

Excuse me?

"I don't appreciate that word or your tone." I'm pissed now too. What the hell?

He leans down toward me, his fury flagrantly apparent.

"I don't give a damn if you appreciate my tone or not. If you think I will ever let anyone touch you, you've got another thing coming."

"I don't belong to you, Clayton."

Clayton's smile is cold as his eyes move over me.

"Want to bet on that sweetheart?"

How did this night suddenly take a turn for the worst? I try to get a grip and act rational even though he's radiating anger and towering over me, doing his best to intimidate me, and let's be honest, it's kind of working. And then I get mad at myself for allowing him to make me feel this way.

"Look," I unleash on him, "he was trying to help me get over *you*. I was a goddamn wreck when I got back from the Maldives. And that's because of *you and Amelia*. You want to know the truth? The truth is that I felt betrayed and lied to and my heart was broken. What do you expect? Did you think my friend would want me to pine after you forever? He wanted me to move on."

Clayton is clenching his jaw so tight it starts to tick.

"You have absolutely no right to be pissed at me right now," I go on as my pent up anger boils over . "And PS Clayton, nothing *fucking* happened. He brought that dress for a situation that could *never* happen because *you* manipulated us into coming here! So I don't know what your problem is, but I suggest you get over it quickly."

I'm practically shaking with rage now and I know, I just know, that people are probably staring at us. It's completely obvious that we're fighting. And I know how much Clayton hates to make a scene. Well, tough, he started it.

I boldly meet his gaze and almost step back in fear. The wolf that is Clayton smells blood and I'm thinking from the look on his face wants to attack me. He leans in nice and close, his face right up in mine.

"*You suggest*?" he hisses into my ear with enough heat to burn Georgie's house down.

Oh shit.

"What *I suggest*, Sophie," he continues in that awful voice, "is that *you* listen very carefully. If I hear Amelia's name uttered one more time from your pretty little lips, I promise you will not appreciate the consequences."

If possible, he leans in still further. "And if you so much as even look at another man, as Erik so unashamedly wanted you to do, I won't be responsible for my actions."

How could I ever look at another man? Is he insane?

Clearly.

"I'm done with this conversation," I grit out and step away from him, trying to give the two of us space to breathe.

My movement fuels him even more and I watch him take a dangerous step toward me, but before he can grab hold of me again, Michael Sinclair magically appears and steps in between us.

"Clayton," Michael says with a warning as he grabs his brother's arm. "I found you."

Brave man. But then they are practically the same height. With the same wolf eyes. And probably the same kind of temper to match.

"Sophie," Michael says smiling at me, "you look beautiful."

"Thank you," I reply as I keep my eyes on his brother.

Michael looks at the two of us then pins his gaze on his brother.

"Let's have a cigar outside," he suggests in a low, warning voice.

Clayton's eyes blaze and I don't think he's going to listen to his brother but then after a second he nods curtly and follows him out.

I watch them walk away and disappear into the crowd.

Well, so much for my romantic evening.

7

"What the fuck just happened?" Orie asks me in concern as he rushes over to me.

"I don't want to talk about it," I tell him stubbornly.

"I totally respect that but you realize you still have to tell me."

I almost smile.

"I will later. I promise. I need to digest it first," I say, then look over to where Abby and her fiancé are seated. At least they're pretending like nothing happened. To be honest, I'm sure Dimitri hasn't even looked up from his game of Angry Birds.

"Where's Erik?" I ask.

"He went to concoct his favorite shots with Georgie," Orie tells me. "He's having them brought over to us."

"Cool," I nod, then take Orie's glass of champagne from him. He watches as I down the entire thing. Maybe not the smartest move considering I've just had a shot, and I finished my own glass of champagne, and I haven't eaten anything since lunch with Clayton.

"You go, girl," Orie smiles. "Just don't throw up. You look too pretty to vomit into a toilet tonight."

"Thanks," I say with a smile.

The alcohol is starting to work its beautiful magic and everything feels warm and nice again. A temporary Band-Aid I know, but I'll take it.

"I'm going to go and freshen up in the ladies' room," I tell Orie.

"Want me to walk you? Do you even know where it is?"

"No, but I'll be fine," I tell him, because I want to be alone. "You stay here and man the fort, maybe try and figure out Dimitri's deal—"

"Oh, thank God you said it first! We have so much to talk about regarding the bride-to-be. I'm so confused," Orie rushes out.

"Me, too," I agree. "Please don't have any of those conversations with Erik without me. I need to be part of everything. I promise I won't be long."

Orie leans down and kisses me on the cheek.

"Remember, fighting always leads to amazing make-up sex."

I wonder.

"We'll see," I say as I clutch my small purse and move through the maze of people. At least everyone else seems to be having a ball. I walk out of the dance room and wander down one of the long corridors searching for a bathroom. I get lucky and spot some girls standing in a line.

I figure this has to be it and just smile politely and wait my turn. And then my night gets even more interesting.

"Did you see Michael and Clayton Sinclair? I passed them as they were walking toward the balcony," one of the girls says in a hushed drunken voice. I'm instantly on high alert. "God, they're gorgeous."

The three giggle together and I'm so annoyed. The woman who spoke sounds blitzed and dumb.

Okay, maybe it's not really fair to call her dumb. But still. Kind of.

"I shagged Clayton a few years back. He's the best I've ever had," the other woman says to my complete and utter horror.

I feel my hands ball into little fists by my side and I try to take a deep breath. She slept with *my* Clayton? *Motherfucker!*

"What I would give," her friend sighs with longing, "when he looks at you with those eyes of his. And his hands. Have you ever seen such great hands? I can only imagine what he did to you with them. Please tell me everything so I can live vicariously through you."

The one who apparently slept with him whispers something that I can't decipher and probably don't want to know, and it sends them into a fit of laughter. I'm so filled with possessive rage that I have to look down and take in a deep breath. So what if she shagged him, right? Obviously he's shagged a lot of women, hence his wonderful nickname, "the wolf," but to be faced with it—to be standing next to someone ... My insides start to burn with jealousy. I become a wild, feral version of myself and I can completely picture myself taking my shoe off and hitting them over the head with it.

What is wrong with you?

Thankfully the door opens and I'm surprised to see all of them rush into the bathroom together, obviously the confined space doesn't bother them.

I'm sick with jealousy. Irrational, ugly, green jealousy. Clayton slept with that woman. She knows just how damn fucking perfect he is. She felt his hands on her body, she felt those kisses. I feel nauseated and I want to throw up.

I hate him.

I want to smack *him* with my shoe.

I don't, really. Okay, maybe kind of. But now I definitely want to wring his handsome neck and scream bloody murder at him. Now I definitely have something to fight with him about—

"Hello gorgeous," I hear as I feel a slimy finger move down my bare arm and I jump away from the touch.

Yuck. It's Davis.

"Having fun?" His voice is slurry and reeks of alcohol.

"Yes, thank you," I say uncomfortably as I step further away from his gross touch.

He's the last person I want to talk to.

"Why are you standing here in the hallway all alone?" He moves closer to me, crowding my space.

I look down the corridor and even though the ghosts of Clayton's past are inside the bathroom I feel very alone. The hall that I walked down seems dark now and the party suddenly feels miles away.

"I was just going to find my friends," I tell him because I really don't want to be in his company anymore.

"Find my friends," he mimics my American accent. Fucker. I notice how bloodshot his eyes are and I wonder how much he's had to drink.

"If you'll excuse me," I say, trying to move past him.

"Why are you running away, little rabbit?" Davis sneers as he grabs hold of my arm and pulls me close to his alcohol-infused breath. "I've only just started to play."

"Please let me go," I tell him as fear slowly begins to takeover and I try to move away.

"I like it when my little rabbits are scared," Davis says as he takes his other hand and yanks on my ponytail. "You don't think we just hired you to paint? The girls he hires are always very talented in many areas. Don't you worry, if you're nice I'll make sure my future brother-in-law gives you a big fat bonus. He's good for it."

I think I'm going to be sick. I'm beyond frightened and I'm pretty sure this delusional asshole thinks he can have his way with me. I try and twist out of his grip but he's strong.

"Let me go!" I tell him forcefully as I try to break free.

"I like a girl with fire. It's so much more fun," he says as he tries to put his gross lips on mine.

I turn my face away from his and before I can really panic, I'm saved by the girls I hated minutes before. In that moment I forgive them for fantasizing about, even for sleeping with Clayton. I just love them. They throw open the bathroom door and rush out in a torrent of drunken laughter, taking Davis off guard and giving me ample time to pull out his grip and rush down the hall toward the party.

I think I hear him laugh.

I can't believe how scared I am. No one. *No one* has ever made me feel so uncomfortable in my life. I know I need to get a grip and calm down but I also know he wasn't joking around. He's some seriously fucked-up guy. And I would be happy never to see him again. I push my way into the crowd, shoving past a million different faceless people, looking for someone, *anyone* familiar.

When I feel a hand on my waist, I practically scream out in fear, thinking it's the hideous Davis chasing after me.

But the hand belongs to someone I know and am beginning to really like. Michael Sinclair.

"Sophie, what's wrong?" Michael looks over me in concern.

My hands are trembling as they come up to grip his black lapel. He navigates through the crowd that's crushing us and pulls me into a relatively empty corner.

I lean into him and am so damn grateful that he grabbed hold of me.

"Your cousin." I begin shakily, then blurt out everything, telling him exactly what just happened. I know it's probably not the right thing to do considering Davis is Abby's brother and Michael's blood relative, but I don't care. Davis scared me and if he's thinking it was some sick, perverted joke, he needs never to do it again. To me or to anyone else, for that matter. I can't even meet Michael's gaze when I finish the story.

He's dead silent so I finally gather the courage to look up at him and all I can think is, oh shit.

He's as scary as his brother.

"What the hell is going on?" My favorite voice in the world interrupts us and pulls me right out of Michael's arms and into his. And I can't help it. I fall into them. I hear Michael speaking quickly to Clayton in French. I don't know why he's choosing to speak another language considering I know exactly what he must be saying, but at this point I don't care. I feel Clayton's body turn to stone. Every muscle tenses. He feels like a steel block. I'm clinging to him now and I realize he's trying to push away from me.

He wants to kill Davis. I'm pretty sure of it.

I look at his face and I'm guessing that telling the Sinclair brothers was maybe a big mistake. However furious Michael was, I think I can multiply it by a million. I don't think I've ever seen Clayton like this. He looks down at what I'm sure is my pale and frightened face in pure rage.

"I'm going to kill him."

Oh my God. I shake my head.

"No!" I rush out. "You can't! He's your cousin. He was drunk—"

Clayton grabs my hands and starts to push me toward Michael.

"Do not leave my brother's side," he commands.

But I still try to cling to him like a child.

"Don't do this!" I plead. "Please! This could be totally me! My fault! Maybe I overreacted."

Not really, but the last thing I want to do is see Abby's party ruined because her cousin murdered her brother.

"I am going to kill that son of bitch, Sophie," Clayton says in a deadly voice.

"You can't!"

The man is completely serious. I turn to Michael, who looks almost as grim. "Talk some sense into him."

"I think my brother has the right idea." Michael pulls me out of Clayton's grasp and holds me in a viselike grip, turns and motions to someone I can't see, then escorts me down yet another corridor in the castle toward a pair of antique double doors. He turns the gold knob and before I know it we're inside some room that I can't even take in because it happens so fast and Sergei has joined us.

Sergei. Where the hell did he come from?

"Sergei will wait with you until we return," Michael commands.

He walks out and leaves me alone with Sergei, who crosses his arms and moves in front of the doors.

"Where did you come from?" I blurt out.

"I always shadow Mr. Clayton Sinclair at these kind of events."

A bodyguard? Sergei is Clayton's bodyguard?

"I would like you to let me out," I say in a stern voice and cross my arms, too. I didn't realize how giant Sergei was. But now he looks damn near seven feet tall.

"I'm sorry, Miss Walker, but that is an impossibility."

I have a feeling he means it.

"If you're his bodyguard shouldn't you be with him, keeping him safe?"

Sergei chooses not to answer this question.

Of course.

I feel like I'm having an out-of-body experience and I suddenly want Erik and Orie. And my mom. Maybe not my mom, but my dad, definitely my dad. I open my purse and pull out my cell phone, so grateful that I brought it.

"Please refrain from using your cell phone, Miss Walker."

I look at Sergei.

"Excuse me?"

"I don't want to have to take it away from you," he tells me. "You cannot use it until Mr. Sinclair is back."

I have a feeling he is completely serious and I have a feeling that I really want to bash Clayton in the head. Why must he have a bodyguard who is just as obstinate as he is?

"I just want to text my friends," I tell him in a small voice.

"You'll have to wait."

Fuck that!

I look at my phone and start to pull Erik's number up but in less than a second Sergei is in front of me and has it in his hands.

"I warned you, Miss Walker."

"This is crazy," I tell him. "Let me out of here. At least let me go to my friends. I won't move. I promise."

"I'm sorry, Miss Walker. You will remain here until Mr. Sinclair returns. Those are my orders."

"I don't work for Mr. Sinclair so I don't have to follow his orders," I tell him.

Sergei acts as if he doesn't hear me.

Before I start having a panic attack I sit down on one of the purple couches that faces Sergei and take a few deep breaths. We can hear the party in full swing outside and the ridiculousness of this situation is not lost on me. Fortunately, I don't have to wait long. In a minute Clayton opens the door and steps into the room. Sergei nods to his boss and leaves us alone, taking my phone with him. I stand up and stare at Clayton.

I search his face and body for any sign of injuries and I'm thankful he's unharmed. His blue eyes beam at me with a heat that robs me of my breath.

"Are you okay?" I ask.

Clearly he is.

"Is Davis—"

"Don't. Say. His. Name," he says harshly. "He's been taken care of."

Taken care of? What does that mean? Do I really even care? Only for Clayton and Michael. I don't want anything to happen to them because of me. That would suck.

And then the impact of everything that's occurred this evening hits me. From our fight about Erik's stupid comment, which nows seems like it happened a million years ago, to the women outside the bathroom talking about Clayton's mad sex skills, to disgusting Davis.

All in one night. In less than a motherfucking hour. Who knew?

"Sophie."

I look at him and I'm trying my hardest to keep it together. I so don't want to cry right now. I wonder if I'm cursed.

"Clayton," my voice sounds hoarse.

"Come here."

At least ten feet of purple and gold carpet separates us. I look at him and know exactly what it will mean if I cross the distance and walk over. I think about the consequence for half a second then slowly make my way to him. I stop just short of a foot from him and our eyes meet.

"I want to hurt Davis again for even daring to put his hands on you."

Again? Oh God. Is Clayton going to jail for me?

"You didn't—"

"Kill him?" Clayton says harshly. "No. But I wish I had. Michael stopped me. Michael and security have thrown him out."

"You didn't have to throw—" I begin to say.

"Didn't I?" he interrupts me. "I keep telling you that you're mine," he says passionately. "I won't let anyone ever hurt you."

My heart thumps loudly in my chest as we stare at each other. The energy between us is electrifying. The tension, palpable.

He reaches out and buries his hand in my ponytail as he steps close to me. He pulls my head back so I have to look up at him. His eyes dance with fire and all I can think about is how badly I want him to touch me.

"You're mine, Sophie," he commands. "Say it."

"I'm yours," I tell him immediately, because it's true. At least for now.

I see a glimpse of satisfaction on his face before he crushes his mouth to mine and I welcome the assault gladly. His tongue sweeps into my mouth and claims complete ownership.

I. Am. His.

My words only solidified what my body and soul already know. I wrap my arms around his neck and he pulls me up toward his body. Instantly my legs encircle his waist as he grinds his pelvis into mine.

He wants me. And I want him.

He tears his mouth away from mine and licks his way down my neck as his hands move under my dress to grip my bare bottom. I moan in response. I missed him. I missed the touch of his skin on mine.

"I need you," he whispers against my neck.

"I need you, too."

"Now, Sophie," he says roughly as he pulls away and looks down at my face.

My answer is to kiss him back and pull that magnificent mouth of his back to mine. His hands, those hands that the women at the party seem to fantasize about push my lace panties aside as he walks with me and pushes me up against the wall. His fingers work their magic, stroking me, and in seconds I'm dying with need and about to come. I grab his muscled shoulders, his hair, anything that I can touch as he makes me wild with desire. It feels like it was an eternity since the last time he touched me.

"Clayton," I beg.

I feel him unzip his pants and I can't wait any longer. I want him so bad, so deep inside me that I think I will scream if it doesn't happen. He rubs himself against me, teasing me, making me moan out for a satisfaction that only he can give. And then he whispers into my mouth.

"What do you want, baby?"

"I. Want. You."

He doesn't make me wait. He thrusts into me and we both moan at the same time from the pleasure of it.

"God, I missed you," he pants into my ear.

I lick his neck, his jaw, any part of his skin that I can get hold of as I revel in the feel of him inside me. Desperate for what is to come. What only he can give me. I feel every sensation. Every part of his body that touches mine heightens my pleasure. It's him. He is my heroin. He's my addiction. Everything about him turns me on.

He starts to move with a fierce intensity, pushing me up against the wall as his thick shaft thrusts so far inside me that I think I might die from the sweet torture.

His hands grip my hips as he moves, teasing me with his fullness before he increases the tempo and I begin to feel like I'm about to come apart.

"Oh, my God," I whisper against his neck. How many nights had I dreamt of this moment? How many nights had I wanted him so badly that I thought I couldn't live from the pain of thinking it would never happen again?

This man is my sweet heaven and hell. All combined in one breathtaking package. He grinds into me and I scream out as my orgasm bursts through my body. I try to hold back my cry and bury my head into his neck to muffle the sounds I'm making. "Clayton."

He throws his head back as he comes and I feel his body tremble into mine. We stay like this for a while. Plastered against the wall. My legs wrapped around his waist, him still inside. Our breath is shallow. He buries his face in my neck and I bury mine in his. I love the way our bodies fit each other, and the way this man makes me feel, and I silently thank god for bringing him back into my life.

"I could stay like this forever," he tells me.

"Me, too."

But all good things must come to an end.

He rubs his cheek against mine then slowly pulls out and we quickly clean up. I pull my hair out of my now destroyed ponytail and run my fingers through it. I'm surprised when he stands in front of me and pushes my hands away and begins to do it himself.

I stare up at the intense look on his face and wonder what he's thinking. A second later I realize that I actually asked the question out loud.

He kisses me on the lips very tenderly.

"It would scare you."

"Try me."

His large hands cup my cheeks as he sapphire gaze burns into mine.

"I'm not going to let you go."

A girl can dream.

I keep my head down and blush past Sergei. I wonder if he knows what we just did. God, how embarrassing. We walk into the main hall where we entered the party, and as luck goes, we run right into Jane. All things considered, I really shouldn't be that surprised. Although I must say, the look on her face is priceless. She's shocked to see me. Like mouth hanging open shocked. Her eyes linger on our entwined hands and I can tell she's pissed.

I'm not going to lie, this makes me happy. Very happy.

"Hi Jane," I say politely. "It's so nice to see you again."

I wonder if I'll be struck by lightning.

"Sophie, was it?"

As if she doesn't remember my name.

"You remember Sophie, Jane," Clayton says forcefully.

Jane plasters a fake smile on her face and brushes back her blonde hair.

"I remember now."

"Are Elizabeth and Eduard with you?" Clayton asks coolly.

"Somewhere here," Jane says, unaffected by his frigid voice, then pins her gaze to me. "So *you're* the Sophie that Abby hired as help for her wedding."

God this woman is a bitch.

"Yes, I am," I tell her evenly. "I'm painting her portrait."

Jane gives me a catty smile. "So you're not attending the wedding with the family."

"She is," Clayton interjects. "Sophie is my date."

I am? I watch as the color leaves Jane's face and along with a feeling of satisfaction, I find myself getting really nervous that Clayton would say that without asking me about it first.

We would be together in front of his family. I'd meet them. His mom and dad. The thought of it makes me nauseated and excited at the same time.

"How nice," Jane grits out. "If you'll excuse me—"

She starts to walk away then stops as if she remembers something and looks over at Clayton. Her smile is sugar sweet.

"Have you spoken to Amelia?"

My heart rate speeds up and I find myself gripping Clayton's hand tighter.

"Why would I?" He seems unaffected by her insinuation.

"I thought you two were back on," Jane says innocently. "You know, she is my plus one."

Motherfucker. Amelia's coming? Or worse, is she already here?

"Amelia and I aren't together anymore," Clayton tells her in an icy voice. "I don't know where she is or what she does, nor frankly, do I care. You'll do well to remember that, Jane."

She shrugs her shoulders, ignoring his cool demeanor. "Come on, Clayton," Jane digs in. "She's the longest relationship you've ever had. *Of course* you care."

And with that she walks away.

I hate the bitch. If Jane had a theme song it would be the same one the Wicked Witch of the West had.

"Sophie."

I look up at Clayton and try to play it cool. Like awful Jane had zero effect on me.

"I'm fine," I tell him.

"I will have Abby tell Jane that Amelia is not welcome."

I'm momentarily stunned that he would do this for me. That he cares so much about my feelings makes my decision easier.

"No," I say shaking my head. "Please don't. She's Jane's plus one. They are friends. It's completely fine. Amelia means nothing."

I lift my chin confidently and meet his gaze.

After a second of analyzing my face to see if I'm telling the truth, he finally smiles.

"You're right. She doesn't," he says.

I'm proud of myself. Not just because I didn't roll into a fetal position and curse the gods for my fate but because it's how I actually feel. I can sense his gaze move over me appreciatively and I'm shocked at how bad I want him again. I want to be alone with him and feel his naked skin against mine. Just us.

"Let's get out of here," he says.

He's definitely a mind reader.

8

I'm acutely aware that I'm in Clayton's bedroom.

And that we're all alone.

It's funny how last night I was perfectly at ease here. But now that he's taking up practically all the space in the room, it's a completely different story. And even though we were just intimate in Georgie's house, during a party no less, I suddenly feel like a born-again virgin.

There's one light on next to the bed and someone from Clayton's staff lit the giant fireplace. My gaze is drawn to the plush rug in front of the roaring fire that looks inviting and extremely romantic.

Besides the occasional crackle it's dead silent, as was our car ride home. Sergei had given me my phone back and I used it to text goodbye to Erik and Orie; Clayton didn't want us to do it in person since he was sure someone would try to convince us to stay. Thankfully, we left unnoticed.

"Can I have something brought up?" Clayton asks politely as he takes off his jacket and throws it on one of the chairs. "Are you hungry?"

I shake my head as I take in his appearance. Without the jacket on I get to see the outline of his chest so much more clearly. God almighty, he's built so perfectly. It's almost unfair to have so much of a good thing going for you. He unbuttons the top few buttons, exposing a part of his tan chest. My mouth waters. Literally. Waters.

I've never seen anything sexier.

And then the earth moves in slow motion and I see him. I really see him. I watch how he lowers his head, I take in the straight line of his jaw, the sensual curve of his lips, and something switches inside and a crazy kind of boldness takes over.

"Don't," I tell him in a surprisingly strong voice.

He looks almost startled as he meets my gaze.

"I want to," I say.

He doesn't say anything. But then he really doesn't have to because I can read him so well.

His eyes light up with desire and I try not to fidget under the intensity I see. He stands perfectly still as I embrace the alter ego I never knew I had until now, *Slutty Sophie.*

I reach behind my neck and grab hold of my zipper and slowly pull it down, all while keeping my gaze firmly locked on Clayton's. I step out of the dress easily and stand before him in my heels, wearing nothing but a black lace thong and bra. My confidence soars when I see his reaction. The way he's watching me makes me feel like a sex goddess. And so I continue. I slowly slink down my bra straps with one thing in mind; all I want is to have this gorgeous man begging to have me.

My bra hits the floor and instead of being embarrassed or shy, I feel more empowered. He takes a step forward, staggers almost, and I put up my hand and shake my head.

"No."

Those beautiful blue eyes of his move over my body and linger on my breasts before meeting my gaze again. His look is feral. Animalistic. I don't think I've ever seen this before. Not even in the Maldives. I walk toward him in a way I've seen women do in countless sexy movies I've watched. I think I'm doing a pretty good job because his mouth is half open and I can see the deep breaths he's taking, I know, to stay in control. When I'm only inches away he tries to reach out and take hold of my hip but I step just out of his reach.

"No touching until I tell you," I command.

My words unleash something raw in him. Barely contained. I know he's going to have a hard time. This hot, gorgeous man of mine who always has to be the one in the driver's seat, the one calling all the shots, now has to try to restrain the caveman in him. I see his hands clench and unclench at his sides as he takes another deep breath, all while keeping his enigmatic eyes pinned to mine.

I reach out and start to unbutton his shirt. I take my time, because with each button comes an extra slice of skin that I get to touch. Skin that I've been dreaming about for a month now. He feels incredible. Hot, so hot and so damn appealing. I feel like a sex-starved addict. Like I've been waiting all my life, when it really hasn't been that long. I continue until it is completely open, then I slowly push the offending material off his shoulders, exposing those muscular arms and letting my hands move over his well-defined chest. I wasn't wrong. I wasn't delusional when I imagined his body back home. It is perfect. Droolworthy perfect.

I hear a hiss of breath as he tries to remain still. It only fuels my fire, giving me more power. I run my hands over his body, lightly caressing every inch of skin, memorizing every line, moving closer to inhale his smell. My hands move to his pants and I unhook them and pull down the zipper. I rub him slowly, intentionally trying to drive him mad, the way he's done to me so many times. I place a soft kiss on his stomach before I am brave enough to look up at him.

His face is etched with desire, his eyes a smoky blue. I know he is teetering on the edge, barely able to restrain himself, just waiting to unleash on me. I can feel this all around me. I pull his pants down and run my hands over his butt, the sides of his thighs to his calves, silently worshipping every magnificent part of Clayton Astor Sinclair.

And then I make my way back to his shaft and rub my hands along the length of him.

"Sophie," he whispers.

I don't respond. I just rub my tongue along the tip before I move my mouth over him. I don't know who I am or what's come over me. I just go with it because I suddenly feel like a porn star, like I was born to do this. I take him deeper, work him with my hands then run them over his legs, over his ass. His hands suddenly reach down to grip my hair and he lifts me in one fluid motion then he picks me up and practically throws me on the bed.

I try to kick off my heels.

"No," he says roughly. "Keep them on."

Fuck.

My legs come up as I lean back on my elbows and look at him. Holy mother of god, he's magnificent. I throw my hair to the side and know my eyes are bright with desire as they stare up at him. His hands now roam possessively over my body.

"You want to play, Sophie?"

My chest heaves before I move my high-heeled leg up a bit higher and stare at him, silently answering. Before I know it, he grabs my ankles and pulls me down toward the foot of the bed and rips off my thong. In less than ten seconds his mouth is between my legs and his hands are holding my bottom, pulling me closer to him as he strokes me. My hands grab hold of the sheets and I try to hold off the tremor that is about to come over my body.

"Clayton," I whisper with longing.

He bites my inner thigh and licks it.

"You want to play?" he asks again before he resumes, and licks me until I'm shaking with an explosive orgasm.

He moves up and takes my breasts in his mouth as his hands continue to rub me. I can't even think straight. I just want him inside me. Now. I want to feel him so fully embedded in me, like he was born to be there.

And at this moment I really think he was.

"Please," I say to him.

He moves above me quickly, robbing me of his magical hands, his mouth now whispering against my lips, the tip of his shaft brushing against me ever so slowly, like he's about to plunge in, but then drawing back.

"What?" he says against my lips. "What do you want, Sophie?"

"You."

"But you left me," he says roughly. "Why should I give you what you want?"

Motherfucker!

"Clayton," I practically beg.

"No," he commands as he leans back. "Open. Your. Eyes."

I do it because I have no choice. His face has taken on a serious look. And he looks heated, almost angry.

"You. Left. Me."

Holy shit. He's going to torture me. I can't even bear the thought of it. I shake my head.

"I didn't—"

"Don't lie."

I close my eyes for a half a second then open them. I know I have to admit why.

"I thought you didn't want me," I whisper.

He thrusts right into me when I say that and I cry out in surprise and from the pleasure.

"Does this feel like I don't want you?" he asks me in a gruff voice against my ear. Nothing has sounded better in my life.

He moves out and I whimper from the loss.

"Does it?" he barely grits out.

I shake my head from side to side.

"No," I say. "No."

His large hands grab hold of my jaw as his thumbs caress my cheeks.

"Promise me that it will never happen again."

I can barely think. My body is screaming with the excruciating sweet pleasure-pain of desire but I know what he wants to hear. What he won't give me until he gets his way. And there's a part of me, some piece back in the recesses of my mind, that knows there must be a reason why he wants to hear me say it. He has to care. More than care. I matter to him.

More than matter.

"Sophie." His thumb moves across my lips. "Promise me."

In my passion-induced coma I lift my hands, cup his face, and meet his gaze dead on.

"I promise."

He drives into me again, so fully and completely that I never want the moment to end. I lift my hips to meet his and before I know it I ride with Clayton to heaven and back.

I wake up in the middle of the night and feel Clayton's arms and legs wrapped around my body, pressed up against my back. I missed this part the most—*okay, maybe not most*, but close. I lift his hand and kiss his palm then rub my cheek against it. I'm not surprised when he leans in closer to me and curls his arm tighter around my waist to kiss my neck.

"What was that for?" he asks me in a sleepy voice.

"Just because I can."

I feel his smile against my neck.

"You can and so much more."

I laugh. "I'm sorry I woke you," I tell him honestly.

"Don't be sorry." He nuzzles my skin.

We're both quiet and I suddenly get a giant whiff of lavender that I've noticed seems to permeate the chateau.

"Your house smells so good," I tell him lamely.

I feel the rumble against my back as he laughs.

"Now that's a first."

I can feel myself blush.

"It's true."

"The woman who takes care of the property puts lavender seeds with oil throughout the house," he admits. "It definitely gives off a peaceful feeling. It's something I miss when I'm in my other residences."

Clayton says this so matter-of-factly that he doesn't make it seem like the big deal I know it is.

"Are your other homes like this?" I ask tentatively.

"In what way?" he asks.

Oh, I don't know. Huge. With crazy expensive furniture. And a vineyard. And let's not forget the other homes on the property that your guests can stay in.

"This big," is what I say instead.

"A few," Clayton replies mysteriously.

A few? I almost roll my eyes.

"Well, this one is pretty incredible, so I can hardly imagine anything else comparing."

"Thank you," Clayton says. "You'll see the other properties, so you can decide which is your favorite."

My heart thumps against my chest. But I force myself not to get too excited or to think about what he's saying and what it means, and instead proceed to have verbal diarrhea.

"The home is really incredible, Clayton," I tell him honestly. "When I was admiring the land I felt as though I was staring at a piece by Monet."

"That's quite a compliment coming from you," he says with pleasure.

"And some of the pieces you have inside are just unreal," I go on. "Of course some aren't quite my style."

"How so?"

"Honestly?" I ask hesitantly.

"Always."

"Well, they're a bit—" I search for the right word.

Clayton waits expectantly so I give him the first word that comes to mind.

"Versaille?"

Sophie! WTF? *I can't believe I just said that!*

He shouts out in laughter. I'm glad that he's amused and not insulted.

"Do you hate me?" I ask him in a mortified whisper.

"No," he's still laughing against my neck. "That's my mother's fault. She designed some of the rooms and went with the style that she's accustomed to, which is a bit dated, I'll admit. My bedroom was most important to me. This one is done the way I like it."

I'm relieved, I'm not going to lie. And I'm touched even more because it's the one he gave me.

"It feels more like you."

"To be honest, it's as much me as any room in any home that I own can be," he admits slowly. "I've been so consumed with my work, with the success of my business, I've usually let other people handle decorating. Well, my mother mostly."

For some reason this really makes me sad. Even the wealthiest people I've known, my parents' friends or just people I've met through school, have always taken time to make their home their own. It's kind of a no-brainer. Your home should be your sanctuary. I can't imagine not caring about what the place that was my own, the place I lived in, looked and felt like. For me it's always all about energy.

"Feeling sorry for me again?" Clayton asks curiously. I can hear the amusement in his voice.

"Maybe," I admit.

And then I remember Abby's remark about his childhood and the little he told me in the Maldives and I want so badly to twenty question him, but I realize that now is not the time or place.

"Why?" he asks as he plants a kiss on my shoulder.

"Why what?"

I can feel him smile.

"Should I be insulted you don't remember what we were talking about?"

"No," I rush out. "To be honest, I was just distracted by my thoughts of you as a child."

I feel his body tense.

"What thoughts?"

"How cute you must have been," I say to placate him. I don't want to bring up bad memories now.

He relaxes a bit.

"According to my mother, Michael was the one with all the looks when we were younger."

"She did not say that," I'm highly offended.

"Yes, she did," he laughs. "I'll show you some pictures so you can be the judge."

I turn around in his embrace and plant a kiss on his lips.

"Did it hurt your feelings?"

He smiles against my lips.

"My ego still cries over the injustice," he tells me sexily.

"What can I do to make you feel better?" I tease.

He proceeds to tell me how and I am very happy to oblige.

Even though I didn't get much sleep with Clayton, I'm surprisingly filled with energy. I'm in what I'm now calling my "art studio," dressed in low-hanging grey sweats and a matching grey camisole, completely comfortable and ready to get started on Abby's portrait. Abby knocks before entering the room. I'm busy taking some pictures of the space, so I don't immediately turn to take in her appearance. When I do, I hope my face doesn't betray what I'm feeling inside.

To say that she looks ridiculous is the understatement of the century.

She is wearing a gold period costume. The period being the 1700s. No joke. She's got a powdered wig on and her face is also powdered white, and to top off the look her lips are bright red. I think she's even penciled on a mole. Oh, God. And that's not all. For accessories she's holding an open bottle of champagne and a plate of cake.

She must have had to start drinking early to make herself put this outfit on.

"Wow," is the only word I can manage. I try to give her an encouraging smile.

Abby snorts derisively and wobbles her way over to the fainting couch. She proceeds to throw herself on it, which is a feat in itself because of her enormous bustle. Once she's settled, she takes a swig of champagne.

"You look," I search for the right word, "cool."

I half expect lightning to strike me right there.

She shrugs her narrow shoulders and looks at me, but with all the powder on her face I can't really tell what she's thinking. I'm about to find out.

"I look like a joke," she says mockingly.

"No," I say to make her feel better. I can tell that she's in a state. Of a nervous breakdown.

She holds the bottle of champagne out to me. "Would you like some?"

I shake my head. "I better not. I'm going to be working."

"Suit yourself," she says as she takes another swig. "You might need it to get through the pains of having to paint me in this get-up."

I finally shake myself and put the camera down, then walk over to her and kneel down. Up close, the white powder on her face is even more ghoulish, like a Halloween costume gone bad.

"Look at me, Sophie." She giggles almost hysterically.

"It is a bit extreme," I say tentatively, glad that she's acknowledging the giant elephant in the room.

Abby waves her hand in the air.

"And the sad part is this outfit is the least of my problems," she tells me. She sounds a bit inebriated now. "Can I ask you something?"

"Of course."

"Is it awful that I found out that Dimitri has a son—" She pauses for a second before continuing. "—just *this morning*?"

Oh shit.

"Yes," I say honestly.

Tears well up in Abby's eyes.

"That's what I thought." She sighs and takes another long sip, then hands me the bottle so that she can concentrate on the chocolate cake. "Dimitri wanted me to hold the cake for effect. I'm going to eat it instead."

I realize I'm watching a train wreck.

"He was handpicked by my mother," she says as she chews a bite of cake. I notice that one of her thick fake eyelashes is slowly starting to make its way off her eyelid.

"Why him?" I ask.

"My mum and stepfather are tired of paying for me. I have no inheritance, everything is being left to Davis, and so I'm really a burden now," she explains to me. "It's like a Jane Austen novel, isn't it?"

Yes, it definitely is, but I'm not going to tell her that. I am still trying to process the fact that they're not leaving their daughter any money. Only that little shit Davis? The creep of all creeps? Are they crazy?

"So my mother picked the fucking Russian oligarch for me," Abby hiccups.

Abby swears?

I decide it's okay to take a swig from the champagne bottle, and I do, then hand it back to her.

"I'll have more brought up," she whispers to me. Now I'm thinking that's probably a good idea.

"He has a child?" I ask, trying to bring us back to the first problem at hand.

Abby nods in disbelief.

"That's what's priceless. Nicholas is seventeen. He's just five years younger than me. He could be my brother. Dimitri called him Little Nicholas. But he's not so little."

"How old is Dimitri?" I ask, shocked by all of this.

"Forty-one."

Okay. I know that Abby is only twenty-two.

"How did you find out about his son?" I ask her, completely bewildered. "And did he tell you why he's never told you about him?"

"That's a great question, Sophie," Abby says with a crazy look on her face. She has definitely been nipping at the champagne for a while. "Do you want to hear how?"

I wouldn't have asked if I didn't. I'm too afraid to say that out loud to Abby in her current state so I just nod.

"The wedding planner was going over seating arrangements and she mentioned that Dimitri's son had changed plans and would now be coming to the wedding. Apparently even *she* knew about his son. Insulting, isn't it?"

I take the bottle out of her hand. There are many bizarre things about this situation. One, Dimitri never told Abby he had a son. Two, his son hadn't planned on coming to the wedding until now? Three, Abby's right. This does have the makings of a Jane Austen novel.

"Did you confront him?"

"Of course I did," Abby says with a snort. "And you know what he said?"

"What?" I ask in a whisper. I'm almost afraid to hear the answer.

"He told me it wasn't a big deal and he hadn't thought to tell me. He didn't think it was important and he didn't understand why I was so upset. In fact, he even told me that he was upset by the accusatory tone in my voice."

Wow. Okay. Talk about having some serious premarital problems. And let's talk about what a dick Dimitri is. I have a sudden urge to punch him in the face.

"And then he said he had business to attend to and that I could call him when I had my attitude under control."

Now I officially hate Dimitri. Like want to get him in a dark alley and beat the crap out of him, hate.

"Do you love him?" I ask her.

"That's a silly question," Abby laughs as she takes another bite of cake.

"Do you?" I press on.

"Absolutely not."

Holy shit. Before I figure out what to say she doubles down.

"I've been in love with someone else my whole life."

I whisper in horror, "Then why are you marrying Dimitri?"

"Because the man I love will *never* love me back. At least not the way I want. That is a fact. I thought I might as well do what a lot of other women do these days and marry for money. But this son thing has thrown me."

There are so many thoughts racing through my mind that I don't even know where to begin.

"Abby, why are you doing this?" I ask her. "There are other choices you can make. You can get a job and be independent of your family."

"I've never worked a day in my life."she says, her lips starting to quiver. "And where would I live, Sophie?"

I'm surprised, even though I know I shouldn't be.

"I don't even know what I'm good at," Abby goes on. "It's so pathetic, isn't it? I'm useless. Completely and utterly useless."

"That's not true," I say gently. "You are so young. There's still time to find your passion."

"But what if that takes me years? I don't know if I'm cut out to be a barista in a coffee shop and I don't mean that in an entitled, privileged way. I mean it like I've never even made a coffee for myself way."

"You can learn."

"But that doesn't solve the immediate problem."

"Well, maybe Clayton or Michael can help you until—"

Abby lifts her hand up sharply.

"I would never ask. Least of all Michael."

"You can't marry someone you don't love," I tell her emphatically. "Someone who's lied to you about having a kid. And then acts like it's not a big deal! What kind of husband will he be? That's completely insane! Are you listening to yourself? Abby—"

Before I can finish my thought we're interrupted by a knock, then the door opens and there stands Michael Sinclair, looking almost as good as his brother, in jeans and a fitted navy t-shirt. His sharp gaze takes in the situation pretty quickly.

"Hi, Michael," I say a bit too brightly.

I saw the flicker of shock, just a quick second of it, as he checked out Abby's get-up, and then the look was quickly covered. I know he must be horrified, but he's polite enough to mask it.

"Ladies," he says.

I smile awkwardly then look over at Abby, who I notice is ignoring him and drinking from her bottle.

Shit.

I take the ball. "Can we help you with something?"

"I'm sorry to interrupt what looks to be a fantastic party but I just came by to invite you to dinner tonight, Sophie," he tells me. "I've invited my brother already and he said it was up to you."

I can't stop my smile.

"That sounds really nice. But if you guys want to be alone that's totally fine as well, I know you don't get to see a lot of each other."

"No," Michael says. "The invitation is for both of you. I don't think my brother is keen to leave you alone for even a minute."

I get a warm and fuzzy feeling inside.

"Alright, then. I'm looking forward to it."

"Perfect. I was thinking around seven," he tells me before his gaze settles on Abby, who's still avoiding eye contact with him.

"Is everything alright, Abigail?" he asks gently.

"What do *you* care?" she says rather childishly.

I'm sure I'm now gawking because of her response.

Michael Sinclair is just as intimidating as his brother. He steps closer to us and narrows his eyes at her as she continues in a haughty voice. "You told me exactly how you feel about me last night and I'd rather not relive that embarrassing moment again, thank you. Especially now that we have an audience."

I turn to Michael, completely riveted. He is pissed off.

"You looked like a slut," he tells her, then stares pointedly at her outfit. "And I'm pretty damn sure Sophie is too kind to tell you that you look utterly ridiculous right now."

I quickly take the bottle of champagne and plate of cake out of Abby's hands as she sits up straight to stare at him in outrage.

"Dimitri's family portraits have *always* been done in costume!"

"You look like a clown."

"You're an ass."

Michael shakes his head in anger. I know he's teetering on the edge. I've seen this look before on Clayton's face.

"Watch your mouth, Abigail."

"I hate when you call me Abigail. You make me feel like a child."

"That's the point, *Abigail.*" His gaze could freeze water.

"You're not my father, Michael Sinclair," she responds coolly. "So don't you dare take that tone of voice with me."

Michael takes a step toward Abby. He's a walking grenade.

I decide to try to divert his attention. "Michael?" I say. It takes him a moment before he looks at me.

"Sophie, I'm sorry you have to witness this," he says with an apologetic smile.

"There's nothing to apologize for," I tell him smoothly. "Family arguments are completely normal where I come from."

"But still," he says, then nods in Abby's direction. "Good luck with the princess."

Then he leaves us alone.

And I slowly start to understand what's going on.

Abby promptly bursts into tears and cries, "I hate him!"

And then I know Abigail is in love with Michael Sinclair.

9

"Try this Pinot. It's from Clayton's vineyard," Michael tells me before pouring a generous glass.

We're sitting at a quaint restaurant in Avignon. Michael was nice enough to invite Erik and Orie and I'm happy that everyone seems to get along great.

"Thank you," I say as I try the wine. It *is* incredible but then I'm not surprised considering who it belongs to.

Clayton waits expectantly.

"It's wonderful," I tell him with a smile. "I didn't know you were in the wine business as well."

He shrugs. "It's a hobby."

A very expensive one.

"You're good at it."

He raises a brow and I can't help but laugh at his arrogance. He leans over and gives me a soft kiss on the lips then pulls back and lets his gaze sweep over my face. I know I have a goofy smile but I don't really care. I'm happy.

"I'll be right back," he says and excuses himself from the table. I watch him walk away. I love the way his broad shoulders fill out the black long-sleeved shirt he has on. He looks good in jeans too. Really good.

Erik brings me out of my reverie. "You're drooling."

I'm about to tell him that I really could care less but then remember that Michael is sitting at the table with us and just watched me stare at his brother like a complete crazy stalker. I look over at him in embarrassment and am caught off guard by the look on his face.

Though he's smiling at me, he seems super shocked. And he can't even hide it.

"This place is great," I say lamely trying to cover.

"You've changed my brother," he says to my surprise

"How?" Erik is the one to ask what I'm dying to know.

Michael pushes back his long hair.

"Believe it or not, I've never see Clayton behave this way with a woman before."

"How do you mean?" The question is out of my mouth before I can stop myself.

"He's usually indifferent," Michael explains. "Not usually. *Always.*"

"Well, our girl is pretty special," Orie says loyally.

I blush.

"I'm just ordinary," I say modestly.

"There's nothing ordinary about you," Erik interjects as he waves me off. "Whether that makes you special or weird is a matter of perspective."

Everyone laughs at Erik's comment, including me.

"I love you, Erik," I tell him.

"I know," he says as he reaches over to squeeze my hand.

"It seems like there's quite a lot of love for you, Sophie." Michael says.

All three of the men stare at me. I'm sure my face is on fire.

"Can we focus on something else?" I ask the guys.

Erik obliges and asks Michael another question that only he would be brave enough to ask.

"So what do you think of Dimitri?"

I watch Michael's demeanor go from completely relaxed to cool in a blink of the eye.

"Abigail's marrying him."

I notice that he uses almost the exact same phrase as Clayton did when I asked him about Dimitri.

"You're not answering the question," Erik says as he picks up his wine glass. I'm surprised he's being so bold considering he just met Michael. But then, he's never one to censor what comes out of his mouth.

Michael's look is guarded.

"It's not my place to discuss Dimitri. Abigial picked him. She's the one who has to live with her decision."

Well, that's not very comforting. I think about how Michael behaved around Abigail this morning and wonder what happened between them.

"She does seem a little stressed out," I say cautiously.

"She's getting married. Brides are usually all nerves," Michael answers.

It's more than just nerves, but I'm not about to argue with a Sinclair. He saw the same thing I did this morning.

"Well, it's definitely going to be a beautiful wedding," I tell him. "Clayton's home is perfect."

"It is," Michael says quietly.

"Then I guess this calls for a toast to Abby," Erik says as he lifts his glass up.

The toast lacks the enthusiasm one would expect for a bride-to-be and it makes me think that everyone at the table must be having the same thought: *What the hell is Abby thinking?*

I take a sip of my wine then excuse myself to find the ladies' room. The restaurant has beautiful views of a vineyard and is really quite romantic. I make my way past a few tables and find a sign that seems to lead me down a hall.

I only spot them because I made what was obviously a wrong turn.

My heart stops in my chest.

It's Clayton and Amelia.

Gorgeous, stunning, sexy as hell Amelia. She's dressed in a long, tan dress with a giant red scarf, which only accentuates her long graceful neck and incredible face. In an instant I feel lacking and underdressed, even though I had tried really hard with the black fitted leggings and high boots to go with the black cashmere sweater and leather jacket Erik had picked out for me. I thought I looked sexy, but now facing this exotic beauty I feel like a wallflower.

And unfortunately that's not all.

Amelia's leaning toward him with a manicured hand on his broad chest, speaking in a low, intimate way. And he seems thoroughly engrossed in whatever it is she's saying. I take a step back and hide behind a large plant, not wanting either of them to see me staring.

"They make such a stunning couple."

Shit.

I turn to stare at bitchy Jane, who gives me an innocent smile.

"They're not a couple," I respond rather harshly, even though I completely agree with her assessment.

"It's only a matter of time," she says as her gaze sweeps over me dismissively, obviously finding me inferior. "They always seem to end up in each other's arms. It's like they're meant to be."

She's right. Clearly. At least as far as I can tell. First in Singapore, now here in Provence. But I'll be damned if I'll give her the satisfaction of showing that I care.

"I'm not worried."

She raises a condescending brow.

"No? Then why were you spying on them?"

"I was looking for the restroom." It's the truth. Well, maybe I did get caught spying but no way this bitch is going to call me out.

"Right," she sneers with a haughty little laugh. "You don't speak French?"

I wish I knew some particular French words because I would use them right now on her. But unfortunately, I don't. So I use another tactic.

"Did you know your face twitches when your lip curls into that sneer?" I tell her casually. "It worries me. You should see a doctor."

I notice with some satisfaction how Jane's face expression goes from normal angry to complete and utter rage.

"You're an American slut," Jane says coldly. "A woman he picked up in the Maldives. A passing fancy. Don't you ever forget that."

Bitch!

Something comes over me.

The world moves in slow motion and then I grab the crazy devil that is Jane by her designer shirt and shove her up against the wall. She looks about as shocked as I feel.

"Watch yourself," I say, my voice strong and aggressive. "Stay away from me or you won't appreciate the consequences."

I let go of her like she's a diseased leper.

"Trust me when I say you don't want to cross me again."

I leave her standing there with her mouth open and make my way back to the table, my desire to use the restroom completely gone. Erik immediately notices my state.

"I need you for a second," I tell him and smile apologetically at Michael. "Wardrobe issues."

"Of course."

It doesn't take a brain surgeon to know something is up. Orie immediately engages Michael in small talk as Erik takes my arm.

"Let's go around the other way," I say to him and lead him toward the door. I want to avoid seeing Jane or worse, Clayton and Amelia.

"What's going on?" Erik's asks in a justifiably worried voice.

"I'll tell you when we're outside."

We step through the front doors.

The cold air is a welcome relief. I immediately spew it out.

"I just went Rambo on Jane and shoved her up against a wall and told her to stay away from me."

It takes a moment to register with Erik.

"Holy shit. That is fucking awesome!"

Erik raises his hand to give me a high five. I slap it

"What happened?" he asks.

"I was looking for the restroom and I don't know, just came across Clayton and Amelia talking by the bar," I explain. "So I did what any normal person would do and hid behind a plant and started spying. And Jane caught me."

I hope I sound calm and not crazy. Because I'm really trying not to jump to conclusions or make false accusations, but seeing them looking so cozy together has really thrown me for a loop.

"They were talking, I guess," I tell him. "But it looked intense. And that's not me reading into the situation, it's what I saw."

Erik crosses his arms. I know he's thinking about what he should say to me.

"How did it make you feel?"

"Honestly?"

"Always."

"Like I'm a fool," I confess.

I wait for him to hit me with an angry tirade about how I have to be more self-confident and get a grip but it doesn't come. The opposite happens.

"Well, that's not good, Sophie."

"It's not?" I'm beyond shocked.

"Even if nothing is going on with Amelia, Clayton shouldn't be letting the bitch put her paws on him. That's just not cool."

I feel a surge of relief.

"Right?" I feel validated.

"Yes."

"And my behavior with Jane?" I ask.

"Totally justified. That girl is a cunt," Erik is blunt.

"I totally agree," I say to him so thankful that he's on my side.

"So should we go?" I ask, and my voice wavers.

"Go where?" Erik asks.

"Home."

He laughs. "Hell, no. You don't run from problems, you face them. Do you want that bitch to think you ran away from her?"

"No!"

"Then we're going back inside. And come what may," he says as he reaches for my hand.

Come what may.

I nod and follow him inside. Clayton is sitting at the table, leaning back in his chair with his long arm sloped over my empty one. He gives me a warm smile and then stands to pull out my chair for me.

"I was about to come and find you," he whispers in my ear, then kisses me on the lips.

I force a smile.

"Is everything okay?"

"Why wouldn't it be?" I ask, knowing full well there's a bit of a high pitch to my voice.

I try not to fidget under the force of his gaze but he chooses not to answer. Instead, his body language responds to mine. I sit down on the chair and manage to scoot it an inch or two closer to Erik. If Clayton notices he doesn't let on. Instead he focuses on his brother and completely immerses himself in a conversation about business. Now he's actually leaning a bit away from me as well, responding in kind to my energy.

"Wasn't it freezing outside without your jackets?" Orie asks as he looks from me to Erik.

"I think that mistral wind that Sergei was talking about is starting to kick in," Erik says as he rubs his hands together then places one on my cold fingers. "Let me warm you up."

"Thank you," I say, trying to fight the sick feeling that is growing exponentially in the pit of my stomach.

"Can we join you guys?" Amelia's voice purrs out of nowhere as she comes up to our table with annoying Jane. She puts her hand on the back of Michael's chair and focuses her gaze on Clayton. I notice with some panic that it's quite intimate.. Kind of like the looks he's always giving me.

Something snaps inside me and before anyone else can answer, I do.

"Of course you can," I say sweetly. "There's plenty of room."

I'm mildly amused when all eyes at the table turn to stare at me in complete surprise. I avoid Clayton's fiery gaze and force an artificial smile.

"The more the merrier," I add.

I wonder whether I'm just a glutton for punishment and am trying to just torture myself by staring at the flawless Amelia for an entire meal, or whether it's the former law student in me who wants to be able to analyze their body language and figure out what's going on. I watch Michael motion to one of the waiters to bring over two more chairs. As everyone is scooting around trying to make room, Clayton pulls my chair up to his rather forcefully. Then he leans down to whisper in my ear.

"What the hell is this about?"

"Nothing," I return, hoping I sound calm. And totally unaffected.

"Nothing?" The way he enunciates the word puts me on high alert. He is definitely pissed.

"They're your friends, right?" I ask innocently.

"Stop playing games," he says coldly.

"This isn't a game," I tell him, suddenly beyond furious. Because it's not. It's real life. *My life.*

I dare him to come back at me. I actually hope he does, but unfortunately he doesn't give me the satisfaction.

Quietly, so that no one can hear, he says, "I'm not doing this with you," and stands up rather abruptly.

"I have to go," he tells the group to my utter annoyance. "I have work to take care of. But you guys enjoy yourselves."

His looks down at me with a sharp, gaze. "Are you coming with me or would you rather stay?"

It's a challenge. I know it. He knows it. And I bravely rise to the occasion.

"I'll stay, thank you," I say with a sugar sweet smile. "Since you'll be working I might as well enjoy dinner with everyone."

His eyes stay on mine for a beat before he nods curtly.

"Enjoy."

And then he leaves. No kiss goodbye. Nothing. Nada. Zilch. I wonder if I just played everything so wrong.

"Sophie," Amelia says sweetly, "it's so nice to see you again."

I'll bet it is.

"Likewise," I tell her with a forced smile.

Jane gives me the stink eye as Amelia continues to check me out.

"When did you arrive?" I ask, trying to fill in the uncomfortable silence.

"Yesterday morning," she says. "I had a shoot for *Vogue* in Prague then rushed right over here to be Jane's date."

Great. The bitch models for *Vogue*.

"What do *you* do, Jane?" Erik asks curiously.

I'm glad he does because I'm dying to know.

"Jane is what we like to call a Sloane Ranger," Michael answers for her.

"Michael—" Jane laughs coyly, not the least bit offended by Michael's description of her.

"What's that?" Orie asks.

"A certain breed of upper-class woman in London," Michael explains with a hint of disdain. "They do a lot of shopping."

"And charity work," Jane smiles.

"That's right. How could I forget?" Michael says mockingly.

"There are some men we both know who fit that bill rather nicely," Jane says pointedly, then, "And there was a time when the Sinclair men would laugh at such a description."

"I don't think it's funny anymore," Michael tells her. "I think it's ridiculous. And that was a long time ago, when we didn't know any better."

I'm really surprised Jane is not offended by Michael's brutal honesty.

"Well, I'm in good company," Jane tells him. "Your beautiful cousin Abigail happens to be a proud Sloanie."

I watch Michael's mood darken.

"Don't remind me."

Jane laughs before continuing.

"But I don't know about that Russian—" Jane realizes what she's saying and stops herself. "Forgive me."

He nods then motions toward the waiter.

"You're forgiven for that slight and for the fact that you've completely intruded on a private dinner."

My mouth drops open.

"I'm not the least bit offended," Amelia says to me with a smile. "Michael doesn't care what he says or who he offends. Clayton at least has a bit more decorum when it comes to what comes out of his mouth and as for your baby brother, William—"

"—he's just kind," Jane finished Amelia's thought. "If he didn't have those Sinclair eyes you'd think he was adopted."

I'm unprepared for the pang of jealousy I feel that these two women I don't particularly care for know Clayton's family so well. I don't even know what William looks like. Until the other day, I wouldn't have known Michael if I walked past him on the street. They all grew up together and regardless of whether or not they really like one another it seems like they'll always be friends because of their background.

"William *is* too kind," Michael agrees. His voice is soft and full of love. "Clayton and I try to toughen him up."

The love he has for his brother is obvious to see.

"You and Clayton got all the Sinclair arrogance," Jane says. "William just got the sweet side. Definitely from your mother."

"When does he arrive?" Amelia asks.

"Late tomorrow evening," Michael says. "My father is working him to death."

"I can't wait to see your parents," Amelia says, digging the knife in.

Now I feel like a complete outsider. Amelia knows Clayton's parents? Why would he ever introduce her to them if she didn't matter?

"Have you met them, Sophie?" she asks with a fake smile.

"No, I haven't." I pick up my wine glass and take a sip.

The thought of meeting Clayton's parents and them not approving of me makes my stomach turn. And let's be honest, it's completely in the realm of possibility, considering I don't have the blue blood this group seems to abound in.

"They're lovely," Amelia tells me, like we're friends. "Rosalind is *so* elegant. Michael, I do believe your mother has the best fashion sense I've ever seen."

"I completely agree," Jane says. "She always looks as if she's just walked off a runway."

I think about my wardrobe and give a silent thank you prayer that I have Erik with me to make sure that everything I put on in front of her is perfect.

"I love a woman with a great style," Erik chimes in.

"Then you'll love her," Jane predicts.

"Everyone does." Amelia agrees. "I hear you're a stylist and costume designer?" Amelia says to Erik, and in an instant Orie, Jane, Erik and Amelia become immersed deep in conversation

I feel Michael's eyes on my face. He gets up from his chair and takes Clayton's. I know he's carefully studying my reactions.

"Why didn't you leave with my brother?" he asks in a low voice.

"You invited us to dinner," I say evenly.

Michael smiles. And again, I note just how incredibly, ruggedly, handsome he is.

"Come on, Sophie," he says. "Honesty between us is a requirement since I have a feeling you and I are going to be great friends."

I kind of have the same feeling. I smile back at him and shrug.

"I didn't feel like listening to his every order."

"But it wasn't an order," Michael says with a laugh.

I raise a brow. "Wasn't it?"

"I guess it was," he agrees. He shakes his head in amazement. "I have to tell you how fascinating it is to see him in this type of relationship. He's usually the one in control."

I lift my wine glass and try to refrain from rolling my eyes.

"I would venture to say that he still pretty much is."

"Is he?" Michael asks.

I look away from his knowing gaze.

"Why did you invite these two vipers to have dinner with us?" he asks me curiously.

I look over to see if Amelia or Jane can hear what Michael just said but they are still deep in conversation with Erik and Orie.

I take my time before answering and lean back in my chair.

"I just thought it was the polite thing to do."

"I don't buy it." Michael shakes his head mockingly.

I can't help but laugh. He's so carefree and easy to be around. I wish Clayton could be so pleasant.

"I won't let up until you tell me."

"You're very much like you're brother in that way," I inform him.

"I take that as the best compliment," he says so solemnly that I believe him.

"Don't allow these women to throw you off balance or make you start playing games with my brother. Or with his feelings," Michael says to my astonishment. "They're not worth it."

His words stump me, I know, because it's hard for me to see Clayton as someone capable of having feelings. It's not a joke. I just think of him as this super-powerful omnipresent man who always gets what he wants and can never possibly get hurt.

"I wasn't trying to play games."

"Weren't you?" Michael asks sharply.

I look away from his gaze for a moment and then decide to tell him the truth. "I saw your brother and Amelia together by the bar. It angered me. She was leaning into him and I felt like I was reliving what happened in the Maldives all over again."

"So you just reacted?" Michael finishes.

"Yes," I say feeling a sudden sense of impending doom.

"I know what happened between you and Clayton," Michael says. "He told me about the article in the magazine and how you didn't believe him and other bits, Granted, he was smashed when he recounted the story, but he told me."

There are no words.

"You don't know our family, Sophie," Michael says slowly. "We are the product of an environment that most people would not know how to comprehend. What we saw between our parents—I can't explain it. Clayton had it worse than William and me because he was old enough to understand what was going on. Those things you see, they shape you," Michael continues as he searches for the right words. "My work is my passion. It's what I live for. The causes that I fight for are what give me hope and reason. Clayton's work isn't the same as mine. Granted, it's fulfilling in a different way, but it's not like what I do. He doesn't get the same joy from it. This is the first time in my life I've seen my brother look so—so exposed. And content. Behind the facade he puts up is a vulnerable man."

Vulnerable. That's the last adjective I would ever think to use to describe Clayton. But Michael looks so earnest I believe him.

"There's obviously something between the two of you," he goes on. "Something big. Don't let these little things get in the way."

I think about Michael's words all through dinner and on the drive home. When we reach the house we quickly say our goodbyes. I head toward my room and wonder if I'll find Clayton there. He didn't text me or call all evening so I know he's still mad. How mad is what I have yet to find out.

I take a deep breath and open the door and my heart slams in my chest. He's sitting in one of the wing-backed chairs in front of the fireplace, sifting through files. He's bare-chested and wearing long black pajama pants.

He looks too sexy for words.

His gaze, however, is glacial.

I shut the door quietly and choose to stay exactly where I am. He just stares. There's a challenge in his eyes.

Crap. I wonder what I've just walked into.

"How was dinner?" he asks.

"It was lovely, thank you."

"Was it?"

I cringe as I hear the sharpness in his voice. I nod lamely. It's all I'm capable of doing.

"The conversation must have been stimulating," he says sarcastically.

"It was," I say with a shrug.

There's a long silence between us again.

"What is this new attitude of yours about?" he asks me coolly.

"I don't know what you're talking about," I say nervously. I think about opening the door and running down the hall.

"Yes you do, baby. And since you're a big fan of games we're going to play one of mine."

My heart drops.

"By my rules," he goes on. "Now take off your clothes."

10

I am paralyzed by his words.

"Take. Off. Your. Clothes."

Clayton drops the files on the floor and leans back in his chair. He picks up the glass of Scotch from the table next to him and continues to watch me aloofly.

This is Clayton, I tell myself. He's mad. Annoyed. Maybe he has a right to be, maybe not. But I know he won't hurt me. It's his way of controlling me. *He's just trying to control me.*

"I don't know if this is a good idea," I tell him.

"Why wouldn't it be?" he asks curiously.

"Because it's not safe," I tell him. "You're angry at me—"

"Not angry, baby," Clayton takes a sip of his drink. "Annoyed."

I remain silent.

"That you would ruin our evening with that irrational insecurity of yours," he says harshly.

My back straightens.

"I don't know what you're talking about."

"Do you think I didn't see you? When Amelia and I were speaking. Back by the restrooms."

I want to die. He saw me spying. I burn from the shame of it.

"I wasn't spying—" Oh shit. Did I just say that out loud?

"I didn't say you were."

Crap. I think I'm starting to hyperventilate.

"Do you have anything to say?" he asks curiously.

It comes down to me having trust issues with him. Right or wrong, I guess I do. And the she-devil was in his arms. I don't know why or how or what for, but she was fawning all over him. So I just went there.

However, I say truthfully, "I don't appreciate the fact that every time I turn around I see that bitch draped in your arms."

Score one for Sophie.

Clayton's eyes widen at my words.

I go on bravely.

"I don't think you would appreciate finding me in Jerry's arms. In fact, I know from experience that you didn't and I would venture to guess that if you found me like that again you'd react a lot more harshly than I did. So in the future I expect to receive the same courtesy from you," I tell him bluntly, feeling empowered by my words and honesty.

I wait for him to speak.

"Fair enough," he says slowly, as if testing out the words or the fact that he is actually agreeing to what I said.

I'm happy he doesn't put up a fight or argue with me over what I saw or how I felt. We stare at one another.

So what now?

"Now take off your clothes."

Shit. I let out the breath I was holding and focus on how handsome his face and body look lit up like that in the firelight.

There's still an unspoken current of anger in the air between us. Everything isn't all better now.

Yet.

But I listen and slowly start to undress. I'm acutely aware of Clayton's eyes on my body, of the way they sweep over me, almost like he's touching me, worshipping me. I tremble in anticipation and am burning with desire when the last piece of clothing is off my body.

"Everything." Clayton's voice is raspy with hunger.

He's referring to the pink lace panties I've chosen to keep on. I scoot them off quickly, willing him to hold my gaze.

He does.

"Come here," he commands.

I do.

Standing inches from him, allowing the heat from the fire and his eyes to burn my skin. He puts his drink down and runs his fingers up my thighs.

"What am I going to do with you?" he whispers as his mouth follows the trail his fingers took only seconds before.

Keep me, I think with longing. *Just like I want to keep you.*

"What do you want to do to me?" I ask him softly as I move my hands to his hair.

I hope he can't see the longing for him that's written on my face.

"Everything."

My heart flutters. He moves his mouth to my stomach and traces soft kisses along my navel. I don't know how it's humanly possible for me to want someone as much as I do this man. But I do. And each time we come together, I crave him more. He stands abruptly and picks me up, wrapping my legs around his bare waist. I don't know how or when his pajama pants came off but they're gone. I pull his mouth to mine and get lost in the taste of him as he slowly lowers us both to the ground.

His mouth nips at mine, his tongue tracing my lips before he pulls back. His translucent eyes pierce into mine and shards of electricity explode through my body.

"You were right about one thing," he tells me.

"What's that?" I know my voice is breathless.

"This isn't safe," he says as he looks down at our naked bodies. He rubs himself against me, his tip teasing me mercilessly.

"It's dangerous."

His fingers fill the spaces between my own.

"It's unpredictable."

His palms my breast, his fingers teasing my hardened nipple until I think I'm going to scream with need.

"It's electric."

I'm desperate with want. With undeniable desire. He does this to me. Always. He brings out every type of emotion possible. Anger. Lust. Even love. Still love. From the second I saw him in the waiting room in the Maldives I was lost. It's like a keg of gunpowder, always on the verge of exploding.

His arm coils around my waist and pulls me closer, making me feel so small and fragile against his large frame.

"And it's never going to end, Sophie."

His mouth takes mine with force. We taste each other; his tongue and mine fuse into one. Excitement courses through my body, eager for the sweet anticipation of what is to come. Of what only he can give me.

"Say it," he commands.

"It won't ever end," I whisper against his mouth. My eyes open of their own accord and I find him watching me in a primal way. The way a man does when he's staked a claim. Like he owns you. And it's the most incredibly seductive thing I've ever seen. His gaze softens. His body leans down toward mine, his hands come up and cup my cheeks as his large thumbs move lightly over my swollen lips. And he enters me, fills me to my core but continues to watch me with that look. I try to hold on to reality as the sweet feeling of pleasure rushes through my body.

There's something on his face I've never seen. An unspoken message in his eyes. I know it. I can feel it in my gut. In my heart. I may be the seduced, he, the seducer, but this look he's giving isn't lying to me. It's there for me to see. A glimpse into his soul. He's fallen for me. He might not know it yet or have accepted it, but I see it right there, plain as day.

"I love you," I tell him softly, before my body starts to tremble.

My words cause him to pull me even closer, thrust even deeper, filling me, moving faster and faster until I explode again from another earth-shattering orgasm. I call out his name and he groans mine.

He gathers me into his arms like I'm a most cherished prize, and we fall asleep in each other's arms.

"I want to apologize for my behavior yesterday," Abigail says to me as we hike up a trail on Clayton's property.

It's a crisp morning. Since it rained last night we're taking advantage of the gorgeous scenery and the views of the fields and vineyards that seem to go on for days.

I was supposed to be doing Abby's portrait. So I waited for her in the studio, but was not that surprised when she came in, not in the Marie Antoinette gear, but in casual jeans and a sweater. She looked as if she had cried all night and my heart hurt for her. I could not imagine what she was going through at this moment. I was the one who suggested a walk, and we grabbed coats and hats and left the villa quickly. I had the distinct feeling that Abby was on the verge of a nervous breakdown.

And if anyone knows how that feels, it's me. And Dr. Goldstein. That poor, poor doctor. I cringe when I think about how many times I must have repeated the same story over and over to him.

"My behavior was deplorable and you must have been horrified by me." Abby says and her voice cracks as she tries not to cry.

"Abby, please," I assure her. "We've all been there."

She actually laughs. "I don't think quite as spectacularly as me."

"Alright," I smile, "maybe not in that outfit and hair and make-up, but in some form or another, trust me. I was there pretty recently, actually. And I know firsthand that it's not a fun place to be."

For whatever reason I don't mind admitting to her that I was in a sad state of mind.

"With Clayton?" Abby asks.

"Yes," I say.

"And now?"

"Now, we'll see where things take us. That's all I can do," I tell her honestly. "But we didn't come out here to talk about me."

"No," Abby says with a sigh, then leans her head back and takes in a deep breath. I hope the fresh air can help ease some of her pain. I take note of her profile—she's really quite pretty, classy and elegant. And innocent. She seems so innocent and young, which is surprising considering the women and the world she grew up around. And also that we are almost the exact same age.

"I don't know why I'm so comfortable talking to you, but I am." She looks at me and her blue eyes are glazed with tears.

"You can trust me," I promise her. "I won't repeat this conversation to anyone."

"Not even Clayton?" she asks with some uncertainty.

"Not even him," I tell her, because I would never betray her trust.

She takes her time before speaking again and I don't push her. The only noise that can be heard is the soft crunch of our shoes on the dirt road. I put my hands in my pockets and wait.

"I don't love Dimitri," she finally says.

I say, "I think you might have mentioned that yesterday."

"I did?" Abby sounds mortified. "I was smashed! I don't even want to know what else came out of my mouth."

"I won't tell you," I say with a smile. In retrospect it was kind of funny. "But I promise it was nothing bad."

"Did I already tell you that I plan to be the runaway bride on my wedding day?" she asks me with some trepidation.

I stop in my tracks and face her.

"No, you did not."

Abby's face is solemn as she nods.

"Since I'm too ashamed to call it off now while everyone is here having a nice time, I thought that if I just leave on the day of the wedding the drama of it will be all that anyone talks about for a long while. And maybe it will lessen the blow to Dimitri."

Not really, but I don't know if I should tell her that. There's so much more I feel like I have to address first. Like ditching the groom at the altar. And I think I'm dramatic.

"I know what you're thinking," Abby rushes out. "I do. But you're wrong. Trust me. These people, this is the only way I can back out gracefully—"

"Gracefully?" I'm shocked she's chosen this adjective.

"Well, somewhat," Abby blushes. "But this is the only way I can get out of here. Dimitri will force me to stay and marry him if I try to discuss my unhappiness with him. He knows, Sophie. He knows that I don't love him and he doesn't care. He just wants me to be the perfect wife and attend society functions and be on the board of various charities, just like all the other wives. He doesn't love me either."

This wedding is sounding more and more like an episode of *Downton Abbey*.

"What about your mom and dad?" I ask her.

"What about them?" Abby looks angry. "Remember, my mum is the one who got me in this situation in the first place. And that pig of a stepbrother I have gets away with murder and stands to inherit everything. All they have done since the day I turned eighteen was talk about marriage. They just want to get rid of me. I guess I must cost too much."

I know she's told me this before, but still I'm totally speechless.

I feel sorry for her. Because I know firsthand that her stepbrother *is* really a pig. Her parents must be blind, deaf, and dumb not to see it. I understand that there is a hierarchy in the system but how can they not leave something for their daughter?

"Have you really thought it all through?" I ask her with concern.

"Yes," Abby says emphatically.

"What will you do for money?"

She pauses for a moment.

"I'm going to get a job," she tells me, sounding extremely unsure. "Or, I don't know... join the United Nations Peace Keeping Operations."

I almost laugh. I don't think Abby really knows what that entails and I'm loathe to be the one to break the news to her. I turn and start walking again and Abby slowly follows. I'm sure she's probably half surprised that I haven't tried to convince her not to do it. And I'm surprised that she hasn't asked for my help, and Erik and Orie's, for that matter, to plan her escape. Which, by the way, I would totally do for her. And I'd bet money that Erik and Orie would think it was fun.

But there's one other question that I have to ask her, even though it's probably not my place to do so.

"And what about Michael?"

I hear Abby's footsteps falter.

"What about him?" she almost whispers.

I wait for her to catch up to me, then I say, "You're in love with him."

Abby's face turns bright red. "Did I admit that to you, too?"

"Kind of, but then you really didn't have to because I could see it all over your face when he walked in the room yesterday," I say gently. "It's okay. Your secret is safe with me."

Abby hugs her arms around her waist and looks at the sky.

"He's never given me the time of day," she says. "He thinks that because we're family by marriage it means we're blood related. And I know he thinks I'm just a toff."

I wince. I've heard the phrase before and I know it's a derogatory way to refer to the British upper class. Considering Michael comes from the same background, I don't think he would use the label.

"I doubt that," I say.

"You don't know him," Abby says. "He hates being back home now. His life is so different. He's out trying to make a difference and he's quick to judge. Or, at least, judge me."

"Maybe that's just you judging you?" I ask her.

"No," she shakes her head. "I know."

I choose not to argue with her because I know it will be in vain. She's not in a place where she can listen to reason.

"So what do you want to do about your portrait?" I ask her.

"I'm definitely not sitting for anything," she says adamantly. "We'll just pretend that we are and if you could be so kind as to make sure Dimitri stays out of that room that would be wonderful. Not that you have anything to worry about because the last thing he will ever do is pretend that he's interested in something that relates to me."

"And Erik?"

"I'll take the wardrobe he bought and all his choices. He and his boyfriend, Orie, are wonderful to be around."

It seems so wrong to continue staying there as if everything is happening as planned when I now know it's not. But there's one thing for sure.

"I will reimburse you the five thousand advance," I tell her.

"Absolutely not!" Abby says vehemently. "You will not do any such thing."

"I can't take money for something I'm not doing," I argue.

"It's for your time. Flying out here to be—"

"In paradise?" I finish her sentence with a knowing smile.

Abby actually laughs.

"Well, yes. But anyway, Dimitri paid for it, and I don't want him ever to know that you knew what was going to happen. Just think of this as a paid vacation that will have one extraordinary end," Abby says, trying to sound upbeat.

"I can't do that," I shake my head. "It's wrong."

"It's not wrong," Abby says firmly. "Please. Just don't argue with me about this."

I nod in agreement but there's no way I will take all the money.

We're so immersed in our thoughts that we don't immediately feel the light raindrops that quickly become pouring rain.

"Oh, my God!" Abby shrieks as we look up at the gray sky and the clouds that seemed to come from nowhere.

We turn around and start down the hilly path, laughing at the absurdity of being caught out in the storm. Abby has a head start on me so I hurry to catch up, which leads me to slide on the mud and trip head first down the small slope. I'm too horrified by my clumsiness to notice the mud that is now plastered all over me, face included.

"Are you okay?" Abby says as she runs over to me and leans down to help me out of the gooey muck.

"Holy cow!" I say as I try to stand up. Then the absurdity kicks in and we both burst out laughing. I slip around a bit as I try to stand.

"Let me help you!" Abby says with a shriek of merriment.

"No!" I shake my head. "You'll just end up covered in mud like me!"

"You *are* covered, Sophie!" She says hysterically. "I'm sorry, but this is the funniest thing I've seen in ages!"

Abby's crying, she's laughing so hard.

"I'm glad I could make you feel better," I tell her with a giggle .

In our suddenly high spirits we don't feel the cold or mind the rain on the way back to the chateau. We walk through the courtyard and find cover and are no longer being pelted by rain.

"I don't want to get mud everywhere!" I tell Abby as we head up to the main entrance.

"Nonsense. Just take off your boots and I'll get you a towel," she says as she looks me over. I'm sure my appearance can't be pretty. "You'll get pneumonia if you stand outside any longer."

And then the unthinkable happens. The double doors open and Clayton is standing there with two people I can only assume are his parents, because he resembles both of them in different ways.

And oh how I want the earth to swallow me whole.

Clayton's mouth drops when he sees me, soaking wet and covered in filth . He pulls me inside quickly and Abby follows.

"You're going to catch a cold!" I can hear the worry in his voice. And I like it.

"It is so nice to see you, Aunt Rosalind," I hear Abigail say, confirming my worst nightmare. Not only is she Clayton's mom, but she is in Chanel from head to toe, literally. And here I am, head to toe in mud. The irony is not lost on me.

"And you, Uncle Harry."

Clayton's father is a silver-haired version of Michael. Wolf eyes and all. His mom is an elegant brunette who must have been stunning back in the day, considering she is still quite beautiful.

"Abigail, you are positively drenched!" Clayton's father scolds her. "What were you thinking being out in such weather?"

"We weren't really paying attention," Abby smiles, then looks over at me with wide eyes. I'm sure she feels sorry for me. "Now if you'll excuse me, I must go run a hot bath. I will see you later, Sophie."

And she leaves me.

Then Clayton says to my and I'm sure his parents complete and utter shock, "Mother, father allow me to introduce you to my girlfriend, Sophie Walker."

They cover their looks of horror quickly.

"A pleasure," his father says politely, masking any judgment he might have made already.

"So nice to meet you," I say with an embarrassed smile. "I took a pretty bad fall in the mud."

"It's a good thing you didn't hurt yourself," Mr. Sinclair says with a pleasant smile.

His mom is way more aloof and much more repelled. "She's going to track the mud through the house," is all she can manage. My back stiffens. She hasn't even acknowledged me.

"No, she won't," Clayton answers evenly.

Before I know what's what, he leans over, picks me up, and cradles me in his arms.

"Clayton no!" I protest, but it's to no avail. In two seconds the mud from my clothes is smeared all over his grey cashmere sweater and jeans.

"I insist, milady." He gives me a wolfish grin.

I blush under the intensity of his gaze.

"Mother, father, now if you'll excuse us."

I glance at his mother with an embarrassed look on my face. I can't help but notice that she's still not said a proper hello to me.

"It was nice meeting you," I say with as much dignity as I can muster.

Rosalind Sinclair looks at me like I've grown two horns.

"A pleasure," she finally manages.

So much for making a good first impression.

"Clayton, we'd love to have you, Michael, and Sophie, of course, join us for lunch," his father says formally. "That is, if you're free."

I feel Clayton's muscles tense up when his father addresses him. He looks down at me.

"What would you like to do?"

I feel the burning gaze of his mom on my face and I'm almost grateful that splashes of mud cover my cheeks. I'm sure I'm bright red.

"I think you and Michael should have lunch with your parents alone," I rush out. "I'm sure they'd like to spend some time alone with you."

Before Clayton can argue his mother chimes in.

"Nonsense," she says formally. "We want you to join us as well."

"Then that settles it," his father says. "Clayton?"

"Perfect," Clayton's voice doesn't sound very enthusiastic. "We'll see you at lunch then."

Clayton turns and heads down the hall to the back stairwell.

11

"I really don't have to join you guys," I say since he's unusually silent as he makes his way to the room.

"I'm not going without you," he tells me. His blue eyes are alight with amusement and he starts to laugh. The rumble in his chest vibrates through my body. "You look utterly ridiculous," he says.

"I'm afraid to see," I whisper to him with an embarrassed giggle. I can only imagine. And in front of his mom, of all people, the woman who's apparently the walking queen of couture. Lord almighty.

"Did you slide down the whole hill?" he asks curiously.

"Basically," I admit with a grin. "By the way, am I supposed to address your parents as Earl or Lady Sinclair? I don't know how that all works."

"Absolutely not," Clayton actually cringes. "We are not formal about our titles amongst family."

Family? My heart soared.

"Other than the torrential downpour did you and Abigail have a nice time?" Clayton asks.

"Great," I tell him. "I really like her."

I wonder what Clayton would think if I told him what Abigail and I talked about. Not that I would ever betray her trust, I'm just wondering what he would do. It probably wouldn't go over so well. Or maybe it would. I'm pretty sure he doesn't like Dimitri. so he might support her decision. Still, it's not my place to test that theory. It's Abby's.

We arrive at his room in no time and he goes straight into the bathroom and sets me down. It's at this moment that I get a good look at myself in the full-length mirror. As they say, ignorance is bliss. Oh. My. God. I am so mortified.

"I can't believe I met your parents looking like this," I say in a strangled whisper.

"It was classic," he says with an amused grin. I can tell he thinks it's hilarious.

"Classically wrong," I mumble.

He unzips my puffer jacket and pulls it off, then takes me beanie off. "Lift your arms," he commands.

I do as I'm told as he pulls my sweater over my head.

His smile is all charm. "I think you'll need some help with getting all that mud off."

I blush.

"Your parents—"

"I'm a grown man," Clayton says with a raised brow.

"But I'm already the American who rolls around in mud for fun. Your parents might not think this is appropriate. Maybe you should go downstairs—"

"Appropriate?" he asks curiously.

"Yes," I whisper. "I don't want them to think—"

"They already do, Sophie."

Right. Hello, reality check.

"They think you're the gorgeous American their son is obsessed with," he goes on to say.

God.

I lose my stomach and my heart. Both fall straight through the floor from the giddiness I feel from those words.

But why stop there, Sophie?

"Obsessed?" I ask.

He lifts his hand to cup my cheek as he stares deep into my eyes.

"What else would you call it?"

My sense of propriety follows my stomach and heart. I reach out to unbutton his jeans. I feel his muscles clench the instant I touch him. It's a heady feeling to know that I turn him on so easily.

I stare into those cerulean eyes of his. They're steamy with desire. All for me.

"You're the gorgeous one," I whisper to him. "Every time I look at you, I—"

I lose my train of thought because he's brought his hand up to cup my breast. I suck in my breath.

"You what?" he asks as he leans down and takes my nipple in his mouth. My head falls back as his tongue swirls over the bud. He uses his teeth and pulls, then licks. It drives me wild.

"You what, Sophie?" he asks again as he moves lower, until he's leaning in front of me and lowers his mouth to taste me. His tongue moves back and forth and if weren't for his hands holding my thighs I would crumble before him.

He takes his time and my body feels like it's being rocked senseless. My hands grip his head, pulling at his hair as he continues the sweet agony.

"Clayton," I whimper.

"Sophie."

"I want you," I confess finally then go on, "when I look at you. Every single time I look at you."

He blows. Licks. Drives me wild.

"You want me to do this?" he asks.

"Yes!"

And more. Everything else he does that makes me crazy with desire and want. He gets up slowly, rubbing his chest and body along mine, until he's towering over me and I have to lean my head back to look at him. I can feel his swollen sex against my stomach and I almost come from the sheer, sweet torture of it. He picks me up and walks in the shower. The hot water feels like heaven. His hands move slowly over my flesh, wiping the mud off my hands, my body, and when he gets to my face, he brushes my skin ever so softly and cherishes me with his touch.

The water rains down on us as he gently kisses my face, his arms locking around my waist and pulling me closer to his naked skin. The way we move against each other is like an erotic slow dance.

"I have a confession to make," he says against my lips.

My hands move to his biceps and I squeeze them as he rubs his lips against mine, his tongue playing ever so slowly.

"What's that?" I whisper and touch my tongue to his.

"Every time I look at you—" he murmurs against my lips.

His fingers make their way down and move in, stroking me until I let out a strangled moan and beg for release. His other hand grabs my hair so his lips can whisper against my ear, his words causing me to want him in a way that his touch never has.

"—I want to be inside you," he continues the assault, his fingers moving deeper until I can bear it no longer.

"Until you're begging me for more," his tongue nips my outer lobe and I can hear the need in his voice, in his ragged breath.

"Until you think you'll die without me," he says as his fingers move out. I cry out in frustration.

He lifts me up in his strong arms and slowly lowers me until his body crashes into mine. I throw my head back and revel in the feel of him, the intensity of having all of him, like this. He moves his hips and pushes further in and walks until my naked back is against the smooth marble wall of the shower. My legs are hooked around his waist and I squeeze him tight. I open my eyes against the warm water that rains down on us both.

God he's so hot. His eyelashes are spiky with droplets of water, his blue eyes hazy with desire. I grind my hips, clenching him tighter so I can push him over the edge the way that he does me. He holds my waist with one arm and takes my hands in the other, holding them over my head so he can pull out and plunge in deeper.

"Clayton!"

"The way I think I'll die without you. Every. Single. Time. " His voice is filled with passion, as his forehead comes to rest against mine.

Connected.

Not just our bodies.

But our hearts.

"So when you met her, you basically resembled a pig in shit?" Erik says. He's sitting on the bed watching me model outfit after outfit. I recruited him and Orie to help me find the perfect look for lunch.

Orie's turned the wingback chair away from the fire to face me and has his legs stretched out on a side table. I'm surprised he isn't sitting next to Erik on the bed. They both seemed a bit off when they walked in. I really hope they're not still fighting.

"Kind of," I nod as I turn in a small circle to show outfit number three. According to Erik, outfit number one was "trying too hard" and outfit number two said "screams we come from two different worlds and mine sucks."

So now I have on a pair of black tights, knee length black boots and a gray, long-sleeved cashmere fitted dress that comes up above my knees. I've left my hair down and put a minimal amount of make-up on, hoping not to come off as overly done up.

"Now this, this, I like," Erik approves.

"I love this whole look," Orie agrees as he checks me out. "You have great legs, Sophie."

"Thank you," grateful the two of them can make me feel so confident. "But are you sure? You don't think I should try anything else?"

"This is it," Erik says with finality.

"You're classy. Stylish. And pretty," Orie agrees.

"Just don't trip over your own two feet in front of the woman or spill a drink," Erik warns. "Especially on her."

"Must you?" Orie asks him with some annoyance. There's an edge to his voice that I've never heard before.

"Must I what?" Erik snaps back. I watch as his eyes narrow in annoyance.

Uh oh. Definitely still arguing.

"Be so negative?" Orie tells him.

"How is what I said negative?" Erik challenges.

"Guys," I say, hoping this isn't about to turn into a full-blown fight.

Erik waves his hand at me, basically telling me to be quiet.

"I'm really tired of you picking on me," Erik says to Orie, his voice raises an octave in anger. "It's getting old."

My heart sinks.

I don't want something bad to happen between them. I love them together. I've never seen them be so aggressive or angry with one another.

Orie stands up. "I don't want to do this right now."

"That's a shocker," Erik mutters.

I watch Orie clench his fists at his side and attempt to get a grip. I know he's dying to lay into Erik, I can totally see it. But he controls himself.

"Sophie, you look gorgeous," Orie tells me with a forced smile. "They would be complete idiots not to fall in love with you."

"Thank you, Orie," I say softly.

"Will I see you tonight?" he asks me.

"Where?"

"They're doing a game night party with board games and everything."

"Sounds like fun," I tell him. "I will for sure be there."

"See you then, beautiful."

He comes over and kisses me on the cheek and leaves the room. I can see the hurt in his eyes and I wonder what is going on. When the door clicks shut I swing around to face Erik.

"What was that about?"

"Nothing," he shrugs. Then, "We're fighting. Isn't it obvious?"

I'm kind of shocked. "Yes, but why?"

"Because he flirted with that French shit the other night." Erik's voice is filled with a good deal of animosity.

"What French shit?" I ask in confusion.

"That Georgie," Erik tells me. "Abby's sad version of me."

"Versace Georgie?" I'm flabbergasted. "He wouldn't."

"Trés." Erik nods his head.

"Are you sure you're not overthinking this and making yourself crazy for no reason? I'm a great example of that," I remind him.

"I'm a man, Sophie," Erik tells me harshly. "I know flirting when I see it. And it sucked."

If he's right, I'm sure it did. I watch him get up and walk over to the bottle of champagne that he and Orie brought in for me, and pour himself a glass. He throws it back like water.

I try to come up with an argument. "Flirting is not cheating."

Erik pins me with his gaze.

"Would you take that same advice?"

"No," I say automatically. "But look at me. I'm a hot mess. I'm still trying to get my shit together.

I'm the last person you should look to as an example."

"You're not a mess." Erik shakes his head then closes his eyes rather dramatically, "I can't believe I'm saying this but you're the furthest from a mess you've been in a long time."

My smile is automatic.

"Really?"

"Really." Erik tries to smile. "But don't get too excited, you could always fall back to your old ways."

He's right, but I choose optimism and get back to the topic at hand.

"Orie loves you," I tell him. "It's so obvious. Anyone can see it. Maybe it wasn't what you thought it was. Maybe you're just reading into things. Never make assumptions, right?"

Erik actually acknowledges my words then sighs. "We'll work through it. I just—"

"What?" I ask as I walk over to sit next to him. I take his hand in mine. Erik's vulnerability hits me hard.

"I've never felt like this before, Sophie," he says. "This is going to sound really fucked—"

"Go ahead," I encourage him when he falters.

"I'm always the one who loses interest first," he says quietly.

I have to pause for a moment. "Why are you even saying this?" I ask.

"I don't know."

I can hear the hesitation and uncertainty in Erik's voice and I'm more than surprised by it. My best friend is the most confident person I know. Insecurity and fear aren't words in his vocabulary.

"Orie is not losing interest," I say with assurance, then give him a teasing grin. "You're just being sensitive."

Erik looks unsure.

"Come on," I tell him. "This isn't you."

"I know," Erik mumbles. "I feel like after all these years, you've finally started rubbing off on me and not in a good way. Like in an Ebola virus way."

I laugh. I'm not offended in the least.

"Listen to me. You're reading too much into the situation. You need to stop and get a grip." I watch Erik's eyes widen at my words. I realize I'm saying almost the same thing he would to me.

I go on like I'm the Dalai Lama. "Let's say he did have a flirtatious moment with Georgie. Can't you just call it that? A moment?"

"Would you?"

"I don't know," I tell him honestly. "But I'm not you."

Erik closes his eyes.

"I don't want to lose him."

I pull him in for a hug.

"You're not going to lose him, Erik," I say. "You're not thinking clearly. That's all. This is just a moment. And it's going to pass, like they all do."

He hugs me hard. I can feel his pain and it hurts to see him like this because he's always the strong one. The force to be reckoned with. The one that I go to with all my problems and issues for him to solve.

I study his face for a second before I make up my mind.

"I won't go to lunch," I tell him emphatically.

"What?" he says as he pulls away to look down at me.

"Let's you and I go into town to one of those markets and shop, hang out, let loose, and go wine tasting." To be honest it sounds way more appealing than a lunch with Clayton's posh family where I'm going to have to try and be the perfect version of myself.

A version that I don't even know exists.

He pulls away to frown at me.

"Are you crazy?"

"Yes," I laugh. "We've established that."

"No way." He shakes his head.

"I don't want to leave you if you're sad," I tell him with concern. "You would never leave me if the tables were turned."

"I'm a big boy. I'm going to be fine on my own for a couple of hours. There is no way I will let you miss this lunch for me," he says firmly. "Go hang with the aristocrats. I'll be here when you get back and we'll get drunk and you can tell me every detail because you know if I could I'd spy on you and point out everything you missed."

"I wish you were coming." And I really do.

"Me too. Beats sitting here and avoiding a confrontation with Orie."

"Maybe that's what you guys need," I say with some encouragement.

"No," Erik shakes his head. "I can't go there yet. Instead, I'm going to pull a Sophie Walker and avoid him at all costs."

An hour later I'm sitting with Clayton and his family at a restaurant in a small boutique hotel overlooking the lush valley of Avignon. It's incredible. The owner of the restaurant knows the Sinclairs and has personally come out three times to make sure everything is okay. Clayton's father is extremely quiet and reserved, especially when he speaks to his eldest son. You can cut the tension between them with a knife. But I notice how his demeanor warms up whenever the conversation is directed at Michael.

"So I hear you're an artist," his mother says to me with an inquisitive smile. I think she's warmed up a bit toward me.

She literally did a double take when I walked up to the table with Clayton and Michael. I'm still embarrassed that I met her for the first time looking like a disaster but since there's nothing I can do about it now, I figure I'll try my best to impress her in every other way and pretend like that never happened.

"Yes, I am," I answer as I rack my brain for appropriate parent small talk. Since I had known Jerry's parents forever I was never uncomfortable or unsure around them. Clayton's parents are another story.

His mom picks at the burrata and tomato appetizer.

"And you dropped out of law school," she goes on to say casually.

I know I can't be surprised she knows, but hearing a parent say it, especially the mother of the man I happen to be in love with, makes me feel like I'm on the defensive. Like I need to prove to her that I'm worthy of her son's affections and I'm not some hoochie mama trying to take advantage of his extraordinary looks and wealth.

"Sophie's an incredible artist," Clayton interjects before I can think of the proper response. He leans over and kisses me on the head. "She was wasting her time in law school."

I don't know who's more surprised by his spontaneous show of affection, his mother or me. Michael beams. I can feel the blush creep up my cheeks but I give Clayton a grateful look.

"I'm sure she is, dear. Clearly." Clayton's mother quickly tries to placate him. "I would love to see her work."

"You'll have to ask her," Clayton says. "But she's usually very guarded about it."

"That's not true!" I say, then look at Rosalind Sinclair. "You can see my work anytime."

As if there would be a chance in hell that I would say no to his mother.

"You wouldn't show it to me in the Maldives," he points out candidly.

"Not my *unfinished* work," I correct him.

He squeezes my shoulder affectionately and winks at me.

I think an alien might have taken over his body. I've never seen him like this. Teasing. Affectionate. What is going on?

"So tell us, Sophie, were you born and raised in Los Angeles?" Clayton's father asks this question.

"Yes," I answer politely. "My father is a criminal defense attorney and has his own practice. I've been in LA my whole life."

"So you tried to take up your father's profession," he deduces.

"Yes," I admit. "But unfortunately it didn't work out quite the way he would have liked."

"I'm sure your father just wants you to be happy," he muses. Then, "Did you ever work for him to try it out firsthand?"

I feel Clayton stiffen.

"Every summer," I answer automatically, before I recall the conversation I had with Clayton in the Maldives. I remember that he told me he wanted nothing to do with his father's business and refused ever to work for him. Crap. I wish I had lied.

"Of course," his father says with a smile that doesn't quite reach his eyes. His gaze flicks over Clayton. I can see the that Clayton still annoys him. "It's what *most* children do."

"Harold," Clayton's mother warns.

He smiles innocently at his wife. "I meant nothing by it, my dear."

I quickly change the subject. "Do you have any vacation plans after the wedding, Lady Sinclair?"

"Please just call me, Ros," she tells me with a smile.

I nod politely, grateful that she's treating me warmly.

"And to answer your question, no, I don't have any vacation plans. I'll just be heading back to our summer home in Montecito."

I look at Clayton in surprise.

"Our Montecito? Near Santa Barbara?"

"Yes, dear," she answers. "Didn't Clayton tell you that we have a family home there?"

I shake my head.

"No. It never came up."

So if the Sinclairs own a home only two hours away from Los Angeles, that means that there's a possibility that he comes to LA at least a few times a year.

"That may be because Clayton hardly ever comes to visit," Ros says drolly. "He's always working."

There goes that beam of hope.

"And Michael," Rosalind smiles affectionately at her son. "You're just as bad. But I never give up faith."

"I have the best excuse possible," Michael says with a teasing grin.

"What's that?" Clayton raises a brow.

"I'm trying to save the world."

Clayton shares a smile with his brother.

"Touché."

"Clayton is quite philanthropic as well," Ros chides. "Just because he's not swinging from vines in the jungles of Costa Rica doesn't make his generous contributions any less significant."

"No," Michael agrees. "But he has yet to come and spend a week with me to really understand firsthand where he puts his money. I can't keep track of how many times I've asked. Even William's come along on one of the trips."

"My schedule—" Clayton begins.

"You can make time," Michael interrupts. "You're the boss. Look at it as sibling bonding time."

Clayton crosses his arms and stares at Michael.

"Sophie can come along for an adventure," Michael tells Clayton, then looks at me, "if it interests you, of course."

"I'd love to," I answer automatically. I'm sure it would be the chance of a lifetime.

"Alright," Clayton agrees, as he reaches over to squeeze my hand. "Send me a few dates and we'll see what we can make work."

I don't miss the "*we.*" I wonder if he's serious about going.

"Are you heading back to Los Angeles after the wedding, Sophie?" Ros asks, then takes a sip of her martini.

All eyes turn to me. The sick feeling of having such a short time with Clayton rushes through me. It was the same way in the Maldives. Whenever I thought about how many more days we had together I was instantly nauseated.

"Well," I stammer, because a part of me is praying Clayton will interrupt again and declare his love for me then and there, but real life never seems to work out that way.

"I am," I tell her almost nervously. "I'll be heading back, but Erik and Orie, my friends who are here with me, they'll be taking a brief tour of Europe."

"That's too bad," Ros says then pins her gaze on her son. "Does that mean you're planning on accompanying her to Los Angeles, Clayton?"

God.

I'd pay to hide under the table right now. Literally. Like a thousand dollars. Maybe two. I don't dare look at Clayton because I can just imagine the look on his face.

"Could you make this anymore awkward for them, mother?" Michael admonishes his mom. God bless him for it.

"I didn't mean to pry," she says as innocently as she can manage. Her statement is obviously a lie but I'd bet a million dollars that I don't have that no one would dare call her out.

"I don't mind the question, Michael. I am actually planning on traveling with her home," Clayton says nonchalantly to my complete and utter shock. He drapes a possessive arm around my chair and gives me a smile.

"I'd like to meet her parents."

12

"That whole thing you said about meeting my parents," I turn to Clayton in the car as he drives us back to his home.

"Yes?"

He takes my hand and lifts it to his lips. The soft kisses make my skin tingle and momentarily make me lose my sanity because I blurt out the question without any thought.

"Were you serious?"

I silently curse myself for asking.

"Why wouldn't I be serious?" he asks in a curious tone.

Insecure Sophie takes over like a fast-moving fungus.

"I don't know," I begin. "I just thought you might be trying to make me feel comfortable in front of your family." I shrug as if it's no big deal and try to pretend that it doesn't matter to me when it *so* matters. Actually, *way* more than matters.

When he doesn't answer right away I go on lamely. "Considering we've never talked about it before."

Clayton is still silent when he pulls off to the side of the road and puts the car in park. He turns to me. His handsome face is impassive. I think my heart is beating so loud he can probably hear it.

"So, let's talk about it." he finally says as he eyes me. His expression gives nothing away so I can't really tell what he's thinking.

It starts to rain again and the soft noise of the drops of water hitting the car is almost therapeutic.

"Is there a problem with what I said to my parents?" Clayton asks.

"Why would there be?" I ask.

"Do you not want me to come with you to Los Angeles?"

Is he crazy? I just don't want to sound overly excited or too eager. I take a few breaths before I answer him.

"It would be really nice," I tell him in what I hope is a cool, calm, and collected voice.

Clayton smiles.

"Have you told them about me?" he asks.

Again. *Is he crazy?* Does he actually think I would tell my parents I had a fling with a foreigner in the Maldives? I haven't even thought about how I'll break the news to them that I'm in love with someone I've known for less than a month. And let's not forget that he lives in another country. Of course if he asked me to move to Timbuktu and live in a tent with him I totally would. But they still think I'm pining after Jerry. Without a doubt my mom and dad will have a nuclear meltdown because they'll believe it will mean that I'm immediately moving out of the country and am kissing any chance at having a career goodbye.

To be perfectly honest, it's a conversation I'm dreading.

"I take it from the look on your face that the answer is no," Clayton says, and sounds almost disappointed.

"Well, when I got back there really wasn't much to tell because we weren't talking," I explain.

"*You* weren't talking to me," Clayton points out.

"Yes, I know." I wave his comment off. "But still. What was I going to say? And to be honest, I don't know how they would feel about it, me jumping from my relationship with Jerry into the arms of a stranger. Especially my dad."

"You didn't have a relationship with Jerry," Clayton says forcefully.

Neanderthal Clayton is rearing his handsome head.

"I did," I tell him emphatically. "For a year. And I've known him forever and my parents love him."

"They're going to have to get over it." His voice is cool and has a definite edge.

"Of course they will!" I rush out to placate him. "They are slowly getting over the idea that we're no longer together but they're still going to be shocked to hear about you. There's no doubt in my mind."

Clayton watches me with an impassive look on his face.

"But I know they will love you when they meet you," I continue, hoping that will make him stop frowning at me.

His demeanor relaxes just a tad. But he still seems pretty stiff so I go on.

"They'll love you because you're you and what's not to love? But most important, they'll love you because I do," I tell him honestly.

I unbuckle my seatbelt and lean over to kiss him on the side of his mouth.

My words worked the magic I hoped they would and I feel his body language change. I smile mile at him.

"So you're really going to come home with me?" I ask in wonder as I let the happiness I'm feeling sweep over me. I can't help it. Clayton coming back to Los Angeles with me is a dream come true.

"I am."

"And then what?" I ask teasingly as I trace my finger along his lower lip.

"Then we'll take the next step," he says cryptically.

I lose my stomach.

Next step? What does that mean?

I don't have the nerve to ask him *that* question and Clayton doesn't even let me go there because he quickly tells me to buckle my seat belt as he puts the car in drive and heads back to the chateau.

I'm left wondering.

Hoping. Wishing. Dreaming.

Longing.

For my own happily ever after.

"During sex I like to think about—" Orie is standing in the middle of one of the lounge rooms in the chateau reading his Cards Against Humanity phrase to a small group of Abby's friends, who are participating in game night.

There are different game stations set up in various rooms in the house, and since Cards Against Humanity is one of our favorites back home, Erik, Orie, and I immediately made a beeline for this station. Clayton and Michael joined us, along with Abby, Georgie, Elizabeth, and Eduard. I was genuinely happy when I spotted Elizabeth, who seemed thrilled to see me.

In fact, she pulled me aside and told me she knew there was something special between Clayton and me in the Maldives, and she was more than happy for us. Eduard had been just as kind and flattering, so it's now become sort of a Maldives reunion. I'm happy to note that Jane and Amelia are nowhere in sight because I don't know if I'm up for another round with those two.

Clayton and I are cuddling on one of the couches and really enjoying ourselves. I lean back in his arms and can't be happier as I sift through my cards to pick an answer for Orie to read out.

"During sex *I* think about pleasuring my partner," Georgie blurts out loud to everyone's amusement as he smiles coyly at Orie.

"Is that on one of your cards?" Erik asks curiously as he eyes him up and down.

Uh-oh.

Georgie shakes his head mischievously and picks up his martini.

"No," he admits with a wink. "But I thought everyone should know how I operate. I'm a giver, *mon cher*. I give so that my lover may feel bliss. Sex is about pleasure for both partners. I try to do my part."

I feel my body tense.

"So we're exactly the same in that regard," Erik says with a great deal of arrogance. "No one has ever left my bed unsatisfied."

The group laughs and there are a few hoots and hollers. I look from Erik, who seems to be sizing Georgie up, to Orie, who's turned a little red and seems very uncomfortable with the whole situation.

My spidy senses go on high alert and I wonder why Orie is so on edge. Can Erik be right? Are Orie and Georgie flirting? I can't believe it because I know firsthand how much he and Erik love each other.

"So who wants to go first?" Orie asks, trying to bring everyone back to the game.

"I'll go," Eduard says and he reads his answer.

I totally zone whatever he's saying out and focus on Erik. I will him to look at me and when he does he just rolls his eyes but I know he's bothered by Georgie's comment, or existence—I honestly don't know what annoys him more.

Clayton absently massages my shoulder as he speaks to Michael, who's just taken a seat next to us on the couch. The two start to talk about the stock market and quickly become immersed in a discussion about the volatility of the economy—a topic that after two martinis has zero appeal for me.

I watch Georgie finish his drink. He must know that I'm staring at him because he turns to me and gives me a smile.

"I'm going to refresh my drink," he says lifting his empty glass. "Would you like to join me, Sophie?"

Perfect. Twenty questions here I come.

"Yes, I would love to," I tell him and turn to Clayton and Michael.

"Can I get you guys anything?" I ask politely.

"I'm fine, Sophie," Michael says kindly. "But thank you."

"I'm alright as well." Clayton takes my hand and kisses it softly. He's being so loving and sweet I feel like I'm in heaven. Or close enough.

"We'll be right back," Georgie says to Clayton as I stand up to join him. "And don't you worry, my wolf, I promise not to tell her your secrets."

"I'll hold you to it," Clayton half jokes, not at all affected by Georgie's words.

I ignore Erik's look of displeasure and let Georgie lead me down the hall to the dining room, which is now set up with a full bar and appetizers. I'm on a mission, and I figure I'll explain it to Erik later.

"What can I get you?" Georgie asks as he sets our martini glasses and picks out several liquor bottles. Obviously he about to concoct something special.

"I'll have whatever you're making," I tell him.

"Famous last words," Georgie smiles as he starts to pour the various beverages into a giant martini shaker.

"Is that Long Island iced tea?" I ask.

"Maybe," he smiles secretively.

"It is," I say.

"Alright, you twisted my arm. I'll admit I've acquired a taste for the drink. It does the trick very quickly."

"Gets you drunk," I say.

"And then the fun begins," Georgie laughs.

"Can you make mine a little less strong?" I ask him, as I watch him pour more than generous amounts of alcohol and very little Cola.

"Yours will definitely not be as strong as mine," he tells me. "I don't want to incur the wrath of *le bel homme*."

He's definitely smart.

"Speaking of which," he continues, "I've never seen him behave like this with any woman before. None of his past girlfriends. You must be very special to him."

Even though I'm annoyed at Georgie for flirting with Orie, his words make me seriously happy. Especially since he's not the first one who's said them.

"I hope so," I say to him.

"Taming a wolf is no easy task," Georgie tsks with his thick accent.

I stay silent because I don't know how to respond to that statement. Have I tamed the wolf?

Highly doubtful, *Sophie*, my inner voice gives me a reality check.

"Especially a wolf with such a varied and unquenchable appetite," Georgie goes on as he starts to shake the cocktail.

The last thing I want to know about is Clayton's sexual history. I'm sure it's long and sordid and filled with enough beautiful women to make me want to throw up. Even picturing him with other women, especially ones like Amelia, is not a path I want to let myself go down because I know nothing good will come of it.

So instead of replying I choose to use his earlier comment for something else.

"So you believe a man can be tamed?" I ask.

Georgie looks me dead in the eye.

"Perhaps."

"Yes or no?" I push.

"Some," he shrugs.

"And the rest?"

"Move from one partner to another," he says. "I'm sure that you're quite aware that life gets boring after a while."

"That's not very romantic," I tell him. "I think if you find the right person life can never get boring no matter what's thrown at you."

"But what if there is more than one partner out there who can show you passion?" Georgie asks me as he pours our drinks out. He stops what he's doing to assess my reaction.

"I guess that's a given," I tell him and shrug my shoulders. "I'm sure there can be many. I won't dispute that. But that doesn't mean those many make you feel the way that one special person can."

"Spoken like a true innocent."

"Like an idealist," I reply.

"A romantic," he says back.

"Maybe."

Georgie raises a brow.

"You have a question, my dear," he tells me. "You followed me here for a purpose."

I should be surprised by his perceptiveness but for some reason I'm not.

I cut straight to the point. "My friends love each other."

"They do," Georgie agrees.

Before I can say another word, Georgie continues.

"*Ma belle,* Sophie, I only tempt what is readily available to be tempted. If you are not open to seduction then you will not succumb."

"Said the snake in the Garden of Eden," I reply before I can stop myself.

Georgie laughs.

"One word would change it all," Georgie says.

"What's that?" I ask.

"*Non.*" Georgie smiles innocently.

I can't believe his blasé attitude. Or what he's implying. That Orie is welcoming the flirtation.

"What are you so worried about?" he asks me pointedly.

"I don't want my friends to be hurt," I say honestly. "They have something special."

"Special cannot be broken, *mon cherie*," Georgie replies. "Special is forever, *non*?"

"It is forever," I agree with him.

"Then why are you questioning me?"

Shit.

Nothing real can be threatened. Marianne Williamson's line from *A Course in Miracles* rings through my head again. Georgie is right. No love, no *real* love would ever be threatened. If it's true and pure and perfect, nothing, absolutely nothing would be able to destroy it. Not even a flirtatious count from France, who throws crazy, amazing parties. And happens to look like an underwear model.

"I didn't mean to," I finally say.

"Sophie," he says, "life is long and made for enjoyment. So just savor the moments."

Clayton breaks the silence as we lie in bed. "You were throwing daggers at Georgie."

Game night is long over and it's way past my bedtime. Clayton and I are wrapped in each other's arms, both exhausted from a long day, just enjoying one another's company.

"I was not," I deny.

Clayton laughs.

"I saw the way you stared at him," he tells me. "I thought you were going to ask him for a duel."

"Pistols or swords?" I tease.

"Pistols, of course."

"What? Really?" I'm offended. "I think I would be amazing with a sword."

"Without a doubt," Clayton agrees. "But I think you'd need instant gratification. You were out for blood."

"I might be a slow and torturous kind of person."

"I don't think so," Clayton says.

He's definitely right. It's a rarity for me to lose my temper, but when it happens, I do go for the jugular for a quick outcome. Luckily, it doesn't happen often.

"How about you?" I ask him.

"Sword."

Completely. He would stalk his prey, anticipating a slow and painful end.

"You should have lived in the Middle Ages," I tease him. "I know you're a fan of the art and your personality fits the bill perfectly."

He laughs. "I don't know if I should be insulted or not."

My fingers draw circles on his chest as my mind wanders and I find myself thinking about his childhood and the strange relationship he has with his father.

"Your parents were really nice," is how I decide to bring the subject up.

"Thank you. My mother is."

I lean back from his chest. I want to see his face, even though he's generally good at hiding what he's thinking. Tonight is no different. His look is inscrutable.

"Didn't I tell you that my father and I have a strained relationship?" he asks indifferently.

"You did," I admit. "But I didn't realize that..."

It was so bad. My voice trails off because I don't want to say this.

There's a long silence between us and then to my surprise Clayton begins to talk.

"When I was younger, I saw things." Clayton seems uncertain. Unsure. Like he's tasting the sound of these words for the first time. "My father wasn't very discreet."

My heart starts to pound. I don't dare breathe too loud because I'm afraid it will make Clayton stop talking.

"He didn't really care about rules or vows. Never mind his own marriage, but his friends' girlfriends or their wives—if my father fancied them it—" He pauses. "—All's fair in love and war, Clayton," he says in a low voice, and with disdain. "You don't know how many times he said those words to me over the years. I lost count of the number of moments I walked in on him with his various flavors of the week, or the extraordinarily special occasions I caught him with my classmates' mothers."

How awful.

"William and Michael?" I ask.

"It's never been something I've discussed with them. Especially with William. He believes the sun rises and sets on my father's shoulders. I won't be the one to break that pretty picture for him. We're very protective of him."

My heart melts for the child he was, to have witnessed what he did. The trauma of watching his father cheat constantly must have scarred him for life.

And scared him away from commitment.

"And your mom?" I ask.

"She knew," Clayton says. "But at some point it stopped mattering to her and she focused on us."

"But how?" I'm horrified at the idea that she stayed with a serial cheater.

"She compartmentalizes things," he shrugs. "I think she likes the idea of being married to him. She has her freedom. He doesn't question her. And he has his."

"But it's so lonely."

"It works for them," Clayton says flatly.

It would never for me. I would go crazy. Hell, I'm pretty sure most women would.

"One night, I was in bed," Clayton continues and I feel my stomach clench in dread. "I was twelve. My mother was in New York and we were with our father and the nannies. He came into my room and woke me up. It was late. He told me to get myself together and meet him in the study."

Clayton's body feels like it's made of granite and his voice sounds like it's coming from far away.

"When I arrived I was met by his mistress and a high-class prostitute," he says apathetically. "My father told me that he was going to watch me become a man and that both women were at my disposal. He was to stay on and make sure I was a real Sinclair. Make sure I could perform."

I feel sick to my stomach and am so appalled that the man I met this afternoon could be capable of something so vile. I can feel my eyes begin to water.

"You can imagine what happened next," Clayton says with a hollow laugh.

The silence is palpable in the room. I know he is reliving the nightmare experience. I wish I could erase the memory.

"Did you ever tell anyone?" I ask him softly.

"Never. Not a soul," he says.

Until me.

"Until you."

"Of course I made sure my brothers would never have the same experience."

My gaze meets his. I wonder what he said to his father. Or threatened. I think about what he went through, the humiliation of it, the awful introduction to sex, and then I think about how special he made my first time. It makes me love him even more. My throat feels thick when I try to speak. I know those damn tears of mine are going to fall.

"I'm so—"

He puts his fingers to my lips.

"Shhh," he tells me. "You are not allowed to feel sorry for me."

"I don't," I whisper. "How could I?"

And I really don't. I have empathy for the child he was, not the man that he has become. He took what happened and didn't let that define him. And rose above it. With demons, granted. But still.

"I see the look of sadness on your face," he admonishes. His voice is soft though, and full of emotion.

"I'm sad that you were robbed," I tell him as I brush his cheek with my hand. "It should have been different for you."

He takes my hand and places a kiss on my palm.

"I'm okay now," he says. "Especially with you."

I feel a warmth move through my body.

"I—" Clayton begins to say in an unsteady voice and my breath lodges in my throat.

I lean up over him, letting my hair cascade around my shoulders and onto his chest. His eyes roam possessively over my face.

"God, you're beautiful," he whispers softly to me, forgetting whatever it was he was going to say, and he pulls me to him for a kiss that leaves me breathless.

13

"Sophie!" Erik calls out as he bursts open the bedroom door.

I was dead to the world. But I sit up in bed immediately as I wrap the sheet around my naked body. The curtains are drawn so I have no idea what time it is. Unfortunately I'm also alone.

I wonder when Clayton got up and left me.

"What time is it?" I ask groggily.

"Past noon," Erik says as he rushes over to the bed.

"Noon?!" I can't believe I slept so late. I take in Orie's pale face as he closes the door behind him.

"What's going on?" I demand as I notice Erik's sad demeanor.

"Something terrible has happened," Erik says.

My heart lodges in my throat. A thousand thoughts race through my mind.

"Tell me."

"It's about Clayton' brother," Erik says, and sits next to me while Orie opens the curtains to allow the sunlight in.

"Michael?"

"No," Erik shakes his head. "The youngest. William."

He takes a moment.

"Erik—" I plead, "I'm freaking out."

"He died last night in a car accident," Erik whispers sadly.

"What?!" I'm stunned into silence.

"It's beyond tragic. The house is in chaos," Orie says as he comes and sits down on the bed too. "Everyone is hysterical. Clayton's mother, is inconsolable. She's been walking from room to room screaming. Literally screaming in pain, Sophie. I've never heard anything like it. And Clayton and Michael have disappeared. We don't even know if they're together."

"And their father?" I whisper in horror.

"He's in the study sobbing."

I don't know what to say. Or to think.

So much sorrow for the family. For Clayton. For me, that I will never get to meet the younger brother who was so protected and loved.

My conversation with Clayton last night seems like a distant memory.

"I have to go to him," I whisper to Erik as tears well up in my eyes. I can't imagine what he's feeling right now.

"He was so young," Erik says as I get out of bed and pull the sheet with me.

"Twenty-five," I mumble. He *was* too young. How does something like this even happen?

I rush into the dressing room and find a pair of jeans, a sweatshirt and my brown Uggs. Orie and Erik follow me into the bathroom where I brush my teeth and wash my face. Orie helps me pull my hair back.

"Sophie," he warns me, "everyone is literally a disaster. William was very loved. I can't imagine Abby and Dimitri continuing with the wedding under these circumstances."

No, I definitely can't either. Especially given Abby's aversion to it in the first place.

"How is Abby?" I ask.

"She's in her room," Orie says. "She asked to be left alone."

"But Georgie is with her," Erik adds pointedly.

Georgie. Now, thinking about the conversation I had with him last night seems incredibly ridiculous.

Orie grabs my hand and squeezes it.

"Have you ever lost someone?"

"No," I tell him. "I mean. I lost my grandparents but I was so young I don't remember."

"This is a big deal," Orie says emotionally. "I lost my dad when I was in high school and it changed my life, made me into a different person. This was Clayton's baby brother. A death like this shifts everything."

Erik rubs my shoulder. "Do you understand what Orie is trying to tell you?"

"Of course I do. I'm not an idiot. I don't care about anything but being there for him. I need to find him."

As soon as I step outside the bedroom I feel the somber mood echo through the house. I get the chills. It is quiet. Too quiet. There are white candles lit everywhere, which only add to the sad ambiance. We walk downstairs and see a picture of the three brothers on a table in the hall with candles flanking the frame.

I look at William's face and see the kindness, the pure innocence, that made him so different from Clayton and Michael. His hair was brown and he had the famous Sinclair blue eyes. He was boyishly handsome. Looking at his picture makes his death more devastating. Here was a man in the prime of his life, taken entirely too early.

"Orie and I will look for Clayton," Erik says. "We'll find you."

I nod absently and continue to stare at William's picture. They leave me there and I'm overcome with an intense wave of sadness. This poor family. What's going through their minds right now? Imagine, having someone here one day and gone the next. And there's no reversing it.

"Do you see my beautiful baby boy?" Clayton's mother sobs behind me.

I turn quickly and am undone when I see her grief-stricken face. The tears come naturally and I step forward and pull her into my embrace she trembles.

"He's gone!" she cries. "My beautiful William is gone!"

There is nothing appropriate for me to say to her. I'm sorry seems like such a ridiculous comment to make.

"What can I do?" is all I can say through my tears as her body crumples into mine.

"Let's go sit down," I say and I wrap my arm around her waist and guide her down one of the long corridors to the main living room where we first met Abigail.

The house is so quiet.

"Where is Harold?" she asks as I take her to one of the couches.

"I don't know," I tell her. "I just heard what happened."

Her head falls back on the couch and I take in her appearance. I lean down in front of her and place my hand on her knees offering any type of comfort I can.

"My poor baby boy," she says. "He was supposed to come with us. But Harold needed him in the office. He should have been with us. We never should have left him alone."

Her voice is raw with pain.

"He was hit by a drunk driver on his way to the airport," she whispers. "A teenager hit his car head on. They're both gone."

I remain silent.

"Oh Sophie, what am I going to do without my little boy?"

"I don't know," I say. "I'm so, so incredibly sorry."

"Have you seen Clayton or Michael?" she asks in a small voice.

"I haven't."

But I realize how much she needs them. She needs to be surrounded by her family and her children, and instead she's all alone—a mother who just lost her child is alone with me, who is practically a stranger.

"Do you want me find them?" I ask her.

"Don't leave me," she pleads almost wildly. "I don't want to be by myself."

"I won't," I promise her. "I won't leave you. Erik and Orie are looking for them. Can I get you tea?"

"Brandy."

"Of course."

I get up and walk to the entryway of the room and notice that a woman is standing quietly near the door, as if she's waiting to see if Lady Rosalind needs something.

"Lady Sinclair would like a glass of brandy," I tell her. "And if you could light the fire and bring her a nice blanket that would be lovely."

"Of course," she says and rushes off to do as I asked.

I walk back in the room and another member of the staff enters behind me and lights the fire. In no time Ros has her brandy and her blanket and a roaring fire. I sit beside her as she cries and offer only my company. The sound of the fire mixed with her tears is something I don't think I'll ever forget.

After a few minutes of quiet she begins to tell me about William.

"He was such a special child," she tells me sorrowfully. "He was so good. Such a happy boy and man. And so pure of heart. He was always trying to make peace between Clayton and his father. Always smiling. Cheerful. Michael and Clayton were so protective of him all their lives. He was so precious. And I was so proud of him. I mean, I *am*—"

She buries her face in her hands.

"I can't believe this," Ros moans. "I feel like I'm in a dream, or a nightmare. Why is this happening to us? Why, Sophie?"

"I don't know," I say as I shake my head in despair. My heart aches for her pain. "I wish I had an answer for you."

"This is just a cruel joke. It has to be," she says, and rocks back and forth in her chair in utter agony.

Moments later Erik and Orie join us. I make eye contact with Erik and he shakes his head, which I know means he's had no luck finding Clayton or Michael. As worried as I am about him, I know I can't leave his mom alone.

Erik and Orie turn to walk out when she says, "I have to arrange my son's funeral," and they both stand stock still.

"You don't need to do that at this moment," I tell her.

"It must be fit for a king," she says as if she didn't hear me. "I need my secretary. She can help me get started. Everything needs to be perfect, just like William. Lilies. He loved lilies. And tulips. Tulips are so beautiful, don't you think?"

"Yes," I whisper, seeing that she was beside herself now.

"I've already made calls," Clayton says.

We all look up and see Clayton standing in the doorway. His gaze is singularly focused on his mom. I take in his appearance and my heart lurches. His eyes are bloodshot and filled with agony. His hair is in disarray. He's dressed in black pants and a sweater and his hands are buried in his pockets.

My friends leave the room quickly.

Ros Sinclair stands up on shaky legs.

"Clayton—"

There is a terrible look of anguish on his face as he walks to his mother and gathers her in his arms.

"My William," she cries. "My William."

His body trembles as he buries his head in his mother's arms, and I know he's crying. Tears are streaming down my face as I stare at them. I realize what I'm watching is an incredibly private moment between a mother and her son, so I stand up and leave the room quietly. Clayton doesn't acknowledge me, not even a look, and even though I know I should have no expectation given the circumstance, I get a tiny feeling of uneasiness.

A death like this changes everything.

Orie's words echo in my head but I push them out of my mind, refusing to go there. All that matters is that I'm here for Clayton during this horrible time.

That is all that really matters.

When I leave Clayton and his mother, I go to find Erik and Orie so we can discuss what our plan should be. Whether we should stay or go. And how we can help out, *if* we can help in any way.

I walk down the corridor that leads to the dining room and run right into Harold Sinclair, who looks just as devastated as the rest of his family. Even though I'm now aware of how mentally perverted he is and cannot forgive him for what he did to his son, I still feel empathy. William was his child. And from the sound of things, the one who followed in his footsteps, worked for him, idolized him. Obviously he didn't know any of his dad's sick secrets.

His handsome face is stricken with sorrow and I say with a full heart, "Mr. Sinclair, I am so, so sorry for your loss."

He lifts a glass in salute and takes a sip.

"Sorry for my loss?" he slurs. It's obvious he's drunk, and I don't blame him. "He was my heir. The only one who understood the business, or me. I worked with him every day. And now he's gone."

He takes a wobbly step forward.

"Clayton and your wife are in the living room. Do you want me to take you to them?"

"By all means," he tells me. "Take me to my loving son and wife."

I put my hand on his lower back and lead him into the living room, where Clayton and his mom have been joined by Michael. All three are now huddled together on the couch in front of the fire. When we walk in, they turn and stare at us. I'm too frightened to meet Clayton's gaze.

"I found him wandering in the hall," I explain softly and look at the only person who safe. Michael.

I hurt for the pain I see on his face but I am reassured by his kind smile.

"Thank you, Sophie," Michael says as he gets up and walks to his father.

"Isn't she lovely," Clayton's dad says. When he reaches Michael, he throws himself in his arms, his body trembling in pain.

"Oh, God!" he says in anguish. "What am I going to do?"

I can't help myself. I immediately start to cry. I look at Clayton in desperation and his eyes are misty but cold as they meet mine. I almost take a step back from what I can only describe as animosity.

"That will be all, Sophie," he says icily.

I hope my face hasn't turned bright red. He's dismissed me like someone who works for him. I nod curtly and leave the room. I can feel the sting of his eyes on my back. I brush away the tears and tell myself that it's alright. He's grieving. I need to let it go.

But I run to find Erik and Orie.

I'm so relieved when I find them in the library. They're drinking wine and nothing looks better.

"Pour me a glass," I demand.

Erik immediately gets up and within seconds I'm holding a glass of red. I find a seat on the couch and Erik joins me.

"We need that magic juice as well," Georgie says as he walks in holding Abby's hand. For a second I forget about the tragedy, because Georgie's outfit completely distracts me. He's wearing bright purple suede pants, a purple leather vest, and an orange T-shirt. But his shoes are what have me really riveted. They are neon yellow. I'm pretty sure they're some designer brand and cost a fortune but they're very distracting. My not-so-subtle best friend whispers, "At least we finally have something to laugh at."

I don't dare glance at him.

Instead, I focus on Abby, who looks pale and fragile. Her eyes are swollen from all the tears she's shed. I go to her and hug her.

"I don't know what to say," I tell her with emotion.

She hugs me back tightly.

"Thank you," she says. "We are devastated."

"It's awful," I tell her as we separate and I return to my seat.

"William was *light*, Sophie," she tells me. "He was so easy and carefree. Always laughing and smiling. He was the one that everyone loved."

Georgie hands her a glass of red wine and she takes a long sip. I do the same. At this point it is almost medicinal.

"As soon as we heard, we postponed the wedding," she tells us, to no one's surprise.

"Clayton got a call in the middle of the night," Abby goes on to tell us, "and waited until this morning to tell Michael and his parents. He sat in his office until six. At least, that's what I was told."

I can't stop the ache in my heart for him. Why did he choose to suffer on his own? Why didn't he wake me up to be there for him?

"What are their plans?" Orie asks.

"I believe they're leaving tonight," Abby says.

"They are?" I say.

Abby turns to me.

"Yes," she says. "I thought you knew."

"I haven't had a chance to really speak to Clayton," I explain. "But I'm not surprised."

"They want to get home quickly to make arrangements for the funeral," Abby explains.

I shake my head and try not to let the sick feeling of dread wash over me again. But my stomach has already dropped straight through the floor.

"Of course," I whisper.

"We can be out of here by tomorrow as well," Erik hurries out.

"There is no rush," Abby promises.

"No," Orie replies. "We'll get it all sorted in the morning so the family can be alone. This is a time for everyone to come together and remember all the great times with William."

Erik takes my hand and squeezes it tightly.

"What?" I ask. I know my voice is hoarse.

"Nothing," he tells me. "I just want to tell you I love you."

"I love you too."

"Don't worry," Erik says.

"I'm not." I give him a reassuring smile.

But that's a lie.

Because I am.

And I'm wondering what the future holds for Clayton and I.

If anything.

After spending the entire afternoon with my friends and Abby and Georgie, and listening to all the tears and stories about William, I need an emotional break and excuse myself to go lie down in my room. I'm devastated on so many levels. And honestly, just exhausted. I take a quick shower, curl up in bed facing the fireplace, and try not to think about what the coming hours will bring.

The time has flown by and I know Clayton and his family will be leaving for London soon. Just as I'm drifting off to sleep the door opens and I know it's him.

I pretend to be asleep because he's just lost a precious brother and I assume the last thing he wants to do is talk about it with me. And I don't blame him. And after the look on his face this afternoon, I don't know what awaits me and I'm not ready to find out. I keep my eyes glued shut as he paces around the room. Every step he takes makes my body tremble in dread.

"I know you're awake," he finally says, breaking the painful silence.

Shit.

I open my eyes and am grateful to find that he's not standing directly in front of me.

Put your big girl pants on, Sophie.

"I am," I say.

I sit up and turn around and take in his appearance. He looks haggard and sad. So sad. So much worse than he did when I last saw him. He pulls his sweater off and I feel guilty for even admiring his physique.

"Clayton—" I begin as I try to come up with the best word to tell him how sorry I am.

"Don't," he says. "If I hear those words one more time I won't be responsible for what I do."

Fair enough.

He is clawing at his hair and begins pacing the room like a caged lion.

"What do you want me to do?" I ask him.

"Can you bring my brother back?" He laughs, a cold and hollow sound, and I shiver from the lack of emotion in his voice.

I try not to get angry. I try to think about his heartache and pain. I know it's not him talking, that it comes from something deeper, something that you can never understand until you go through it. But the woman in me still balks at the offensive nature of his words. At the way he's treating me when all I want to do ease his suffering.

"I think I should leave you alone."

"Yes," he says, the answer I dreaded.

God.

That hurts like hell. I can feel the tears well up in my eyes. I push back the covers to get up and he comes to stand in front of the bed.

"Where the fuck are you going?" he practically snarls at me.

"You told me to leave," I tell him as I try to keep up with his volatile emotions.

I watch as his hands curl up into fists at his side. "Goddamnit!" he roars.

I don't know where to go.

"He was supposed to be here already!" he howls in anguish. His eyes are bright with unshed tears and I forget my fear and have only empathy for him. I watch him, unable to move and afraid to even take a breath as I wait for him to speak.

He walks over to the table where he keeps his decanters of whiskey and pours himself a glass.

"*My father*," his laugh is empty. "My beloved father told him to stay and finish a goddamn contract."

He throws back the shot.

"The gall of him, forcing William to stay," Clayton continues. "And my baby brother always wanted to please him—"

Then he grabs a decanter and throws it at the fireplace. I jump back as the glass shatters all over the room.

"It's his fault!" Clayton roars. "He killed him! He killed William."

I'm shocked into silence, but force myself to take a step toward him.

"Don't come near me," he warns me.

I stop.

"I don't know what you want me to do," I whisper helplessly, then stand against the wall in fear as he systematically destroys the room. Seeing Clayton lose control like this is unreal. This man is always in check. Always. And I'm watching him break. The man I love is losing a piece of himself, a piece that he may never get back. And I ache for him.

I begin to cry uncontrollably.

When there's nothing left to throw he punches the wall and I finally cry out. His knuckles are bloody from the impact.

"Clayton—" I plead with him through my tears.

He snarls as he takes a step toward me. I stand my ground. Even in this epic rage I know he won't physically hurt me. Emotionally, maybe. Verbally. But he would never lay a hand on me. This I know.

"Talk to me," I whisper.

"I don't want to talk to you, Sophie. I want to fuck you."

I feel like he's slapped me across the face.

"No," I tell him.

"You like it when I fuck you," he says.

"Not like this," I say. "You can't touch me like this."

"Can't?"

The gauntlet is thrown. There is nowhere for me to go. He advances toward me, this angry, beautiful man, towering over me, and runs his bloody knuckles against my cheek.

"I think you know I can," he tells me in a heated voice.

Before I can respond the door bursts open and Michael rushes in, takes in the scene, and grabs hold of his brother.

"Clayton!" he yells, and shakes him, then turns toward my bloodied face in horror.

"Are you alright?" he asks urgently, still holding on to Clayton.

"I'm fine," I tell him. "It's his blood."

The look of relief on Michael's face is staggering.

"I think you should go, Sophie. Let me be with him."

I don't argue.

I walk past Clayton and see the raw pain in his eyes. I want to hold him but I know it's an impossibility.

Before I can close the door he utters two words that almost bring me to my knees.

"It's over."

14

It's morning and I'm in bed cocooned between Erik and Orie. I'm numb to the pain now.

When I left Clayton's bedroom last night I hurried to my friends who were thankfully in their room and cried my eyes out. For once, neither of them told me I was delusional or acting crazy. They just held me and didn't say a word. Their silence spoke volumes, which was perhaps even worse than their usual censure.

Michael found me hours later and asked to speak to me privately. We went to Abby's dressing room, Just thinking about the conversation makes me sick to my stomach. He looked haggard, like he had been crying forever and was just so worn out.

"He's not good, Sophie," he told me solemnly. "No one is, but he's taking it the hardest. He's the oldest, and always took on a caretaker role—especially with William."

Clayton had told me that he protected William from experiencing what his father had done to him. If only Michael knew the half of it.

"How can I help?" I asked softly.

Michael gave me a sad smile. "You can stay away."

I was floored. That was not what I was expecting.

"What?" I shook my head. "No. I want to be with him. I need to be there for him-"

Michael stopped me. "I saw his eyes, Sophie. I know my brother and I don't want you to get hurt. God only knows what he said to you before I got there. You were scared."

"I'm not afraid," I told him, even though I was.

"But I am, for you," he said gently. "He will tear your heart to pieces. There's a part to him—you saw it—I just—"

He searched for the right words.

"I just don't want you to be broken."

I knew the part he was referring to. The wolf in him. The animal side that didn't think. Only attacked.

"Everything is different now," he went on. "We, the immediate family, we're leaving tonight to arrange my brother's—" He couldn't go on.

"I know," I said to him. "Abby told me."

I stepped toward him and he gladly embraced me, welcoming the comfort I offered. So different from Clayton.

"I keep asking God why it couldn't have been me," he said in agony.

"Don't say that," I whisper. "William wouldn't want you to say that."

"He was so special," Michael said through his tears. "He was good. He didn't deserve this."

No, he didn't. But these things, these tragic things that happen never have rhyme or reason. They just occur without warning and change lives forever.

I had lived a charmed life until then, never experiencing such horrible grief. And watching this family mourn a man I never even knew was a horrific thing.

Michael had pulled away from me and kissed me on my cheek.

"Take care of yourself."

Those were Michael's last words to me.

As if that would be so easy to do.

And so they had left.

And I'd stayed hidden away with Erik and Orie in their room. We'd gone to bed and decided to deal with our flights and departure from the chateau in the morning. The day had been too emotionally exhausting. A small part of my heart had hoped that Clayton would seek me out and take me with them, or at least say goodbye. But that hope died when Abby informed us that Sergei had taken the family to the private airport and they had departed.

Now this emptiness.

Heart broken by Clayton Astor Sinclair. Again. For different reasons. Ones that seemed irreversible in a more profound way. As Michael had said to me, everything was different now with Clayton. Opening up about his childhood, talking about his father, finally allowing me in, it all seems like a dream now. Like it never even happened.

"So Erik and I have made an executive decision," Orie tells me, interrupting my sad train of thoughts.

He rolls to his side in the bed and takes my hand.

"What's that?" I ask.

Erik leans into me on the other side and rubs my arm.

"Should you tell her or should I, Erik?" Orie asks with a mischievous grin.

"Go ahead, you can give her the news," Erik offers but before Orie can utter a word Erik spills the beans.

"We're taking you on a whirlwind tour of Europe," he exclaims happily.

"Unbelievable," Orie says to Erik. But he's smiling at him with love. I'm glad to see that everything is back to normal between them. I'm sure William's passing had something to do with them letting things go.

"You're what?" I ask.

"It's a gift, Sophie," he explains. "We are going to get on a plane, then a train, and do the whole we're poor backpacking thing, except not in a poor way, because god forbid we stay at a hostel and catch some goddamn disease. We'll do it at hotels. Five-star ones. And eat well. Really well. And drink. Heavily."

"I think she gets the picture," Orie says as he rolls his eyes at me.

"And we're going to pay your way," Erik continues. "Because we love you. And it's our Christmas present to you since that's coming up even though it doesn't feel like it right now. And most importantly, because you *are* poor."

Goddamnit.

The guy actually makes me laugh.

"You are unbelievable," I say.

"You are lucky you know me. And that I call you my best friend."

"I am," I tell him as I take his hand and squeeze it. I take Orie's as well. "And you," I say.

"We're like Three's Company," Erik explains. "It will be shit hot. Think of all the Instagram posts."

I smile.

"Sounds great."

But it doesn't. Not really. At all.

"This is going to be hard, babe. There's no way around it." Orie is the one to address the elephant in the room.

P.S. it's a giant fucking elephant. It might be a dinosaur even. Like a Tyrannosaurus Rex.

"I don't have a choice," I say to Orie.

"Can I be real with you for a moment?" Erik asks me.

I roll my eyes.

"Like you pretend with me or ever sugarcoat?" I ask him.

"You like my honesty," Erik says unaffected. "Remember?"

"Umm, sometimes it would be nice to have some things laced with a bit of sweetness to take out the sting," I reply honestly.

"But that's boring and fake," he tells me. "Like designer handbag fake. Like if you're carrying a Valentina instead of a Valentino. Or a Channel instead of a Chanel. Or a Hermeez instead of an Hermès. Or a—"

"Would you get on with it," Orie interrupts dryly.

"Fake is so rock bottom," Erik continues .

"Okay, be real. Go ahead," I say as I lean back into the pillows with a sigh and prepare myself for whatever onslaught is coming my way. "You're going to anyway so I might as well give you permission."

"This situation is fucked," Erik says bluntly. "Like F-U-C-K'ed—fucked."

"Tell me something I don't know," I retort.

"Oooh. I like that fire, Sophie," Orie says appreciatively.

"Give her a second, babe, and she'll be in goddamn tears again," Erik waves off Orie's comment.

"Maybe not—" Orie replies.

"Watch," Erik turns to me. "You and Clayton are over, babe."

Fuck.

My eyes start to fill up. Goddamnit! They're welling. The tears. One slips. Erik nods knowingly as the flood is unleashed.

"That's not fair," I say as I wipe them away. "That's devastating to hear."

"It's reality," Erik says harshly.

I sit up, in anger.

"That's a terrible thing for you to say."

"What did you expect me to say? You want me to lie to you?" Erik goes on. "He told you it's over—"

"Erik, don't be so harsh," Orie chimes in.

"She needs harsh," Erik snaps back. "She needs honesty. She needs *real.*"

"But there's a way to go about things, and a right time—" Orie's voice becomes background noise to everything going on in my head. I hear them arguing but I don't actually *hear* their words. Because for whatever reason something starts to take over inside my heart. Something profound and moving. And life-changing.

Hope.

"I don't accept it," I blurt out.

"What?" Erik and Orie say at the same time.

"I don't accept it." I say again. More forcefully. With conviction.

"Say it, babe." Suddenly Erik has a knowing glint in his eyes.

"That's it over between Clayton and me," I tell him.

"And why would you feel that way?" he asks.

"Because how can something so special be over? How can something that moved my soul and made me love so much be done? I felt him the moment I saw him. I knew him," I say passionately. "Everything about us is different, unique. Once in a lifetime. How can once in a lifetime ever be done? It's supposed to be forever."

Erik smiles at me with respect and it dawns on me. I understand his game. How he pushed me into this.

"There it is," he says proudly. "Your fierce."

And it *is* here. I don't want to let go. Or give up. I want to fight. For Clayton. For me. For us. For our future. For everything that life is supposed to be. A fairy tale. Where you meet your true love and you live happily ever after.

Why can't that be my story?

It can.

I just have to believe it.

"You're so brave," Abby says.

She's in my room watching me pack . She looks forlorn. Devastated. I don't know what is causing it—William's passing or Michael leaving. Or the Russian oligarch she still has to deal with. She's got a whole list of awful that I don't envy. After I had my revelation with Erik and Orie that morning I sought out Abby and told her I was going to pack up and go find Clayton. She was getting ready to leave as well but she would be going through Paris with Georgie to stay a few nights there with some of his friends.

"I'm not," I tell her. "It's all a façade."

"I don't believe that," she says.

"You're the brave one," I reply as I fold a pair of jeans. "I don't think I could ever be a runaway bride. I would have married into misery. Especially if I had a houseful of guests and my parents watching my every move. If I had gone as far as you have down the road, I would have forced myself to the finish line. And then regretted it after."

"But we don't know if that's the decision I would actually have made at that moment with my dress on," she says back.

I raise a brow.

"And I still have to end it with him," she goes on. "Of course he understands why everything has been postponed, but now I have to actually break off the engagement."

"It will be easier than being a runaway bride, Abby. Trust me."

"Will it?" She doesn't sound like she believes me.

Which she shouldn't. I think about how hard it was for me to break up with Jerry face to face. Not a situation I would like to relive. Running away might be a better bet.

"I don't know," I sigh. "It's not going to be easy. But it's better for you. In every way. That I *do* know."

I hope she believes me now.

"What about you?" she asks.

"You know what I'm going to do."

"But what if he rejects you?" Abby asks, voicing the question that I've been wrestling with in my head since I made the decision this morning to get on a plane and go to London and not accept the generous vacation that Erik and Orie offered me. I was going to find Clayton and fight for us. To help him see through the grief and sorrow of his loss. To be there for him. To hold his hand. For him to know that he has someone who loves him and will help him through this awfulness. And any other he might face in his life.

"Well?" she insists.

"I don't know." I shrug. "I haven't thought about that. Honestly. I guess I'll just have to deal with it as it comes. I don't have a crystal ball to predict what he'll do. I can only hope."

"How can you put yourself in that situation?" Abby asks in awe.

I see the respect she has for me and I almost laugh. How did this ever happen? How am I the fearless one? How am I suddenly the one who's going to follow her heart and let the chips fall where they may?

Who would have thunk it?

"I don't know," I tell her. "I don't understand the need that's come over me. But suddenly I just—I just feel like this is what I need to do. For me. Or I'll regret it. And I don't want that."

Wow.

I said it. Because it's the truth. I do feel brave. A foreign feeling, no doubt. But one I like.

"I wish you could rub off on me," Abby mutters.

"Maybe I can?" I smile.

"My situation is completely different than yours."

"How so?" I ask.

"He's my cousin—"

"By marriage," I interrupt. "And there's definitely something between you guys."

"There is?" I see the longing in her eyes.

"Yes," I tell her honestly. "I don't know what it is. Or what it could be. But it's for you to find out."

Abby is pensive.

"And what if my heart is broken?" she asks softly.

The million-dollar question. One I'm facing right now, even though I'm being gutsy chasing after Clayton.

"Then it is." I think I say these words for myself as well as for Abby. Because there is nothing I can do but try.

"Abby, all you need to do is look at what happened to William."

Her eyes go wide.

"Life is short," I tell her the obvious. "It can be gone in a blink of an eye. Do you think he woke up that morning and thought he'd get in a car accident—and die? No. He was just going to catch a plane and come to his cousin's wedding."

Her eyes well up with sadness.

"It's the truth," I go on. "A fact of life that we never really take into consideration until it happens. So how can we not follow our hearts? In the end, what do we have to lose? It's all about now, and living in this moment."

What the hell was I thinking?

Yes, this is the thought that is racing through my mind as I sit in the cab in London on the way to Clayton's home in Hampstead. I sat on a soapbox and regurgitated all the information I had read in the dozens of self-help books I've read over the years, acting holier-than-thou to Abby. And now I feel like I'm going to pee my pants out of anxiety.

Abby was the one who gave me his address and assured me he would be here today because William's funeral would not be for four more days. I thought about coming after it was over, but I was afraid that he would disappear to some location that neither I nor Abby would be able to discover. I also knew that there would be no way Clayton would leave his family right now. But just to be sure, she enquired for me and confirmed me that Clayton was holed up in his home not seeing any guests. Just grieving.

It's been less than a day since I've seen him.

Which is not long at all.

I left Erik and Orie at the airport. They were flying to Italy, and had graciously accepted that I couldn't go with them, as wonderful as their offer was. As expected, the car ride with them was more than memorable.

Erik had turned to me and stared inquisitively. "So you're really going?"

"Yes."

"I fucking knew it!" he said. "Orie and I made a bet on whether you'd get chicken shit and change your mind at the last minute and come with us instead."

The idea had merit.

"And then what?" Orie asked, ignoring Erik.

"And then I don't know," because I didn't. The only thing I did know is that I wanted to be with Clayton. And I was going to gamble and see where that want left me. Who knew if he'd even see me? The thought of having the door slammed in my face was sickening.

"Well, you have our numbers," Erik told me in a comforting voice. "If anything goes wrong—"

"You sound like my parents," I laughed. But let's be real, they *were* on my speed dial in case the shit hit the fan.

"We feel like them," Orie told me.

"Do you believe—" my voice was tentative, unsure.

Erik interrupted me with a reassuring smile. "I believe you have to do this for you, because if you don't, you'll regret it forever."

I didn't want regrets.

The cab pulls up in front of a striking Victorian home. It's posh and exactly where I picture him living.

"We're here, miss," the driver says as he gets out to help me with my luggage. He opens my door and takes out my bags and puts them on the curb. Then he turns to me and gives me a curious look.

Probably because I'm not moving. I feel like my butt is glued to the seat. I just stare at the home and wonder.

Am I crazy?

What if Clayton tells me to leave?

What if he sends me away?

What if he doesn't care about me anymore?

"Are you getting out, miss?" he finally asks.

15

I'm standing on the doorstep of Clayton's home.

The taxi is long gone and I've actually been contemplating ringing the doorbell for give or take fifteen minutes. Yes. That's right. That long. Even though it's beyond freezing, it's dark out and snow covers the ground and I'm not dressed to be standing outside like a crazy person, I haven't quite been able to bring myself to ring the bell.

Shit. What to do?

When all else fails, text Erik.

I pull out my phone.

ME: I'm outside his door.

Thank God I don't have to wait long for him to reply. It's like he has ESP or something. He must have been waiting for me to message him.

ERIK: Is he not home?

ME: I have no idea. I haven't rung the doorbell yet.

ERIK: (sigh, eye-roll, etc.) Have you thought about the fact that a man of his caliber might, just might, have a security camera watching you? #yourecrazyandyouknowit #dothemath #tres

Oh shit!

Startled, I look up and around the door and sure enough there's a round, black, glass-looking device that I can only guess is a camera.

Oh. My. God.

Has he been staring at me this entire time?

ERIK: Are you there, stalker? Or is your mouth hanging open? #howarewefriends

ME: Hanging open. Totally ajar. #tres

ERIK: Well close it because you most certainly are not on candid camera.

ME: Fuck. Me.

ERIK: No thanks. But you're hot. Ring the bell before this gets even weirder. #howdoyoufunctioninsociety

I sigh.

ME: Okay. I love you.

ERIK: Don't forget to text me with updates.

ME: I won't.

I put the phone in my jacket and try to fight off the completely mortifying feeling of being caught on the security camera. I'm sure someone from his staff has told him that I've been standing here for a quarter of an hour with my luggage staring at the door like a lovesick lunatic.

You are a world-class idiot.

Whatever, I tell myself. *I was gathering the courage.*

And now, my subconscious snorts derisively, *you're talking to yourself, which makes you look even crazier than you already are.*

I wish I could shove my foot up your—

Before I can finish my thought, the door opens, to my horror. Embarrassment. Humiliation.

Thankfully, it's only Sergei, Clayton's bodyguard. Hired to protect him against people who talk to themselves and stand outside his home. People just like me.

"I was worried you were going to turn into an ice statue," he says dryly. "I didn't know how much longer you'd last."

Who knew he had a sense of humor?

"I was just thinking," I tell him lamely.

"I think you should 'think' inside," he tells me. "Or you will catch pneumonia."

"Good idea."

He gives me a knowing smile and steps outside to take my luggage. When he turns back inside I follow him tentatively and take my first look at Clayton's house.

I can only describe it as classically beautiful.

The floors and walls are white limestone. There's a mix of contemporary art and beautiful antique pieces that come together incredibly well. The foyer is done in shades of pale blue, which, combined with the limestone and the art, makes it feel warm and welcoming.

"Follow me," Sergei says and shows me into what looks like the living room.

He helps me out of my jacket then says, "Wait here. I will get Mr. Sinclair."

I'm sure you will.

I nod nervously then try to concentrate on the glorious room that I'm standing in.

There is an enormous stone fireplace that must be hundreds of years old. He has the same kind in his chateau in France, and I bet he had it sent from there. Thankfully, there's a fire blazing that immediately warms my numb fingers. I hadn't even realized I didn't have feeling in them anymore.

White linen couches flank the fireplace and between them is a huge coffee table that's a giant shell with a glass top. It looks like it dates back centuries, too. It's like art. Every piece in the room is perfectly placed. An oil painting almost covers an entire wall of the room, and I move closer to it. It's a beautiful ocean landscape in pale blues and greys. It reminds me of scenery you'd see on the East Coast.

And then it happens again.

The energy in the room changes, and I know he's here even though he has not made a sound. I can feel his eyes on my back. I have to take a moment to gather my courage before I can turn around to face him. I'm dressed casually in jeans, a black turtleneck, and my black knee-high boots with a heel. I figured that I needed the extra height for an advantage. I don't know why I thought that would change a thing because just being near him, smelling him, *feeling* him, instantly puts me at a disadvantage.

"Sophie."

My heart flutters.

God.

His voice.

The way he says my name.

I slowly turn around and his sapphire blue eyes burn into mine.

I quickly take in his appearance.

He looks tired and worn out. Grief stricken. He's dressed in blue jeans and a long black thermal shirt. And he's barefoot. I try to keep my thoughts purely PG- or G-rated but it's hard when I'm staring at well over six feet of male perfection.

"Clayton."

On cue, a crackle in the fireplace.

I try to remember what I was going to say. What I had planned on the plane, in the taxi over here, and it all goes out the window. I can't remember anything.

"How are you?" I offer.

Shit.

Dumbest question ever, Sophie! How do you think he is? I brace myself for a cutting response. But he surprises me.

"I'm devastated."

My heart aches. But the relief I feel from him not shutting me out again is overwhelming. He continues to stare at me. I watch as his eyes roam possessively over my body and that single action reassures me in a way that nothing can. He still wants me. I affect him. That's all the courage I need.

"I know you are," I tell him softly.

There's an awkward silence between us as I try to think of at least one of the great lines I had come up with on the short flight over.

"What are you doing here?" he asks guardedly.

"I'm here for you," I say as I take a step toward him.

He watches me silently so I continue.

"I'm here because I can't see you like this. In this much pain. All alone. My heart is breaking for you. *With you.*"

I watch how his eyes waver and he looks down. Like he's fighting his emotions. Fighting for control.

"You don't have to be brave in front of me," I continue. "You loved your brother. You *love* your brother."

He runs a shaky hand through his hair.

"Sophie—" his voice is choked up. "Please—"

"No," I say as I courageously make my way to him until we're standing face to face.

"Look at me, Clayton."

He doesn't.

"Look. At. Me," I command, using the same words he always says to me.

His gaze finally meets mine.

There's an angry fire in his eyes. I know it's because of the authority in my voice. Until now he's always been the one in control and I know he probably doesn't appreciate the role reversal. But I continue and speak my heart.

"I love you."

So much it hurts, I think.

I watch him take in a breath.

"You shouldn't," his voice is rough with emotion.

"Really?" I challenge. "Do you want me to go find someone else to give my love to?"

Clayton is silent.

"Do you want me to let someone else touch me?" I press on and watch with satisfaction as his eyes flare in fury.

But he still doesn't answer me.

"I can, you know," I continue in a serious voice. "I can walk out that door and go find someone—"

I can't even finish my sentence because he grabs me by the hair and pulls me to him. His gaze sweeps over my face.

"You're pushing me."

"You didn't let me finish my sentence," I say as I bring my fingers to his lips to silence him. "I can find another man, Clayton—"

His jaw flexes.

"—but I don't want to," I plead with him. "I just want you. I will *always* want you."

There is a brief second when I wonder if my words have even had an impact. If he's going to let go of me and tell me to walk out of his life. I can feel him fighting me, or himself. But then there's a change, something happens.

And his lips crash into mine.

It's not the type of kiss I'm used to from Clayton. It's different. It's frantic with longing. And need. Maybe he craves the warmth I can give him. Maybe he's looking to escape from the grief. And I'll give him whatever it takes.

We rip each other's clothes off, touching each other with maddening need, our lips barely breaking apart. Desire tingles all over my skin I want him so bad. I need him so bad. He picks me up and takes me to the sofa, comes down on me, and runs his hands through my hair as he stares into my passion-filled eyes.

"I can't wait." His voice is raspy.

"I don't want you to." I feel just as demanding. I *need* him.

I'm given exactly what I need as he plunges into me, filling me so completely.

"Oh, God," I moan.

"Oh God, what?" he whispers against my mouth as he moves inside me.

It's rough. Hard. But I still come apart in his arms. We both find our climax at the same time. Our hearts pound together. Intertwined in their beat. Like one.

"What are you doing to me?" he whispers against my mouth as he kisses me, still buried deep inside.

He leans up on his elbows and looks down into my eyes. The raw pain is there. I take my hands and cup his face.

"Please just listen to me," I whisper to him as I hurry to tell him my jumbled thoughts. "I just want to be here for you. I don't expect anything. I don't need anything. I just want to be with you through this."

As quickly as I'm given a glimpse of his pain, it's gone. And he's hiding from me again. The barrier is back.

"Don't do that," I plead as I hold on to him, not letting him move.

"Do what?" he asks aloofly.

"Go cold on me," I tell him. "You need me right now."

He closes his eyes.

"Use me however you like and I'll deal with the consequences of what will come," I say with a shaky breath. "But don't push me away now when more than anything you need someone to hold your hand."

He doesn't answer me. Instead, he gets up and grabs a throw from one of the couches and wraps it around my body. I have a fleeting moment of panic that someone from his staff or even Sergei might have witnessed our intimacy, but I brush it aside because I know he would never compromise me. He picks me up like I'm the most precious thing in the world to him and heads out of the room and up the stairs.

"Be careful what you wish for," he finally utters.

I answer by wrapping my arms around his neck and pulling myself closer to his body.

"I always am."

I wake up the next morning alone in his giant bed. The sheets and comforter feel like butter and are winter white. His room is very similar to the one in Avignon except that the palette is grey instead of navy blue. But the style is almost identical.

I get out of bed and find my purse on the grey linen couch next to the fireplace. I explore his room and find the master closet, which is beautifully done in dark wood. All my belongings have been unpacked and are hanging neatly opposite Clayton's clothing. Someone had obviously made room for my things. The fact that I slept through this is astounding to me but then Clayton kept me up for most of the night and I haven't had much sleep since arriving in Europe.

I get my phone from my purse. I have about five missed calls from Erik and twenty text messages that basically say, "*What the F is going on? We are dying. Details. Now bitch,*" in one way or another.

I quickly text him.

ME: I'm alive. I'm at Clayton's home. Obviously I slept here. My stuff is unpacked so it looks like I'm here for a while.

ERIK: Took you long enough to respond.

ME: Sorry. I slept in.

ERIK: Loverboy keep you up all night?

I blush.

ME: Maybe.

ERIK: Whore.

ME: Takes one to know one.

ERIK: Better believe it. We're just sitting down to lunch so I'll call you when I can talk.

ME: Love you.

ERIK: Me more.

I put my phone down and go about the business of getting ready.

Once I'm showered and dressed in a pair of dark black skinny jeans, ballet flats, a grey sweater and my hair in a ponytail I venture out the door.

Clayton's home is *very* English. The architecture is just like the homes I'd picture when I read books that took place in eighteenth-century Europe. The kind English high society would have and throw fancy balls in. Everything is so posh and perfect. It looks like it was just photographed for a high-end magazine.

I go downstairs and explore some more until I find the kitchen. There's an attractive woman in her sixties cooking in a white kitchen that looks like it is the domain of a world-class chef. There are two sub-zeros, six stoves, an enormous wooden island that is pristine even though she's chopping away. It's completely unreal.

She smiles when she spots me.

"You must be Sophie," she says in a lovely English accent. "My name is Ariana."

"Nice to meet you," I reply.

"Mr. Sinclair has left for the day but he wanted to make sure that you eat," she tells me to my surprise.

Left for the day?

"What can I prepare for you?" Ariana asks.

"Did he say when he would be coming back?" I ask in a small voice.

Ariana shakes her head. "No," she informs me. "And I never inquire."

When she sees what I'm sure is the crestfallen look in my eyes she tries to reassure me.

"As you know, everything is chaotic right now," she says sadly. "I'm sure he is taking care of things." She looks down as if she is trying to contain her emotions and begins chopping again before she says, "William is sorely missed. He was a joy, a pure joy. This is a devastating blow."

"Yes, of course," I respond immediately. "You don't have to make anything for me. I guess I'll just do some sightseeing until he comes home, and I'll grab something along the way."

"Perfect," she answers kindly. "But I *will* make you something before you go. I think you're very brave to go out in this weather. I'd suggest indoor activities. Stay inside as much as you can. The cold can get you."

"I was thinking along those lines," I smile.

"So what would you like for breakfast?"

"I'll just have some eggs and toast, thank you."

"Where would you like to eat?" Ariana asks.

"Right here is fine," I say.

"Are you sure you wouldn't prefer breakfast in the dining room?" She asks me.

"Not alone," I reply quickly because it's the truth.

She seems surprised at first but covers with a friendly smile.

"After your breakfast I'll call the driver to come and get you. He'll take you anywhere you like."

"Oh no," I tell her. "I don't need a driver."

"Mr. Sinclair insisted on it if you leave the house."

"I promise you, I'll be alright," I say, touched by his kind gesture. "I'd really rather explore on my own."

I can see that she's unsure for a moment, but then shrugs.

"Very well, " she says and begins to prepare my breakfast.

I feel a bit useless sitting there waiting to be served. "Can I help?" I ask.

Apparently this is a ridiculous question because Ariana waves me off like I'm joking.

I try not to be too disappointed that Clayton left without a goodbye or even a note. Or a text. I know he has to deal with his brother's funeral and his family right now. They're probably all together. I just wished he would have told me. At least when he'd be coming back home.

After eating Ariana's to-die-for eggs, I quickly leave Clayton's house, again assuring the chef, housekeeper, or whatever she's called that I will be okay on my own.

She gives me directions to the Tube, which are easy enough to follow, and I get a map of London at a shop near the station, and am off. Then I have an epiphany. This is the first time I've ever been on my own. Whenever I've traveled in the past it was always with Erik or my parents.

I've never ever explored a city completely by myself. Many of the self-help books I've read over the years have always encouraged having a "date" with yourself, so to speak, and for some reason I've never actually done it.

I reach into my bag to text Erik this revelation and realize I left my phone at Clayton's house.

Do I need it? Maybe.

But why not have a full day of liberation?

Just completely me, with a map of a city I've been dying to see. Clayton is either with his family or working and I'll be there for him when he gets home. It's actually liberating and it makes me feel so excited.

I decide my first stop is going to be the British Museum.

And when I arrive, I know it was the right decision because even the building that houses all its art wonders is awe-inspiring.

I explore the marvels of ancient Egypt, the Renaissance era, Greek, Iranian, and Indian art. I'm lost in the different cultures, in the different forms of beauty that have excited me over the years and do so even more now, when I'm faced with the actual pieces. Hours go by and I lose track of time and even forget to have lunch.

My growling stomach is my only reminder.

So from there I manage to find my way to the Wolseley to have high tea. It's a beautiful location and I understand why so many people love to have the experience. And the fact that it's the holiday season only adds to the appeal.

Christmas time in London is really magical. The entire city is decked out with decorations that only make it more special. I do a quick mental countdown and realize it's less than a week away. I figure I'll use this time to buy gifts for my family and friends.

And for Clayton. It has to be something beyond special and I'll know it when I see it.

I enjoy the scones and small bites and people-watching and I truly feel like a tourist looking in on a life I've only read about.

I'm fully immersed in Clayton's world. This is how he grew up. He was raised in this city, and this is my way to learn more about him, his culture, without having to ask, or beg as is usually the case, for information. I walk down Piccadilly Circus and do the tourist thing and buy a few souvenirs and find some fun Christmas presents. I hardly notice the cold because I'm enjoying myself so much. I walk past Buckingham Palace . It is spectacular and regal and I stop to stare at the changing of the guards. I find the engraved markers on the ground they have for Princess Diana and can't help but think about what love did to her.

Positive thoughts, Sophie. *Only positive vibes!*

I stroll around some more and pass many tourist sights that I want to linger in but I know I'll go back at my leisure.

I find Harrods and walk inside the giant store in shock. It's so busy and posh, and is literally Erik's wet dream. I buy him and Orie a small Christmas teddy bears with the logo on it, which is beyond touristy but I know they'll get a kick out of it. And then I find myself parked at a cute café enjoying a glass of Sauvignon Blanc, staring out the window at the busy city. Suddenly I feel the way Carrie did in *Sex in the City* when she went to France with the Russian and was left wandering around alone. Not that I'm as glamorous or well dressed but I feel just as lonely.

My thoughts drift to Clayton, to his family, and then I think about my own parents. I miss them and will call when I get back to the house. I realize how badly I need to hear my dad's voice. He always makes me feel secure even when I'm doing something that pisses him off. It's something I never take for granted.

Time flies and before I know it, it's dark out.. I know the sun goes down early in the winter so I don't think it's *that* late. I'm a little bummed that I wasn't able to find a Christmas present for Clayton but that means I'll just have to return. I make my way to the Tube station and it takes me a good thirty minutes to figure out how to get back to Clayton's house. Sense of direction has never been my thing. A half hour later I arrive in Hampstead.

I step outside and the cold air hits me hard, and I dread the walk to his house.

But I'm saved.

Or in trouble.

I don't know which.

"Sophie!" Clayton's voice bites harder than the cold.

I turn around, bags in hand, arms crossed over my chest from the frosty air, a cold-hot mess of disaster, and find Clayton striding toward me. The black Range Rover is parked across the street. Sergei stands beside it.

Clayton has on a long black wool coat and his gorgeous face looks like it's carved out of stone.

"Hi," I say with a tentative smile as he reaches me, even though I have a good idea that I'm in trouble for something.

"Hi?" he practically snarls at me.

"What's wrong?" I ask.

He closes his eyes for a second.

"Do you have any idea how worried I was? Do you know what time it is?"

"Five or six?" I say, unsure. I don't have a watch or my phone and it's the first time in my life I never bothered to stop and ask someone.

"It's seven o'clock at night!" he grits out. "I called you a thousand times!"

Shit. Time certainly did fly by.

"I left my phone at your house," I rush out. "I'm sorry."

"You didn't think to call me to check in?" he goes on, clearly livid.

"I don't have your number memorized," I explain.

He towers over me.

"Why didn't you take the driver like I wanted you to?"

"You didn't tell me," I inform him.

"Yes—"

"No," I interrupt and watch his eyes flare. "You told Ariana. Actually, you had a conversation with her, but left me without a word."

He doesn't look too happy about me pointing this out.

"Did you forget what you told me last night?" he asks softly.

Right. My willingness to let him navigate the waters of this time without a peep from me. Of course he has to bring that up now.

"No," I shake my head, but I don't back down. "But the rules should go both ways, right? Seems only fair."

I watch in fascination as the muscles in his jaw twitch. Not once, but twice. I hope I'm not giving him some sort of affliction or something.

"Now, are you going to help me with my stuff or do you expect me to stand here and argue in the freezing cold?"

His bright gaze widens in shock then his manners kick in and he steps forward and takes the shopping bags from me.

"Thank you."

He doesn't answer. He's still pissed. I follow him to the car in silence, where we sit next to each other in stony silence. You can cut the air with a knife it feels so suffocating. And I'm exhausted from my long day in town, though I feel energized by all that I saw and experienced on my own.

We get to Clayton's house quickly, and Sergei pulls into the up in front of the house.

I move to open the car door but Clayton's viselike grip on my arm stops me in my tracks.

I look at him in alarm, but the look he gives silences me as Sergei quietly exits the car and shuts the door. Clayton watches him make his way inside before he turns to look at me and unleash hell.

"Never behave like that again!" he roars.

My ears ring.

"Do you hear me?" Clayton goes on.

"I think your neighbors can hear you," I say with growing anger. I face him head on. Confidently. "And I don't think I like your tone."

He's shocked. Totally. Completely. Shocked.

"This isn't medieval England," I go on. "You don't get to tell me what to do or how to behave. I decide on my own."

He closes his eyes.

I know it's to gain control. He probably wants to strangle me, control freak that he is.

"You don't get to make the rules, Sophie," he says in a voice that is so dangerously soft, my guard goes up. *"I do.* Remember?"

I swallow audibly and reach for the door handle.

"You're clearly in a mood and I don't want to have this conver—"

He hits a button on the side panel and the doors lock.

Oh shit.

I press the buttons on my panel and try to open the door.

"I control *all* things," Clayton strong voice rings through the car.

I start to panic. I remember the last time I experienced a Clayton Sinclair type of sexual torture-punishment-agony and it was hell. Pure hell. I have a feeling this is what he has in store for me now.

"Let me out," I say.

16

"Not yet," Clayton tells me.

"Remind me why you came here," he says.

"To be here for you," I say, my cheeks reddening.

"And by that you mean gallivanting around London all day?"

"That's not fair," I inhale sharply.

"Really?" he says harshly. "I came home for lunch to experience some of that comfort and peace you offered yesterday and instead of finding you waiting for me, you were gone. Without a trace or a note."

His words sting and I feel an immense sense of guilt.

"Instead of comfort, Sophie," he goes on in a cold voice, "I was overcome with worry. With a feeling of helplessness. Wondering if I would get another call like the one I received about William."

"I'm so *so* sorry!" I interrupt him in a whisper.

I didn't even think about that side of it.

"Sorry doesn't take away how I felt while I pictured every horrible thing that could possibly befall you in town," Clayton replies angrily.

"I didn't know when you'd be getting home. I thought you'd be gone all day," I plead with him. "Please understand,"

He turns to me with lightning speed and takes hold of my jaw and I stare into his beautiful, tormented face.

He looks intense. A fire rages inside him. An angry inferno that I'm not so sure he can control.

"You know what I don't understand?" he finally says.

"No," I whisper.

"I don't understand why—" he leans in to whisper furiously against my lips.

"Why I can't—"

My heart pounds.

"Let. You. Go."

He closes his eyes. "I want to push you away," he goes on in an anguished voice. "I *wish* I could push you away."

I don't dare utter a word.

"I was supposed to be with my family today," Clayton rages, "and I left them to spend time with you. I spent all day obsessing about you. All I wanted was to be with *you*."

I know he's furious with himself. This gorgeous man is angry that he finally needs something.

And that something is me.

It's an unbelievable idea to wrap my head around.

"I should be thinking about William and instead—" His breath hitches "All I think about—"

His thumb moves over my lips.

"All I want—"

I wait.

"All I need is—"

I hold my breath.

He's so close he puts his hand on the passenger side window behind me.

And then the car alarm goes off.

We jump away from each other.

Sergie appears within seconds. I don't know where he came from. Once he takes in the scene and knows that everything is okay he pulls out a key and clicks the alarm in the direction of the vehicle.

The moment is over.

Clayton opens the car door. "Let's go inside,

And just like that the intensity has evaporated along with whatever Clayton was going to tell me.

The next two days go by in a blur. The routine that develops begins to irritate me no end. I see Clayton around seven o'clock. We have dinner together. The conversation is stilted and is usually about what museums I went to during the day (with a driver of course, because he insists). He makes love to me all night, then leaves again the next day to be with his family or go to work, I don't know which because he doesn't share this piece of information with me.

When I ask him how his day was or if he needs anything, he's distant and gives curt responses. It's a hard pill to swallow, but I since I don't want to give up on him, *on us, I should say*, I try to bite my tongue and take it easy. To let things just flow and be.

I have been here for three days and the funeral is tomorrow. and I know Abby is back in town from Paris since she texted me. But today Clayton's told me he will be spending the entire day with his mother. Even though I'm dying to call Abby and see if she would like to have lunch with me, I choose to stay home in case he comes back and needs me, especially before the funeral. In fact, since the day I had a date with myself, I've pretty much stayed in for most of the time, only doing a little sightseeing and Christmas shopping in the morning, hoping that Clayton would come looking for me like he did the first time I went out. But as my luck goes, he's stayed away. Not shocking, right?

The only adventure I had was yesterday, when I asked the driver, whose name is Paul to take me out to a store where I could buy art supplies, determined to busy myself with sketching and painting. Anything to keep my mind busy and not obsessing about Clayton and my unknown future as an artist, which I realized I haven't even thought about at all.

Clearly my career is not a priority in my life right now.

I called my parents a few times and lied about my whereabouts. They still think I'm in France for the wedding and will be home next week before Christmas. I figure it's better this way so they don't freak out and come after me. I'm relieved neither my mom nor my dad is on social media because if they were they'd see Erik and Orie's excellent adventure. Sans Sophie.

The two post on Instagram all day long, and from the look of things they're having the time of their lives. In love. Laughing. Happy. I gather that the whole Georgie flirting thing is completely in the past. I'm so relieved by this. I don't know if I could handle another crazy relationship in my life right now. And with Erik I know it would be beyond.

Sometimes I wish I were with them touring through Europe. But then I think about how I felt when I thought Clayton had betrayed me in the Maldives, and the loneliness of being away from him, and I know I'm making the right decision staying here.

Without a doubt, I would be a big ball of depression if I were with Erik and Orie. I'm pretty sure the pictures would not be the same. They'd be a series of shots with two hot guys and Debbie Downer.

I sigh and get back to my task.

It's late afternoon and I'm in Clayton's living room sketching a photo I took from the hill above the chateau in Avignon, one of my favorite spots on his estate. It's a view of mist settling over the beautiful valley.

"Has anyone ever told you that you look beautiful when you work." Michael Sinclair startles me as he walks into the room.

I turn quickly and see Clayton's tall, handsome brother confidently stride into the room. He's dressed casually in black jeans and a hoodie and is sexy as hell.

I set my sketchpad down and get up happily. I must be starved for company, because I'm just so pleased to see someone I know in person, and not on social media.

I walk over to him and give him a hug.

"It's nice to see you," I whisper as he embraces me in his strong arms, practically lifting me off the ground.

I don't blame Abby for being in love with this guy. I think a nun would be. Or a monk, for that matter. Talk about a tall, rugged, extremely masculine, body of sexy.

He gives me a brotherly kiss on top of my head.

"You didn't listen to me," he half jokes as he pulls away to watch my reaction.

"I didn't," I admit ruefully.

Michael's quiet. I wonder what he's thinking.

"How's your mom?" I ask him.

"Stronger than expected," he tells me.

"And your dad?"

"Not great." Michael looks so sad. "To be honest, I thought it would be the opposite."

If I had to guess I would say that the eldest Sinclair is feeling beyond guilty since he had William stay behind. I can't imagine what must be going on his head.

"And you?"

I watch the shadows come over his bright blue eyes that remind me so much of Clayton. He runs a shaky hand over his face.

"You know," he begins, "I don't know how I feel. Sad, of course. Devastated. Like there's a void that can never be filled. Which it can't. Ever. My baby brother—"

His voice breaks and he turns away from me and walks over to the fireplace. I stay quiet. He stares down at the blaze. My eyes are glued to his handsome profile.

"And then there's this part of me that understands," he tells me. "You know, I'm a voracious reader. I have been since I was a young boy. Philosophical books are my favorite. I'm trying to take what I've retained over the years and apply it to my situation now. Maybe that's what's helped me be able to bear this more than the rest of my family. I don't know. But I feel like it has in a way."

He seems embarrassed by his admission. "Do I sound like a lunatic?"

Hello? Look who you're talking to! I want to say. But thankfully I don't.

"Not at all," I say calmly. "I'm actually a big self-help reader myself." I notice the look of surprise on his face. "But obviously I've got a ways to go," I rush out awkwardly, since it's blatantly obvious that I am not the picture of Zen. Most of the time, I'm the exact opposite.

Michael laughs.

"You're very funny," he says.

"Unfortunately it's not intentional," I admit ruefully.

Michael shouts with laughter now.

He has a great laugh. Like his brother. And I'm happy that I've made him smile even if it's at my expense.

"Can I ask you something?" I say.

"Anything," he says with a smile.

"Tell me what's going on with Clayton."

He looks at me inquisitively. "How do you mean?"

"He doesn't really talk to me," I explain. "Or tell me what he's thinking. And I don't want to push him, so I'm quiet and just— just here with him. *For* him. But I wish he would open up to me. Do I make sense?"

"Yes, of course you do."

I wait.

"I think he blames himself," Michael says after a while.

"But how can this be anyone's fault? And why would he even think that?" I demand. It's the most ridiculous thing I've ever heard.

"He thinks he should have pulled William away from our father," he explains. "He wanted William to work for him. I've tried to tell Clayton that it wouldn't have changed anything. That this awful loss probably would have happened regardless. At least, that's what I believe."

I'm surprised Michael is looking at this in such a open–minded way. It makes him even more attractive.

"I believe that, too," I admit.

We look at each other and there's an understanding between us. A recognition of sorts. In that moment, I believe our bond is made forever.

"My brother is lucky," he whispers.

I can feel myself blush. But before I can respond—

"Am I interrupting?" he says in an annoyed voice.

Clayton is there, dressed in an expensive black suit, his face, even though chiseled in grief, alarmingly handsome. He takes my breath away.

"No, you're not," Michael replies with narrowed eyes. I'm sure he didn't miss the tone in his brother's voice.

Clayton looks from his brother to me in an almost accusatory way. His look doesn't even dignify a reaction.

"I didn't expect you so early," I tell him.

"Really?"

I can't miss the cynicism in his voice.

"No," I ignore his tone. "I was sketching when your brother surprised me. Is there something wrong?"

I watch the struggle.

I know it's hard for him. He wants to go there. He's probably looking for a fight more than anything right now. I'm sure that the only reason he's restraining himself is because he doesn't want to look crazy to his brother.

"We need to talk now, Michael," Clayton says. "There are some things we need to go over."

I watch the way Michael's eyes light up in annoyance by his brother's commanding tone, but he too holds himself together and nods.

He looks at me. "If you'll excuse us, Sophie."

"Yes, of course," I say to him.

"I'll see you tomorrow," Michael tells me.

The two walk to the door. When Michael exits, Clayton lingers to turn and stare at me.

"I won't be here tonight," he says to my surprise. "I'll be in Bath, where we will be laying William to rest."

It's sad that I don't even know where the funeral is going to take place. But it's another pill I just swallow.

"We have a family estate in Bath," Clayton explains. "It was William's favorite place."

I don't know what this means for me. Does he not want me to go the memorial? Is he going to shut me out completely?

Thankfully, he quickly relieves my worries.

"Sergei will drive you tomorrow morning, the service doesn't begin until four-thirty pm," he says. "We'll stay in Bath for the night then come back the following day."

The surge of relief I feel is staggering.

"Alright," I say. "Are you leaving now?"

"Yes. With Michael."

We stare at each other.

The distance between us seems greater than the few yards.

Because I know he won't be the one to bridge the gap, I do. I walk over to him and don't allow a second for him to hesitate. I get up on my tiptoes, since I'm barefoot, and pull him into my arms.

He pauses for a moment before he gives in and lifts me up off the ground. He buries his head in my neck, his lips pressed against my skin. I feel a shiver of desire race up my spine.

"Sophie," he whispers.

"Clayton," I say back.

He doesn't kiss me on the mouth as I would like, but instead pulls away.

"I have a surprise for you."

I lift a questioning brow but he gives me the hottest smile.

"Patience," he tells me. "I'll see you tomorrow."

He walks out and I'm left alone.

Again.

It's been a little over an hour since Michael an Clayton left and I'm now sitting alone in Clayton's family room in front of a giant flat-screen television and channel surfing. It's dark out already so I'm just going to stay in for the rest of the evening. I'm looking for something on the Discovery Channel or History. My secret addiction, besides self-help books, KitKat, and pizza (in no particular order), are shows about aliens. Yes, it sounds crazy. It probably is. But guess what? I love it. And yes, I believe!

They are so coming down to wage war one day.

Ariana made me a tray of tea sandwiches, chocolates, and wisely included a bottle of rosé on ice that I plan on indulging.

"Yo, bitch. Get out the way..."

Just like that, my life is perfect.

Erik and Orie are standing in the doorway posing like supermodels. Looking fabulous. And ready to rock and roll.

I can't help it. I scream in joy!

Then I run to Erik and throw myself at him.

"Jesus. You act as though we haven't seen each other for months," he say as he pulls me into his strong embrace. "You know it's only been three days?"

"Seems like forever," I tell him.

"You've lost weight," Orie says as he smacks me on the ass.

"I've been eating," I tell him. "It must be nerves."

Erik spins me around.

"Thank God for those," he says. "They do wonders for body fat."

"What are you guys doing here? I thought you were in Majorca?" I ask them after we get over the hugs and kisses.

"Clayton called us," Orie says.

I pull away from Erik.

"What?"

"He called Erik, actually, and said that he thought you might like the company."

"He sent a jet for us," Erik informs me. "A fucking, crazy-ass, Lear motherfucker, what's up, I'm rich kind of jet. When I saw that thing on the runway I knew we made the right decision to come to you."

"You're speaking a foreign language," I tell him with a smile.

"Yeah, I figured," he says. "It's called *luxury*. And you need to become fluent in it real fast. I don't think they have a Rosetta Stone for it so you're gonna have to learn it on your own."

I burst out laughing.

"I missed you!" I tell him.

"I know." He's completely unaffected by my words. He spots the rosé and walks over and fills my glass and takes a healthy sip.

"Before I get into the whole how-fucking-nuts this home is, how are you?" Orie asks in concern as he comes over to me and rubs my hair.

I take a moment before I reply. I wish I could hide from Erik and Orie but they are too good at sensing my moods. They can read me like nobody's business.

"I'm okay," I say.

Erik raises a brow.

"Don't look at me like that," I tell him. "This is not an easy time. I can't tell you I'm happy and perfect and we're riding off into the sunset, because we're not. This situation is not good. I'm only here for Clayton. I want to support him during this awful time. I don't expect anything from it."

"Bullshit," he answers..

"What?" I'm annoyed.

"Of course you expect something from it." He waves at me like I'm an insignificant fly. "You can't lie to me."

"I'm not lying," I say.

Am I?

You are so lying.

"Okay!" I admit. "But right now isn't about us, it's about him and his loss."

"Yes," Erik admits. " And after tomorrow?"

"I haven't even thought about that," I tell him honestly.

"Don't think about it now," Orie says.

"But you will think about it the day after tomorrow," Erik warms. "You can't stay here forever and sit in his house and just drink wine, have tea sandwiches, and be waited on hand and foot. I mean, you could do that, but it won't make you happy. It would make *me* happy without a doubt, but not you."

I almost laugh.

"You have to be Sophie," he goes on dramatically. "The Sophie I know. The artist. And you have to make decisions, even if they're not going to be the ones you like."

I give him a sad smile.

"I know this," I say softly.

"Do you?" He doesn't believe me.

"Yes," I say. "I do. But for the time being I just want to think of Clayton."

Erik looks like he wants to give me a stinging reply but Orie hits him in the gut and prevents him from doing so.

"Fine," he says. "I hear you. I'll give you forty-eight hours before I start on you again."

Instead of having Sergei drive us we decide to take the train into Bath that morning. This way we'll safely get there with enough time before the memorial and we'll have some privacy to talk. The countryside is absolutely beautiful and I fall in love instantly. I wish I was here under different circumstances, but when we reach the historic city, I understand why William was drawn to the area. You can't help but fall in love with the buildings and trees. The history that oozes from the place. And there are the ancient Roman baths here that I know the city is known for and I'm dying to explore.

We get a taxi to our hotel. Clayton's assistant had Ariana tell us this morning that Erik, Orie, and I have reservations at The Royal Crescent Hotel, which I guess was someone's home in the eighteenth century. She doesn't say whether Clayton is staying there as well or at their family estate and I don't ask. I like the idea of experiencing something very English.

Clayton hasn't called since he left yesterday.

I try not to dwell over this but it's hard. I know he's with his family. I know this is an awful time. But the part of me that loves him so bad wishes he would accept my embrace and compassion. And most important, love. I want to help him feel at least somewhat, better. That's the only reason why I came to London. But with each passing day, it seems like less of a possibility.

He did warn you, Sophie, my inner voice creeps up on me.

You suck! I silently say back.

You do realize you're talking to yourself?

Whatever.

I'm officially going crazy. Or I have been but it's seriously inching up on me now.

The three of us check into the hotel, which I really can't believe was someone's home in the eighteenth century. The grounds, the sheer size, it's all so epic.

Erik and Orie love the hotel and their room. Clayton booked them a suite, which is large and beautiful. There's a living area that is done in pale yellow colors with silk couches, combined with crown moldings and gorgeous oil paintings, the room is to die for. My suite is is just as jaw dropping. It's bigger than theirs and a good distance away. The front desk gave me only one key and hoped that I would enjoy my stay. This can only mean that Clayton is not staying with me. He had his secretary book it, so he's obviously staying at his family estate.

We get dressed in conservative black attire and we're picked up at four pm for the funeral. William's mass is held in a small old church that is not over the top at all, the opposite of what I expected given the stature of Clayton's family, but it's extraordinarily charming. And perfect.

Erik, Orie and I stay at the back of the church, even though many ushers ask who we are and urge us to go to the front pews. I reject this notion because I'm acutely aware that I'm an outsider. And I don't want to sit with the immediate family and impose myself. Clayton is surrounded by mourners and I give him his space. I'm sure he knows I'm here so he will find me if he needs me. I just accept what is. I know the family is in deep pain and just hope that my presence is enough.

The mass is beautiful. The eulogies are incredibly touching. When Clayton speaks, I am proud of him and overcome with emotion. He reads a poem from Henry Scott-Holland titled "Death Is Nothing at All." The verses bring everyone to tears. The he talks about his relationship with William. Their love for on another. His older brother persona and how overprotective he was. It's humorous and poignant, and I find myself crying through his entire tribute.

After the service, I don't see Clayton in the crowd of people, so can't tell him how beautiful I thought his speech was, but I bide my time. I don't want to intrude and I want him to be able to talk to whomever he must and be with his family.

Then everyone retires to a pub in the city that William particularly loved. There they serve William's favorite food and drinks. Erik, Orie, and I order wine and take a seat in a small booth in the back that allows us to see everyone who comes in the room, including Clayton, who isn't here yet.

"I'm glad we decided to sit and chill," Erik says.

"I concur," Orie says.

"Good decision," I agree.

Eventually Georgie and Abby come and join us. Georgie is wearing all black suede and actually looks chic as shit. I watch as Erik gives him an admiring once over.

"I need wine," he says as he moves his way into the booth to sit with us.

"C'est tellement triste," Georgie goes on. "William was the best of the Sinclairs."

"Don't say that, Georgie," Abby says as she scoots into the booth with us.

She looks pale and gaunt and I worry instantly.

"Are you alright, Abby?" I ask in concern.

"Yes, Sophie," she tells me. "I'm just tired. Too much going on and—"

"She dumped that fucking Cosack," Georgie finishes for her.

My mouth drops open. Abby flushes.

"Georgie!"

"I couldn't wait to share the good news," he says. "It is cause for celebration. Even William's ascension into the afterlife is a cause for a party."

"That's bold," Erik says.

Georgie raises a brow.

"Is it not? Our *belle homme* William has left the earth and will now be an angel with the giants. That is cause for happiness, not grief."

"We still miss him," Abby says sadly.

"Yes, of course," Georgie agrees.

"But we celebrate him," Michael chimes in as he appears out of thin air.

I watch the color race back into Abby's face. And I don't miss the concerned look that Michael gives her.

"Are you alright, Abigail?" he asks. "You look like you need to eat something."

"I'm not hungry," she says with a shrug. I can tell she's trying hard not to be affected by him. But I understand her dilemma. The Sinclair men are hard to ignore.

"I'll order you something," Michael says, ignoring her response.

I almost snort.

Typical.

He turns to me. "Have you seen my brother yet?"

"No," I say as I shake my head.

He reaches over and squeezes my hand.

"I'm glad you're here," he says. "He needs you."

I know, I want to say. But I hope Clayton realizes it, too.

Later that evening, I stand on the small balcony of my hotel room and look out on the manicured grounds. .

I feel like I've been transported back in time as I look out on the landscape. It is so dream-like. That's the only way to describe it. A wild land that lived for thousands of years and has seen so much and now, me, little old Sophie Walker, is taking it all in. A feeling of great renewal seems to come over me.

I mourn William Sinclair, the man I didn't know. I send a quick prayer up to him. I mourn the past. I mourn all that was and all that was beautiful that I never recognized. There is something that's been changing inside me since I arrived in England. I feel reborn in a way. Even now, looking out on the history and the magnificence only reinforces the feelings I have. No matter what happens, life is going to be okay.

The door rings. I've ordered room service so I'm not surprised.

I tighten the belt on my robe and hurry to open it.

I'm shocked to find Clayton there. I had barely seen him at the pub. In fact, I thought he was avoiding me.

His black tie is loose around his neck. The top buttons on his crisp, white shirt are open, and his black jacket is draped over his shoulder. His thick brown hair is messy but that only seems to bring out the beauty of his face, especially his eyes.

His eyes brush over me.

I feel acutely aware that I'm naked underneath my robe. My toes curl in the carpet.

"Clayton," I say.

"Sophie," he replies.

But he sounds smashed. We stare at one another. "Aren't you going to invite me in?"

17

"I didn't think you needed an invitation," I tell him.

"Touché."

I stand aside and allow him entrance. He walks in and takes in the luxurious surroundings. Since I had nothing to do with booking it, I know I shouldn't feel self-conscious, but I do. I can't help it.

"The room is too small," he says after a moment.

"It's a suite. And it's actually perfect," I insist. "Thank you, it's enough for me."

"But it's not just you," he informs me.

My heart thumps.

"I thought you were staying at your family home," I tell him.

"Why would you think that?" he asks curiously.

"I hadn't heard from you—" I begin.

"So you assumed."

"Yes," I say.

He walks over to the minibar and takes out a small bottle of whiskey.

"How do you like Bath?" he asks me as he fills a glass.

"What I've seen is absolutely beautiful," I tell him. "Would you like me to order you some ice?"

"This is fine."

Clayton throws his jacket on the chair, walks over to the bed, and sits down. He places his drink on the side table and begins to unbutton his shirt.

It's extremely sexy so I try to distract myself.

"Your speech today was so moving," I tell him. "It brought everyone to tears."

"I don't care about everyone," Clayton replies as he takes a long sip of his drink and leans back on the pillows. "Only William."

I feel a pang in my heart.

"I know he loved it."

There's a knock. He looks at me questioningly.

"I ordered food," I explain as go to open the door. A woman from room service enters with a wheel in table and sets it up for me.

"I've got some soup and salad," I say to Clayton. "Would you like something as well?"

"Not so boring," he says. "I want bangers and mash and fish and chips."

I try not to smile. He must be smashed. Two meals?

I look at the woman. "Can we order that as well?"

"Of course," she says.

After she leaves, I sit down to eat, but I can feel Clayton's eyes on me. I try not to get nervous but it's hard. I lift the cover off the food.

"Can I offer you anything," I ask politely.

"I'll wait for my fish and chips," he tells me as he takes another sip of his drink. "But please, eat before your food gets cold."

Awkward.

I put the napkin on my lap. The last thing I want to do is slurp my way through this unnerving silence. I wish the TV was on or something.

I know he's watching me.

"Do you plan on staring at me while I eat?" I ask nonchalantly as I lift a spoonful of soup, trying my best to be as delicate as possible.

"Is it bothering you?" he asks curiously.

I bet he loves this.

"It's a little disconcerting," I admit, then begin to eat. The soup is delicious. My stomach growls in pleasure. I didn't have a bite all day so this is like heaven. What I'd like to do is dip my bread in the soup and go to town. But I continue to eat as demurely as possible.

"Must you?" I finally say as I put the spoon down and look him square in the eyes.

He laughs.

"Watch you?" He drawls.

"Yes."

"I must," He says with enough heat to light the fireplace.

I lean back from the food and try to figure out his mood.

Drunk? Check.

Playful? Check

Brooding? Check.

When in Rome—

I go to the minibar and take out a bottle of red.

"Do I drive you to drink?" he asks with amusement. I can tell he's happy that I'm so affected by his presence.

"I don't think you want me to answer that," I retort. I pick up the wine opener and insert it in the cork and start to twist it.

Within seconds Clayton is standing next to me, invading my space with his warmth, and takes both items out of my hand.

"Allow me," he says politely.

I look up at him and sigh. I wonder when the sight of him won't cause for me to feel so overcome by his utter hotness.. His muscles flex as he uncorks the wine, and it takes all the effort in the world not to lick my lips.

If he I can use one word to describe him right now it would simply be *yum.*

I'm pretty sure my dad would be disappointed by my inability to find another word in the English language to describe him. And the fact that I'm lusting after a man who's deep in mourning. What does that say about me?

Clayton picks up a wine glass and pours for me.

"I don't know how good this will be," he says as he studies the bottle.

"I'm not a connoisseur like you, so I'm sure it will do," I reply.

"That is irrelevant. I want you to have only the best," he answers. "Let's order a bottle from room service."

I snatch the glass he's filled out of his hand.

"This is fine for now," I tell him. "Cheers."

Clayton acquiesces. He picks up his glass and says, "To my brother, William."

We clink glasses.

It's a difficult balance to be on edge all the time with him. Not to know where his mood will take me from moment to moment. I'm literally at his beck and call. Completely in his territory. Playing by his rules. Unsure of what tomorrow will bring.

What the next second will bring, for that matter.

This man I've fallen in love with is dark and dangerous, perhaps out of my league or even my reach, especially now, when he's in a fog of grief that is taking him on a journey he refuses to share with me.

One thing I know for sure. There will be a time of reckoning in the near future.

Clayton's sensual mouth is parted as if he knows the direction of my thoughts.

"We're going away tomorrow," he says.

"Away?" I ask. "You mean, back to London."

"To Gstaad."

"Switzerland." I'm confused as to why.

"I have my eye on a chalet there," Clayton explains. "I feel like now would the perfect time to take another look at it."

Or to escape, I think. I don't blame him. If I had the money he has at my disposal I would do the same. I'd probably take a year off real life.

"We're booked at the Alpina," he brushes the back of his fingers along my cheekbone. "I think you'll like it."

Shit.

"I have to go home," I tell him.

I think of what Erik said to me. That I wouldn't be happy just being a woman of leisure at Clayton's beck and call, and I know my best friend is right. That's the last thing I want in my life. The more time I spend with him, the more attached I'm becoming. I know it will be easier for me to let him go now, no matter how my heart feels about it.

I did what I thought was right and I was here for him during the hardest time of his life. However much he let me in or will let me in is irrelevant. I tried. And that's enough.

"I'd like you to join me," he cuts into my thoughts.

And then what? I want to ask but I don't.

"I don't know if it's a good idea," I finally say.

"You are finished being here for me, you mean?" He drawls softly.

I explain. "I just think it might not be very smart for me to stay longer. I need to get back to my life in Los Angeles. Get home for Christmas like I promised my parents. Figure out my work situation. I can't be on perpetual vacation. And that's what it would be."

"But I want you to come with me," Clayton insists.

Room service arrives again and they push in another trolley next to mine.

"Clayton," I begin when we're alone.,"I just can't–"

He turns to me, his harsh indrawn breath the only indication of his annoyance.

"You *can*," he tells me. "It's just three days. You can make it back for Christmas."

But it's three more days to become even more attached to you than I already am.

"I won't take no for an answer."

No, he won't. He's the man who always gets what he wants. I have no doubt that I will not win this argument. I close my eyes for a second and think of all the reasons why I shouldn't go with him, but as usual I can't resist him.

"Just three days," I finally say in a small voice.

Clayton gives me a sexy smile.

"You won't regret it."

So he says.

There are definite pros to traveling with someone who has what I perceive to be an unlimited bank account. Going private, for instance. It's decadent. Truly unbelievable. You don't have to go through airport security. You don't have to take your shoes off or take out all your electronic devices, and you're given unlimited champagne and food on the plane while sitting in the most comfortable seats known to man.

The other plus?

The fact that Clayton can book a suite for my two best friends and have them fly with us to an expensive ski chateau in the mountains of Switzerland.

Yes, that's right. Erik and Orie are with us. And I'm so happy. And relieved that I'm not on my own. Clayton surprised me in the morning when he told me he'd asked them to come along the night before he came to our room. I can't say how happy I am for the moral support. Thankfully, Erik hasn't talked to me about my do or die deadline with Clayton yet. The end is looming before me and it's hard not to cringe when I can picture myself crashing and burning.

I will enjoy myself though on this little holiday and try not to think about my own stress, but instead, help Clayton. He has moments of light, where it's as if nothing happened, and then it's like a cloud comes over his face and he remembers the grief and sadness. I know there is nothing I can do but be here and try to distract him. I wish he'd talk to me about what's going on inside of him, as Michael has, but he's not there yet, and may never be.

We are picked up from the private airport by two black Range Rovers and I absorb the gorgeous scenery as we drive through the town on the way to the hotel. Gstaad is absolutely stunning. The small winter town sits in a picture-perfect valley. The snow powdered trees are symmetrical and it looks as though the whimsical city was painted this way by a master artist.

As we pull up to the Alpina I'm awestruck at the luxury we're immediately surrounded by even in the driveway. I look over at Clayton, who's dressed handsomely in knee-length black wool coat, blue jeans, and a thick sweater. He's wearing a pair of scruffy black boots that I find extra hot, and leather gloves.

Clayton says, "I usually stay at the Palace but I thought we'd try this out together."

"I'm sure it will be fantastic," I tell him as I patiently wait for him to open the car door.

"Isn't the Palace famous for their diamond parties?" Orie asks excitedly.

"Those two words in the same sentence is as good as an orgasm," Erik says, then changes his mind. "Okay. Maybe not quite. But close."

I can't contain my laughter.

Clayton says, smiling at me, 'I don't agree. Doesn't even come close.'

I can feel my face turn red as Erik and Orie whistle.

The cold air hits us hard when the doors are opened by our driver.

"It's freezing!" I squirm.

"We're going to have to take you shopping," Clayton says.

Does he find my clothes lacking? They're certainly not high-end designers like I'm sure all the women at this resort are decked out in, but they're nice. Erik picked them.

I shake my head. "My clothes are just fine."

"But we're going to ski," he explains.

Ski? The last time I skied I was fifteen and Erik dragged me to Bear Mountain, because he happens to be an incredible athlete. He took me on some black diamond run and I was so scared I ended up sliding down the entire slope on my butt, which in turn caused a giant hole on my outfit. I don't know if I've ever seen Erik laugh so hard.

"Sophie's a great skier," Erik says playfully.

Clayton looks surprised. I don't know if I should be insulted.

"You are?"

Awkward silence.

"Yes, I grew up skiing."

What's the harm in lying?

"That's fantastic," Clayton seems thrilled. "After we get you guys some gear, we'll go out today."

Erik pulls Orie in for a hug. Probably to laugh in his embrace.

I want to kill him. I figure I'll just let Clayton fly down before me and I'll just fake it.

Like all little white lies, this one came to bite me in the ass.

What the hell was I thinking? Pretending to be an amazing skier? Who do I think I am, Bode Miller?

I blame Erik. This is all his fault and I plan on cussing him out once I find a way to get down the monstrosity of a hill that I'm climbing up on the lift with Clayton. *It's really steep.*

We shopped for clothes, which I would have found fun if I hadn't actually seen the price tags on some of the ski items he bought for me. Clayton insisted and I just gave in. He left Erik, Orie and I in a boutique and gave Erik orders. I argued the entire time about everything because I didn't understand why I needed six different ski outfits when we'd only be in Gstaad for three days.

Before I knew it, not only did I have a new ski wardrobe, but a whole winter one as well. Shoes and all. It's astounding how much money Erik can drop in one hour. When I commented on it to him, he simply said, "It's a gift. You'll thank me later."

Now, I'm dressed in a white ski outfit that costs more than my entire wardrobe, goggles and all, and am headed up the lift with the man of my dreams. He looks ruggedly handsome in his black ski pants and simple jacket. Let's face it, he's just too cool for school. Erik and Orie are behind us on the lift, probably laughing their faces off over how terrified I must be and how this situation is about to turn into a comedy. Or a tragedy. Depending on how you look at it.

I really hope I don't break my leg. Or worse, neck. That would totally suck.

Clayton reaches out and takes my gloved hand in his.

"It's beautiful up here, isn't it?"

I haven't really been paying attention at all because my thoughts have been solely centered on how the hell I'm going to get down. Oh, my God. Worse, I have to get off the lift first. That part always freaks out. Last time I got off a ski lift I slipped and the chair hit me in the back of the head. Erik almost wet his pants he laughed so hard. I tried a couple of times after that but I was ruined for skiing. I send a silent prayer to God asking that at the very least I get off the lift chair okay.

"It's breathtaking," I finally answer.

"It's one of my favorite places in the world," Clayton says wistfully as he looks out over the slopes.

"Gstaad?" I ask.

"No," he shakes his head. "This lift."

He closes his eyes.

"I'm free up here. And when I ski down the hill, it's liberating."

"It sounds like you have way too much stress in your life," I say to him.

He gives me a smile. "It's nothing I can't handle."

"No, if your one moment of relaxation comes from sitting on a ski lift in Switzerland, there is much to be desired any way you look at it." The words come out before I can stop myself.

I wait for his teasing response but I don't get one. Instead he looks away from me and out toward the endless pine trees.

"Perhaps."

I'm surprised he admits it.

"It's hard not to get caught up," I tell him gently. "But you need to have more moments for yourself. Ones that liberate you and make you feel good right at home. I think now more than ever."

"*You* make me feel good." I look at him and his passionate gaze burns into mine.

His words make me so happy that if I could I'd run around the snow-covered hills in joy like Fraulein Maria in *The Sound of Music.*

"And there are times when you make me really mad," he goes on.

The Sound of Music scenario comes to a screeching halt.

"Like when?"

"Now," he answers.

I look at him in surprise.

"Wearing that outfit that fits your body so well it's like a second skin," he says with passion. "I saw the way the men were looking at you."

My skin tingles.

"You have got to be kidding me—"

"No," he continues. I fidget under the fire shooting from his eyes. "Do you know how it makes me feel? To see their desire?"

"For now, I'm with you," I remind him.

"For now?" He lifts a brow.

I turn away from him and look out on the valley.

"Let's not ruin our time," I say.

He reaches out and takes hold of my ponytail and turns my head to face him.

"You belong to me."

God.

I love it when he says that to me. He leans forward and captures my mouth for a kiss that leaves me breathless.

When he finally pulls away we're reaching the first drop-off point.

"We'll get off here," Clayton tells me.

"Go the right," he orders as he holds on to his poles. I grip mine like my life depends on them, which it kind of does. I'm not going to lie.

My heart pounds as the lift rounds the corner and we're forced to get off.

I can't do it.

The lift is moving too fast. Oh. My. God.

"Now, Sophie." Clayton gets off and skis to the left. He thinks I'm following him. But instead, I freeze.

And the lift keeps on going up.

I close my eyes before turning around and watching as Clayton waves at me in surprise from the side of the hill. I look behind me and see that

Orie's gotten off but Erik has stayed on the chair and is coming up with me.

He lifts his hands in the air like I'm a complete moron.

Mortifying!

"That was classic!" he yells out.

I give him the finger and turn around. My face is so hot it might go up in flames.

Cat's out of the bag, Sophie.

How am I ever going to get off this lift, I think to myself. I can feel my heartbeat race uncontrollably as we near the top. I'm going to have to jump; there's no other choice.

When the lift reaches the landing I close my eyes and practically throw myself off. I ski-stumble unceremoniously off the lift and toward the take-off point. Since I can't seem to stop, I squat down until I'm fully seated on the ground.

I feel the slush of the cold snow against my bum.

Erik expertly skis right up to me.

He's bent over, laughing hysterically.

"It is so not funny," I tell him in anger.

"If you saw what I saw, you would think it was," he tells me.

"You should have seen the look on Clayton's face when you didn't get off the lift," he says in glee., "I don't think he's ever seen someone do that before."

"I hate you," I reply.

How am I going to face Clayton?

The bigger question is how are you going to get down the mountain?

"It's all your fault," I remind him.

"I thought you'd be smart enough to just stay at the lodge," Erik fights his smile.

He reaches out his hand.

"Let me help you up."

"What's the point?" I say as I look down the monstrosity of the hill.

"If I attempt to ski down that thing I'm going to break my neck and die," I tell him. "I might as well slide down on my butt."

"Why not see if you can take the lift back down," Erik says.

"I'm terrified of the lift," I tell him. "I don't like it."

Erik bursts out laughing again and has to lean on his knees.

"It moves too fast," I mutter.

It starts to snow.

Just great.

We're going from bad to worse.

"I wish you could see yourself right now!"

"Thankfully, I can't," I tell him as I firmly sit down now in between my two skis.

"Just leave me here," I say dramatically. "I'll find my way down, and if I don't, think of me fondly."

Erik rolls his eyes. "You are ridiculous."

"I'm mortified," I tell him. "Clayton must think I'm a complete idiot. How am I going to face him again?"

"Well, you're going to have to in about ten seconds," Erik says as he looks past me.

Oh no. Just great.

Clayton skis up to us and takes one look at Erik then at me and bends over in laughter. Erik practically falls. I don't dare look at either of them.

"Are you guys done?"

"No," Erik tells me as he wipes away tears.

I've never seen Clayton laugh so hard. I'd be really happy about it if it wasn't at my expense.

He squats down next to me, perfectly balanced in his skis, takes one of his gloves off and rubs his knuckles across my cheek.

I'm too embarrassed to look at him.

"Sophie," he says huskily. "You holding onto the edge of the lift and refusing to get off was the cutest thing I've ever seen."

His chest rumbles with mirth.

"I'm sure," I say in embarrassment as I finally look at him. When I see the joy on his face I can't hold back my smile.

"So you can't ski?" he deduces.

"No," I'm forced to admit. I look over his shoulder and give my best friend the stink eye for putting me in this situation in the first place.

"Why did you pretend you could?" Clayton asks curiously.

"I wanted to impress you," I say truthfully.

"I don't think you could impress me anymore than you already have, Sophie." His voice is gruff as he leans in to kiss me on my lips.

18

A few hours later, I'm dressing in one of the outfits Erik made me buy at the shop today. It's just a simple pair of skinny black jeans and a fitted black turtleneck, but the material is wonderful on the skin. I put on a pair of my new thick Moncler puff boots over the jeans and grab a jacket. Since I'm all alone now, I'm going to take my Kindle and go down to the lodge, read, have a drink, and hopefully forget about my cringe worth experience attempting to ski.

Poor Clayton was forced to help me down the hill. It was slow and painful. He tried to teach me some moves, to help me let go of my fear of falling and breaking my neck or leg, but I was too cold to pay attention. And I told him as much.

He finally gave up and had ski patrol (how embarrassing) help us both down. He didn't have to say it but I know he wasn't too excited about getting in the ski patrol vehicle with me. When we were finally back at the lodge I begged him to go enjoy himself and I promised I'd go straight to the room and take a bath. Since I knew he was dying to have some proper runs, he left me and joined Erik and Orie for real skiing.

I leave a note telling Clayton where I am, grab my stuff, and head down to the hotel bar where everyone seemed to be congregated when I came in. I take a look around at the crowd and decide I'll take the opportunity to check out the famous Palace Hotel. I have the hotel car take me over.

When I arrive, I'm happy with my decision. I remember to text Clayton, Erik, and Orie to let them know that I changed locations.

The hotel is more old school and there's a great vibe. I find one of the older, cozy bars and sit down on a comfortable couch, order a drink, and start to read.

I'm thoroughly immersed in a book that was recommended to me by Michael Sinclair, *Dying to Be Me* by Anita Moorjani. It's the story of a woman who had stage four lymphoma and went to heaven and came back. And completely cured herself. It's one of the most inspirational books I've ever read.

"If it isn't my favorite American." To my horror, it's Davis, sneering at me from the couch opposite me.

He looks just the same as he did when I last saw him. Drunk. Except this time he has two friends tagging who both also seem to be wasted.

"Hello, Davis," I say politely.

"Hello," he responds snidely. "Funny, I don't remember your name. 'Hired help,' was it?"

I try not to laugh. He's so lame.

"Why, yes, it is," I reply with a smile.

It would feel so good to throw my drink at his arrogant little face.

"I'm flattered you remember," I say as I lift my glass of red wine and take a sip.

My dad always taught me the best way to respond to someone who insults you is to laugh it off. When you outwardly seem so unaffected by someone's mean words you take away the satisfaction the person gets from the sting of their cruel words.

And it works, because Davis looks annoyed that I'm not the least bit offended by his comment.

"Clive and Douglas, please meet Clayton's latest plaything," Davis says.

"Stop!" I laugh. "You're flattering me, Davis."

Davis' face turns red with anger. It's fun to watch.

His friends look a lot like him. And have the same awful disposition. "What's your real name?" the one with the short brown hair, Douglas, I think, asks. He has beady eyes. I hate beady eyes.

"If you're not comfortable calling me 'hired help,' Sophie works just fine," I reply straight-faced.

The two men laugh.

"She's a fetching one," the one I think is Clive says. "And she's got a sense of humor."

"Yes, she does," I say with wide eyes. "Imagine that?"

Clearly they find me vastly amusing.

I decide that it's probably a good idea for me to leave and go back to our hotel. One thing is for certain, I don't want to be in Davis's company anymore. And two, remembering how furious Clayton was the last time I mentioned Davis's name I can't even imagine what he'd do if he found him sitting across from me. Given Clayton's current state of mind, I'm pretty certain that Davis would take the brunt of his aggression.

"Gentlemen, if you'll excuse me," I say as I motion for the waiter to pay my bill. "I must leave you to your own devices."

"Why so soon, little rabbit?" Davis says with a challenge.

" "Clayton and my friends are waiting for me," I answer.

"We can see you back to the hotel," Douglas suggests.

In your dreams, I think to myself.

"That's quite alright," I tell him. "You guys enjoy yourselves. I'll be sure to tell Clayton I saw you."

I only say the last part to get a scare out of Davis and from the way his eyes round I can tell that it works. I don't like the way his friends are staring at me and now I'm getting scared that they might follow me to the hotel. Or worse, accost me again.

Just as the waiter brings me my tab I catch a glimpse of Clayton, Erik, and Orie entering the bar. The handsome trio turns some heads. I'm glad to see they seem relaxed. Clayton even has a look of contentment on his face. Given my last encounter with Davis, and his entourage, I am really relieved to see them. Now I don't have to worry about being followed or stalked by him and his awful friends.

I wave at Clayton and he sees me and gives me a seductive smile that makes my heart pound and the three head my way.

And then he catches sight of Davis.

Oh crap.

In less than two seconds he goes from looking like he's in a good mood to looking furious. The anger etched on his face has me worried.

"Clayton just arrived," I say. I hope Davis runs.

But the little shit doesn't. His face just contorts in rage.

Sorry asshole, I think to myself, I tried to warn you. I almost pity him.

Almost.

"Sophie," Clayton says as he reaches the couch. I stand up and walk right into his embrace. I feel better instantly.

"Hi," I reply as I wrap my arm around his waist. "Look who I just ran into."

His body feels like it's made of stone. I hold him tightly.

"Davis." Clayton says him name with a great deal of contempt.

To his credit, Davis starts to look uncomfortable by the looks Clayton's giving him. I watch with satisfaction how he seems to squirm.

"What are you doing here?"

"I'm sorry?" Davis says with mock surprise. "I hadn't realized you bought the Palace Hotel. I don't remember reading about that."

I smile nervously at Clayton. "I was sitting here and Davis and his friends sat across from me. Small world, huh?"

"Small world?" he grits out to me. He's seething. It's oozing from his body. He obviously doesn't believe me.

I take Clayton's hand in mine.

"Everything is okay," I assure him.

I look over at Erik and Orie for support but because I told them about my experience with Davis they don't look like they will be much help in containing Clayton.

"Davis, have you ever seen the show *To Catch a Predator*?" Erik asks in a cold voice.

Oh shit.

"Erik—" I begin, but the look he gives stops me cold.

"I'm sorry?" Davis has the audacity to look offended.

"*To Catch a Predator*," Erik repeats. "Have you seen it?"

Davis's eyes are cold with fury.

"I don't like the question."

"What I don't like that is you being in the vicinity of my best friend," Erik says protectively.

I lean over and take Erik's hand in mine and squeeze it. "Let's just—" I begin.

"Sophie," he turns angry eyes on me. "Don't even start."

I'm sure that my surprise is written on my face. I've never seen Erik look so pissed off before. Or aggressive. He is usually calm and collected. Even Orie, who is usually the voice of reason, looks like he wants to bash Davis's face in.

Davis stands abruptly in outrage and his two friends flank him. They look like the axis of evil. He takes a menacing step closer to Erik, who thankfully is a good head taller and looks down at him.

"Are you insulting me?" he asks.

"Took you long enough," Erik smiles. "Not the brightest tool in the shed, are you?"

In less than a second Davis grabs hold of Erik's shirt and shakes him in fury. Clayton pushes me behind his body, moves forward, takes Davis's collar, and literally lifts him off the ground.

"Clayton!"

I grab hold of his muscular arm. A quick look around confirms that the entire bar is staring at us. I see the bartender motion to the discreet-looking security.

"Let me," Erik begs Clayton.

"Let you what?" Clive sneers.

Erik narrows his eyes.

"That's just rich," Clive says, then he looks at Erik and starts to laugh.

Oh no.

In a second mayhem breaks loose.

I watch in horror as my best friend throws back his arm and punches the douche right in the face. Clive hits the ground and Douglas clumsily rushes Erik. But before Douglas can get in a punch, Clayton shoves him into a piece of furniture.

I jump up and am ready to get in on this and kick Clive in the shin when I'm roughly pulled back and forcefully shoved aside by security. Unfortunately for them and for me, I crash right into a table face-first, feel drinks spill over me, and black out.

When I come to, I'm lying on a bed in a clinic. It takes me a few moments to remember what just occurred.

Oh no.

I sit up quickly and wince from the pain in my shoulder and chin.

"Thank God!" Orie says and jumps up from his chair and rushes over to me. He looks down at my face with wide eyes.

"You won't need plastic surgery," he assures me. "But that bruise on your chin is deadly. But I have some good cover-up for it."

"Bruise?" I say as I touch my chin and feel the god-awful pain.

"They gave you good drugs, don't worry."

"Where is everyone?" I ask him when realize that we're the only two in the room.

"If by everyone you mean my man and yours—" Orie says.

I nod.

"They're in jail."

"Oh my God!" I sit up again and try to swing my legs over the side of the bed. The wave of nausea is unreal.

"No sudden movements!" Orie warns. "Don't worry, Clayton's attorneys will have them out in no time, just as long as he pays for the damage to the hotel."

"You're not joking, are you?" I ask Orie as I hold my head. I feel like someone punched me in the face.

Not someone.

A table.

Orie puts his strong arms around me. "Do I look worried?"

I look at his countenance.

"No," I shake my head. "You don't at all."

"Because the entire police station is filled with people Clayton called who I guess are at his beck and call here. And they're going to crazy town. They are mad."

"Mad? How can they?" I ask in confusion. "Clayton threw the first punch."

I mean, I hate to say it, but it's the truth.

"Mad because the hotel security guard pushed you, which caused you to fall, hit your head, get bruised, and possibly suffer from concussion."

"Oh, God." I close my eyes in misery. "Do I have CTE now?"

"Bite your tongue," Orie chides. "Girl, you should have seen Clayton's face and the guttural roar he let out when you were unresponsive at first. It was like he was possessed by a hundred crazy animals or something."

"Really?" I ask breathlessly.

Orie rolls his eyes. I don't blame him. But still.

"He freaked out," Orie goes on. "Like legit. And let me tell you something. My man? I am so goddamn impressed and turned on by him at the same time. He went just as bat shit crazy as Clayton. The two of them went at the security guard. I went to you or I'd have been arrested as well."

Wow. I missed a whole lot of action.

"Davis?" I ask.

"No idea," Orie shakes his head.

I stare at him for a beat.

"Orie?"

"Yes, babe," he says.

"Do you think I'm prone to disaster?" It's a serious question.

Orie takes his time before responding.

"I don't know if I should answer that," he finally says.

"So, yes," I say to him. "The answer is yes."

"Maybe."

Great.

"Well, we've gotta go see what we can do to help them," I tell him.

Orie holds his hand up.

"First, I have some bad news."

"I thought I just heard the bad news?" I ask in horror.

"There's more."

My heart sinks.

"I have a blood clot," I whisper in dread.

Orie lets out a breath and rolls his eyes.

"Now I know how you and Erik are friends. You guys are both so dramatic!"

"Tell me," I say. "I can handle it."

"The doctors called your parents when you were brought in."

Oh. My. God.

The blood drains from my face. I feel nauseated. I want to throw up. I want to run away fast before my dad gets here. He's going to kill me.

My mom. I can't even think about what my mom is going to do.

Holy shit.

My life is over.

"It's not that bad." Orie tries to make it sounds like we're discussing the weather.

I stare at him with round eyes.

"Okay," he concedes. "It's really bad. Like fucking awful. God-awful. The doctors said that since you're American and single and they are your next of kin, they had to call. Now you might have to run away or something."

I slowly lean back down on the bed. I forget about Clayton and Erik being incarcerated. Right now, that actually doesn't seem too bad compared to the shit storm that I'm about to face.

"I can't breathe," I whisper.

"I know," Orie says.

"I lied and told them I was still in France," I say in a small voice.

Orie is silent.

"I'm dead," I say.

"You are," Orie agrees.

And then my stomach falls through the floor and sinks down into Middle Earth.

"Are they on their way here?" I gasp.

Silence.

"Soon," Orie finally says. "But they've got to find tickets. The time difference is working for you because it's way early morning in LA."

"I want to die!" I practically screech.

"I tried to tell them you were okay but because your dad couldn't talk to you he didn't believe me," Orie rushes out. "He is so fucking pissed at Erik and me. He let me have it—"

"When did you talk to him?" I ask.

"Like forty-five minutes ago, after the doctors spoke to them."

"Give me the phone!" I pant. "I need to stop them."

Orie can tell how serious I am. He hands me his cell phone.

"The call's on me," he says.

I almost laugh. But then I dial my dad's number.

It barely even rings once.

"Orie?" My dad's strong voice echoes through the phone. "We're packing now and my secretary is looking for flights."

He sounds worried and it makes me feel terrible.

"Daddy?" My voice sounds like a shell of itself.

Silence.

Then—

"Sophie Elizabeth Walker!" he yells.

Literally. Yells.

"I'm okay." I state the obvious then ramble on. "It was a total accident. The bartender shoved me into a table but I'm completely fine."

"Don't you lie to me, young lady." my dad says sharply. "Your *boyfriend* was picking a bar fight."

I look up at the ceiling.

God, if there is any time to just cut my life short, now totally works.

"Dad—" I begin slowly.

"Don't you dad me!" he roars through the phone. I hold it away from my ear.

"You lied to us!" he continues. "You lied about where you were going, who you were with—about everything. Did you even lie about getting a job, Sophie?!"

Orie stares at me in fear.

"Of course not!" I say back. "I was at the wedding to paint a portrait, and things got cancelled because someone passed away, and then things changed and—"

"You ran off with a man?"

I know this voice. This is my dad's 'I'm going to go to town and kick your ass in court' tone. I am so dead.

"It's not like that," I finally say. "Clayton's—"

My dad fills in the blank. "A man who gets arrested for punching people."

Oh. My. God.

How does he know this?

"Daddy?" I don't even know what to say.

"Sophie," he says in a dangerous voice. "Your mother is on the verge of a nervous breakdown. You almost gave me a heart attack tonight. And more than anything, I'm just so, so disappointed that you lied to me. I know what time it is in Switzerland. You will go straight to bed and call me in the morning from the Alpina and let me know what flight you'll be on."

Crap.

"Do you understand me?" he says.

"Yes, daddy." I feel like I'm a five-year-old again.

"And Sophie?" he continues.

"Yes?" My voice can barely even carry.

"When I call in the morning, you'd better have your own room. Use the emergency credit card. And be aware, young lady, that I might call periodically during the night to see that you are in a hotel room that *I* am paying for. And that you're alone."

I can hear my mom shrieking in the background. Lord only knows what she's saying.

My face is four hundred different shades of red. I am sure of it. How embarrassing!

"Daddy, " I try again, "please let me explain."

"I don't have the heart to listen right now," he says. "I'll speak to you in the morning."

He hangs up.

I stare at Orie.

My life is over.

19

I did listen to my dad.

I was actually deathly afraid that he would fulfill his promise and call a hundred times. When the doctor was ready to release me, Orie drove with me back to the hotel, helped me get a new room and then went to the police station to deal with the situation alone. He said that after the fall I had, the only thing I should do was rest. And since there was no way I could handle going to jail to see Clayton and Erik, I took him up on his offer. To be honest, they had injected me with some painkillers that were flowing through my veins, making it virtually impossible for me to stand up straight without closing my eyes. He promised he would text me when they got out.

I texted Clayton and let him know that I changed rooms and that I was doing this because of my parents. I knew he probably didn't have his phone yet but when he checked at least the message would be there. Since Orie was aware of the whole story, I left it at that. I was sure he would fill him in. By the time my stuff was in the significantly smaller room, I could barely even stand. I threw myself on top of the bed, the medicine kicked in, and I completely passed out.

I'm having an incredible dream.

Clayton's in my room and is undressing me, slowly making love to my body and waking me up from my deep sleep. I don't realize that I'm not dreaming until I feel his strong hands grip my thighs and lick me awake.

I lean up on my elbows and stare down at him, my eyes barely open.

"You're here," I whisper.

He doesn't speak.

Instead he brings me to a quick orgasm, using his fingers and mouth, and before I can even utter his name, he kneels, pulls me up, and thrusts into me.

The pleasure is so intense. It's everything and more.

"Clayton!" I call out.

His mouth nips at my neck. He's mad with passion and something else.

"You belong to me!" he whispers in my ear.

I can't stop the moan when he pulls out.

"Say it, Sophie," he commands.

I pull his lips to mine. Crush them with a kiss that speaks to all my longing for him.

"I'm yours," I tell him.

The sun shines bright in the room. I forget where I am. For a second I think I'm back home in Los Angeles but the tan, masculine arm draped around my waist brings me back to reality.

The situation I'm in washes over me like a tidal wave.

Shit.

My parents.

"They know!" I whisper in horror as my eyes pop open and I contemplate all the scenarios that await me.

Clayton's arm pulls me close to his body.

"Go back to sleep," he whispers in a groggy voice.

Sleep?

Is he crazy?

I move out of his strong grip and get out of the bed. I find a T-shirt to slip on over my naked body.

When I turn around, Clayton is on his elbow watching me.

His face goes from sleepy to angry. He sits up quickly.

"Come here!" he orders.

"What?" I say, not comprehending.

"I'm going to kill them," he says. He throws the cover back and gets up, naked, and strides over to me.

God. His body.

Before I even have a moment to blush he gently lifts my chin so he can study my face.

It's at that moment that I remember I slammed it into the table the night before. Just like that, the pain comes back in full force.

I wince. His gaze goes from being tender to looking even more furious than before.

"Does it hurt?" His voice is almost strangled.

"No," I lie unconvincingly. "It's okay, I promise."

He doesn't believe me.

"It will be once I take an Advil or two," I say.

Or four.

I place my fingers on the cut on his lip.

"Are you okay?" I ask in concern.

"Fine," he brushes my question off.

"I'm sorry I didn't make it to jail to visit—" I begin.

That actually makes Clayton smile.

"Words I never thought I'd hear," he tells me.

"Orie wouldn't let me," I explain, "and the pain meds they gave me—"

"Sophie," Clayton says. "If I had seen you like this at the police station I would have gone crazy and without a doubt I'd still be incarcerated. You're lucky it was too dark for me to see your injury when I came in the room last night."

"Clayton, is it all resolved?"

"I'm in the process of pressing charges against the security at the hotel."

"Are you crazy?" I ask him.

"He pushed you," Clayton says. "That is not allowed."

"Clayton," I begin, "I don't want the man to get in trouble. He thought he was doing his job."

Granted, he was a little rough, but maybe I would have been too given the circumstances.

"Don't," he says sharply.

I try to talk but his look silences me.

"You will let me take care of this."

Clearly, there is no use arguing with him.

"How did you get my room key?" I ask him.

He gives me a look.

Right. *Because you're you.*

"I had to get my own room," I explain even though I texted him as much.

"Orie told me everything," he says.

"My dad wants me on a flight home today," I tell him.

"And you?" he asks me. "What do *you* want?"

To stay with you forever, but we both know that's a losing battle.

"I'm torn," I say honestly.

I can't read his face and wonder what he's thinking.

Before either of us can say any more, Clayton's cell phone rings. He walks away from me and picks it up.

"Do you have news?" he says quietly.

Whoever he talks to on the other end gives him a mouthful. He runs a shaky hand through his thick hair and turns to stare at me. I watch how his eyes narrow when they sweep over my face.

"I'll be there," he says ominously before he hangs up.

"Who was that?" I ask.

"My lawyer," he tells me. "I have to meet him downstairs. I'll call you after."

He dresses quickly and walks over to me.

"Don't do anything until we talk," he says as he leans down and kisses me gently on the lips.

He leaves the room.

Now might be a good time to look at your face, Sophie, I think to myself. *It's clearly a disaster zone.* I gather the courage and walk into the bathroom.

Thankfully I'm alone.

Arghh! I look like I got into a real honest to goodness fight! And no one even threw a punch at me. I hit a table!

A dark, black, hideous bruise covers half my lower right cheek and jawline, and my eyes are way too bright. That I know must be because of the meds I took the night before.

"I look crazy," I whisper in horror as I pull back my hair to study the damage more closely.

Before I start thinking about what I'm going to do and panicking about whether or not my face will return to normal the phone in the room rings.

I have no doubt who it is.

I walk over to the bed and sit down to pick it up.

"Dad?"

"I'm happy you listened to at least one thing I said," he tells me.

I look over at the crumpled sheets and blush when I think about the passionate night I had with Clayton. I am so happy for the distance from my father.

"Sophie," my dad begins to speak, but his voice breaks. "I'm so worried about you."

In that moment, my heart breaks, too.

This is my dad. My hero. The man who's always fixed everything in my life, who was there when anything was wrong.

"Talk to me," he says.

And I do.

I tell my dad everything. About the Maldives, about my job in France, about Clayton's brother. I leave the intimate parts out, but my dad is smart enough to know. I just put it all out there. Even about my insecurities, about my love for Clayton and my fear of the unknown. And the relief I feel is staggering.

When I'm finished, I'm in tears.

"What do you want to do, baby?" he asks me after a long minute.

I'm shocked. I was expecting him to weigh in, to unleash that side of him that always argues for what's the logical thing to do, and I don't know what to say.

"I don't know, dad." Then I say softly, "What do you think?"

"I'm not going to tell you what to do," he says in a voice filled with love. "But I'm going to tell you what I know about the beautiful daughter I raised."

I swallow a few more tears.

"My Sophie is strong. Is capable. Is brilliant. She's the best of the best. And she doesn't wait for any man or anything to dictate how she lives her life. She's fearless. A fighter. She's passionate. And kind. She is everything a man could want in life, but the beauty is, that doesn't define her," my dad says with love. "She is her own woman. She was raised to stand on her own two feet and make decisions for herself. To know the difference between right and wrong. To follow her heart but to know when the journey has come to an end. My Sophie is a warrior."

My Sophie is a warrior.

My dad's words echoed through my mind and heart for the next few hours. He was incredible. After our long talk, he told me that he trusted me and that he knew he had raised me to make the right decision.

But the responsibility of making the decision on my own weighed on me. All I wanted was to make the right choice.

Now I'm in the restaurant at the Alpina with Erik and Orie. I'm happy to see that Erik doesn't have a scar or blemish on his body (as far as I can tell) and he seems exhilarated by the night's experience.

I really don't understand men.

"I have a man crush on Clayton," Erik tells me candidly.

I smile.

"Orie's totally fine with it," Erik waves at him. "Because he does, too."

"That's nice," I say with a laugh. "Is it because he can throw down?"

"Yeah," Erik nods. "And not only that but he dresses fucking unbelievably and is rich as shit and looks like a supermodel. I get it. He has that dark brooding thing going for him, which is a plus in my books."

"Totally agree," Orie says nodding.

"Great," I say. "But where does that leave me?"

Erik takes a moment.

"You still don't get it, do you?"

"Get what?" I ask.

"That this guy is head over heels in love with you," he says.

"Thanks for the vote of confidence," I tell him. "But he's actually never told me that. And to be honest, he's so commitment-phobic that I don't think he's ever going to be capable of it."

"Sophie," he says, "tell us what more you want."

"More?" I tell him. "More? I want to know that I'm safe, Erik. That he's my man, that I don't have to worry about some other woman from his world, someone who fits him so much better than I do—"

My voice trails off.

"I just want to feel secure," I finally say. "And I don't. Not at all. I don't know what tomorrow will bring and the longer I'm around him, the more invested I become. And I'm already so far down the rabbit hole I don't even know how I'm going to crawl out. I have to at least try to protect myself now."

I wait for the Erik attack but it doesn't happen quite like I expect.

"First, you're fucking hot and amazing. And he knows it," Erik tells me. "That's the most important part of this. You're not lacking in anything, Sophie. I don't want you to ever think you are."

Silence.

"But—"

I feel sick because I know Erik is going to agree with me now. And that means I'm going to have a big choice on my hands.

"I get it," he finally says. "I want you to feel safe, too. You deserve to be in a secure relationship. I want that for you."

"What does that mean?" I ask.

Erik reaches out and takes my hand. He squeezes it hard.

"It means, I understand you, babe," he says. "I love you. I want you to be happy. And whatever makes Sophie Walker happy makes me happy."

My eyes fill up with tears.

"So what should I do?" I look from Erik to Orie.

"We can't tell you that," Orie says gently. "We can only be here for you no matter what. But you've got to make whatever decision you want to make on your own."

"Well, that sucks," I tell them. "You both usually have an opinion about everything."

"This one is all you," Erik tells me.

I go for a walk in the town. I buy some souvenirs for my parents. I take my time and stroll around and study the people. I take some pictures. I sit at a café and soak in the ambience. I think about my life. How much has happened in the last few months.

How much I've lived.

And I give thanks for everything. No matter what the future brings for me, I'm grateful for all these incredible experiences I've had.

I mean, I am so lucky. I think it's the first time in my life I actually realize this. And I'm so incredibly thankful.

I take a sip of my cappuccino and contemplate my future. *There is only today*, Sophie, my mind repeats like a mantra. Only today.

I pick up my phone and text Clayton.

ME: Where are you?

He writes back immediately.

CLAYTON: In my room.

For some reason, him saying "my room" makes my heart hurt.

ME: Do you have a minute?

CLAYTON: Always for you.

I feel sick.

ME: I'll see you in a few?

CLAYTON: You know where to find me.

I don't respond. I pay my bill quickly and head back to the hotel. I go to my room first and freshen up then pick up my sketchpad. Since I never found a Christmas gift worthy of Clayton, I had started a 14x17 sketch of his brother, William while in London. It was done in black charcoal and it was a profile shot of him I found while looking around Clayton's home. It was the only gift I thought would mean something.

I was proud of the piece and I hoped he would like it as much as I did.

I leave my room and make my way to his and knock.

The door opens almost immediately.

Clayton looks worried.

"Why didn't you use your key?" he asks.

"It's your room," I say. "I wanted to respect you."

His body tenses when I say that. He walks over to the floor-to-ceiling window overlooking the ski slopes and leans his shoulder against it. I take his beauty in and admire everything about him. He is so sexy. And wonderful. And generous. I'm so blessed he was my first time. My first experience with passion and love. Even with all his flaws—Lord knows I have more than him—I couldn't have asked for a better lover.

And that's what he is. This man dressed casually in jeans and a long-sleeved white thermal shirt, has been my first lover. I'd die happy tomorrow knowing he was all I'd experienced.

"How was your morning?" he asks cautiously..

"Great," I tell him. "I took a walk. It's really beautiful here."

"I'm glad you like it." He pins me with his gaze.

We stare at each other quietly.

"So what now?" he asks guardedly.

I'm thrown. I'm not going to lie. I was half expecting him to pull me into his arms and tell me that I belong to him, like he always does when we make love, but clearly, that's not on the agenda.

That could just be what he says in bed with women, Sophie, my mind tells me.

But my heart refuses to believe this, even if it might be the ugly truth.

"I looked up some flights," I say. "There's one tonight with a layover in Frankfurt."

He stares at me in stony silence.

"I think I should go," I finish awkwardly.

"That's what you want to do?" He asks.

No.

It's the last thing I want to do.

"Yes," I say instead. "It's what I want to do."

"Do you want me to beg you to stay?" he says, but his voice is distant.

"Clayton," I say as calmly as I can, "I know you. Or at least I know as much of you as you've allowed—"

"You know me," he says gruffly.

"So I know you don't beg," I say softly. "I'm not expecting you to."

"Then what are you expecting, Sophie?"

"Nothing," I whisper.

His eyes widen.

"Nothing," I say again. Because it's not only the truth, it's the reality.

"So this is it?" Clayton asks.

My insides just turn in knots. I feel like my stomach is going to come out of my mouth. I can't believe that this is where we are.

I try to smile.

"It is," I say in a shaky voice.

I put the sketchpad down on the coffee table.

"What's that?" He asks me.

"Your Christmas present," I say. "You can look at it when I'm gone."

"I didn't get you anything," he says.

"You've spoiled me enough in every way," I reply.

He crosses his muscular arms and continues to stare at me in that possessive way of his. It's too much for me to handle. I should leave the room before I break down and cry and ask him why he can't give me more.

"Clayton," I begin.

"Please don't," he whispers and closes his eyes for a moment.

"I must," I say as I take a step toward him. This is something I have to do. I walk up to him and reach out, cup my hand against his cheek, and smile even though the tears are forming in my eyes.

"I think you're a beautiful man," I say with emotion.

"Sophie," his voice sounds muffled and he looks away from me.

"Look at me," I insist..

He does. "Please—" he says.

And I get my strength.

"No, I'm not finished." My voice trembles but there is nothing I can do to help it. "You are so incredible. Inside and out, Clayton. You have so much to offer someone. To life in general. I never knew William—"

His eyes look glassy as they meet mine.

"But I know that he'd want you to be happy. To find love. To move on and honor him. So do that."

He closes his eyes.

"Will you promise to do that for him?" I ask as I blink back my tears.

He doesn't answer me.

"For me?" I plead.

His eyes open and they are bright with unshed tears. His hand moves to cup my cheek.

"I wish—" he whispers.

"No," I stop him, because I don't want to hear whatever it is he is about to say. Because I know it will be like a thousand knives in my heart. "Just promise me."

"I promise."

20

It hurts to be smart.

It's the only phrase that seems to echo in my head for the next few hours. I walked away. The smart thing to do.

But holy shit, my heart hurts like hell now.

He let me go.

He let me walk out of his ten thousand dollar suite and out of his life. There's a part of me that can't believe it.

But then I can.

I understand him. All his deficiencies. He's incapable. I was praying for a miracle that was never going to happen.

When I get to the airport, I find out that I've been upgraded to first on Lufthansa. I know Clayton did this and, to be honest, I'm actually grateful because it will be way more comfortable on my long way home.

Erik and Orie were not surprised by my decision. They drove with me to the airport and checked me in. They decided to stay another week and promised they would text me and send me pictures of all their adventures. I put a brave face on because I was tired of being the downer in their life. And I promised them that I would be okay. Because guess what? There's no other choice for me.

I get on the plane to Frankfurt and when it takes off I cry my eyes out. I feel like I've left my soul behind. That beautiful man has taken it from me and I don't know how I'm going to be whole again.

Maybe not how, but when.

The flight to Frankfurt is quick and I fill the three-hour layover shopping in Duty Free. I splurge on make-up and perfume and buy wine for my dad. I use his credit card, but who's checking? The time goes fast because I intentionally keep my mind occupied.

I avoid the magazine newsstands at all costs (we know where that got me the last time) and I just shop. Literally until I want to drop.

When they call the plane, I'm beyond relieved and ready to go home.

Maybe if I get a dog when I get home that will fill the hole that Clayton's left? I'm totally going to research different breeds and find an animal.

Once I'm safely settled on the plane and have taken the first of what I know will be many glasses of champagne from the stewardess, I allow my mind to wander and go over everything that's happened in the past few weeks.

There's a book in this, I think to myself. Or maybe a movie. It's completely crazy.

Since I'm next to the window seat, I busy myself by daydreaming and staring out. I don't notice who comes or goes. I'm just lost in my own thoughts. And tears. Yes, I'm crying. I'm Sophie. I have to cry!

Someone holds out a tissue for me.

Since I can barely see, I just take it and wipe my eyes.

"Thank you," I say.

"Rough day?"

I look over quickly.

The voice I know as well as my own.

It's Clayton.

Seated next to me.

I don't know what to say so I just nod.

"They say you can always find a silver lining," he tells me.

"Who's they?" I ask out loud.

"I wish I knew," he shrugs. "But does it even matter?"

No. It doesn't.

I stare at him with all the love in the world.

"You're here," I whisper in awe.

"I'm here."

"Is this real?" I wonder.

"So real," he smiles at me.

But there's something there in his eyes. Something more. Something I've longed for since the moment I met him.

It's love.

"What now?" I say.

He takes my hand in his and brings it to his lips.

"Now we live."

-THE END-

Made in the USA
San Bernardino, CA
04 April 2018